CW01497998

The Man Who

DIED SEVEN TIMES

The Man Who DIED SEVEN TIMES

YASUHIKO NISHIZAWA

TRANSLATED FROM THE JAPANESE BY JESSE KIRKWOOD

Pushkin Press
Somerset House, Strand
London WC2R 1LA

Original text © 2017 Yasuhiko Nishizawa. All rights reserved.

The *Man Who Died Seven Times* was first published in 1995 in
Japan as *Nanakai Shinda Otoko*, by Kodansha Ltd., Tokyo.

Publication rights for this English edition arranged through Kodansha Ltd.

English language translation © Jesse Kirkwood 2025
First published by Pushkin Press in 2025

ISBN 13: 978-1-80533-543-6

All rights reserved. No part of this publication may be reproduced,
stored in a retrieval system or transmitted in any form or by any
means, electronic, mechanical, photocopying, recording or otherwise,
without prior permission in writing from Pushkin Press.

The authorised representative in the EEA is
eucomply OÜ, Pärnu mnt. 139b-14, 11317, Tallinn, Estonia,
hello@eucompliancepartner.com, +33757690241

Designed and typeset by Tetragon, London
Printed and bound in the United Kingdom by Clays Ltd, Elcograf S.p.A.

Pushkin Press is committed to a sustainable future for our
business, our readers and our planet. This book is made from
paper from forests that support responsible forestry.

MIX
Paper | Supporting
responsible forestry
FSC® C018072
FSC
www.fsc.org

www.pushkinpress.com

1 3 5 7 9 8 6 4 2

CONTENTS

CHARACTER TREE

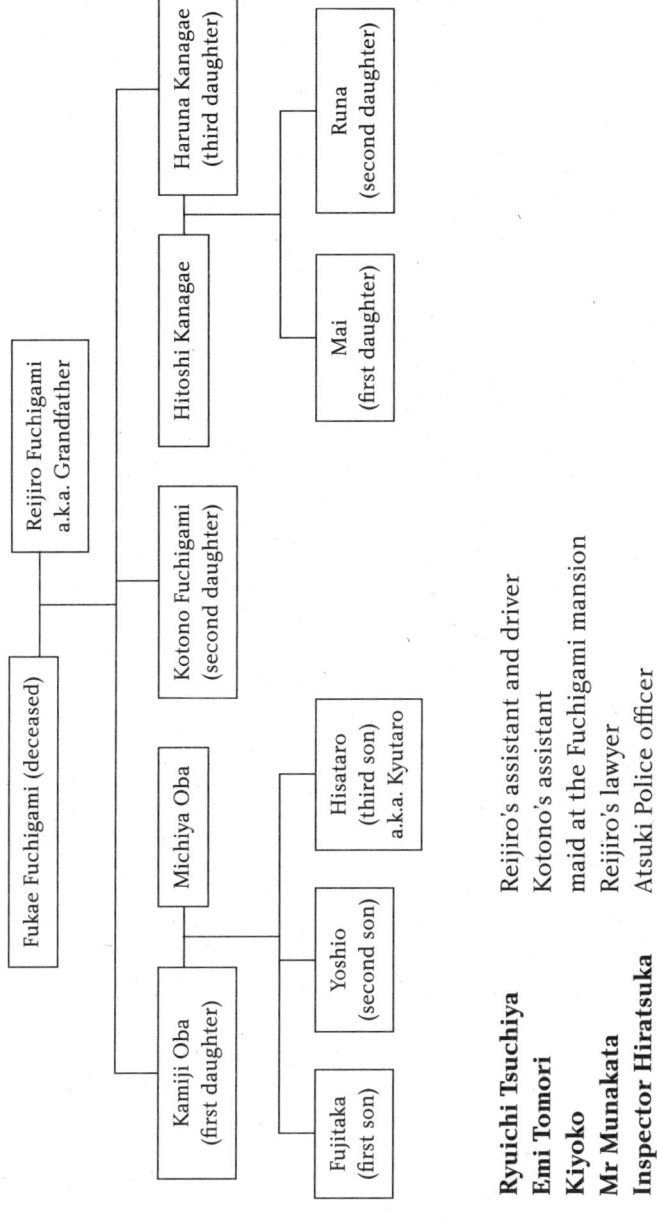

Fukae Fuchigami (deceased) — Reijiro Fuchigami a.k.a. Grandfather

Kamiji Oba (first daughter) — Michiya Oba
- Fujitaka (first son)
- Yoshio (second son)
- Hisataro (third son) a.k.a. Kyutaro

Kotono Fuchigami (second daughter)

Haruna Kangae (third daughter) — Hitoshi Kangae
- Mai (first daughter)
- Runa (second daughter)

Ryuichi Tsuchiya   Reijiro's assistant and driver
Emi Tomori   Kotono's assistant
Kiyoko   maid at the Fuchigami mansion
Mr Munakata   Reijiro's lawyer
Inspector Hiratsuka   Atsuki Police officer

1

A FIRST GLIMPSE OF THE MURDER

We found Grandfather lying in the attic. It was a small, six-mat room, dark even during the daytime, its only window about the size of a piece of A4 paper. In the middle of the room, under the naked light bulb that dangled from the ceiling, was the futon mattress I'd left out that morning.

My grandfather, Reijiro Fuchigami, was sprawled face down on the futon. His left arm was trapped under his belly; his right hand grasped at the tatami mat. Just beyond his reach lay a large sake bottle. It must have been almost empty even before it fell over, because the spilt contents formed only a small dark patch on the tatami.

The few white hairs Grandfather had left, a sort of candyfloss-like swirl at the back of his head, were spattered a dark red. Lying in front of his face, hiding it from view, was a copper vase. Its former contents, a bunch of out-of-season moth orchids, were strewn across the tatami. Emi had bought them as a present for Aunt Kotono, knowing she liked orchids. So, really, they should have been in Aunt Kotono's room. Not here.

He's been hit with the vase. That was the thought that crossed my mind, and presumably everyone else's. But no one—not

Mother, not Fujitaka, not Yoshio, not Aunt Kotono, not Kiyoko, not Aunt Haruna, not Mai, not Runa—moved an inch. Even Ryuichi and Emi seemed to have frozen in the face of this momentous event. Everyone just stood there, jostling around the cramped doorway, barely able to breathe.

Eventually, after who knows how long, I found myself stepping forward into the room. This was my bedroom whenever we stayed at the mansion—a fact that seemed to have instilled a strange sense of duty in me. In any case, no one stopped me as I went to kneel at my grandfather's side.

I took his wrist. It felt like a cut of ham that had been left out too long. There was no pulse. So he *was* dead. That much had been obvious from the moment we saw him lying there, but the confirmation still came as a shock. Or rather, it filled me with a fresh sense of despair.

I turned to look at my family, who were still peering through the doorway. I had no idea what you were supposed to do or say at a time like this. I must have had a pretty idiotic look on my face, but nobody was laughing. Instead their expressions were blank, as though all the emotion had been scoured from them. Watching them, I began to feel like bursting into hysterical laughter. For one thing, with the exception of Kiyoko, they were all clad in the bizarre combination of brightly coloured tracksuit and sleeveless chanchanko jacket that was the standard 'uniform' whenever we stayed at my grandfather's mansion. Given the circumstances, there was something almost grotesquely hilarious about the mismatched outfits.

It was Emi who recovered first. She seemed to have received the silent message I was trying to convey, because she abruptly turned and clattered off down the stairs—presumably to phone the police.

Her departure broke the spell. There was a sort of collective sigh. Then, as if this was the cue they'd been waiting for, my mother, Aunt Kotono and Aunt Haruna suddenly turned on the histrionics. *Father, Father! Oh no! How could this happen!* That sort of thing. Sobbing and wailing as if trying to make up for all the time they'd been dumbstruck.

'You mustn't touch him!' exclaimed Yoshio, restraining Mother as she tried to embrace my grandfather's body.

'We have to preserve the crime scene until the police get here!' shouted Runa at her own mother, who was trying to do the same.

'What crime scene? What are you talking about?'

I couldn't even tell who shrieked these words—my mother or Aunt Haruna. In the close confines of the attic, all hell was breaking loose.

'Isn't it obvious?' said Yoshio urgently. 'Look at him. Just look at him! He's been *murdered*!'

Murdered. That one word from Yoshio was enough to make everyone freeze again. *Murdered*, their fearful eyes said. *Murdered, really? But how… how could something like this happen to us, of all families? This can't be real. A murder, among upstanding citizens like us…?*

But I was shocked for a different reason. The question on my mind was the same—how could this have happened?—but in my case it wasn't just rhetorical. I really wanted to know *how*.

On this day, the 2nd of January, no murder was supposed to take place at the Fuchigami household. Its non-occurrence was something I'd already established as fact. Yesterday—or more precisely, on the 'first' 2nd of January—nothing untoward had happened. The day had ended without incident. And yet today—or rather, on this second version of the same day—my grandfather had been murdered. Why?

As these thoughts swirled through my head, my eyes briefly met Runa's. She didn't seem to register my gaze. She was too busy staring fearfully back down at Grandfather's body.

Even at a time like this, I couldn't help noticing that she wasn't wearing her earrings. When had she taken them off? Yesterday—the real yesterday, that is, the 1st of January—I was sure she'd been wearing them. Like everyone else, she'd been obliged to change into the 'uniform' when she arrived at the mansion for our New Year's gathering. Worn with her bright yellow tracksuit and blue chanchanko jacket, Runa's earrings always looked utterly out of place—and yet she made it a rule never to take them off. Which, of course, only made their absence all the more noticeable…

2

THE PROTAGONIST FILLS US IN

It was in the early years of elementary school that I first became aware of my 'condition'. Not that it started then. My memories are a little vague, but I have a feeling I was born with it. It just took me a while to notice.

My name is Hisataro Oba, but not many people actually call me that. 'Hisataro' is a fancy way of reading the characters, and most people opt for the simpler 'Kyutaro' instead, which they combine with my last name to get 'Obakyu'. Which is fun. 'Obakyu' also happens to be the name of a character from a manga series that was popular in the sixties, one my generation has barely heard of, which means the older folks get to have a good chuckle at my expense, too. In any case, I wish people would leave my poor name alone.

I'm sixteen now, and I attend the Kaisei Academy, a combined middle and high school in the city of Atsuki. I'm in my first year of high school. It's one of the more prestigious schools in the prefecture, with a good track record of getting its pupils into top universities, and if you walk around with your Kaisei uniform on, the adults tend to treat you with respect. I attended a local middle school until last year when, in accordance with my mother's wishes—maybe 'orders' would be closer to the mark—I took and passed the entrance exam and transferred to Kaisei for the high school portion of my education. When I reveal this to most people, they tell me, with obvious admiration, that I must have a good head on my shoulders, but actually that's pretty far from the truth. In fact, it would be more accurate to say that I have quite a bad head on my shoulders. Proof of this can be found in the fact that, when it comes to my grades, I consistently rank among the lowest-performing pupils in my year.

You often hear about kids who manage to get into elite schools and then, through a sort of recoil effect, start slacking off and underperforming. That's not what happened with me. The truth is, I've never been very academically gifted. And if you're wondering how I managed to pass the entrance exam for a school as exclusive as the Kaisei Academy, well, that's where my 'condition' comes in.

When asked to describe me, there's a phrase people love to fall back on. *Old for his years.* Apparently, talking to me feels like sitting opposite some elderly man sipping green tea on the veranda and telling yarns about the old days while he soaks up the sun. This can only be described as an accurate assessment of the situation, the reason being that, despite my tender biological age of sixteen, my mind is at least thirty years old. Just to clarify, this is not a figure of speech. It's a mathematically provable fact.

It was food that first made me aware of my condition. As a young child, the only thing I showed much interest in was filling my belly. And even at that age, I'd found the occasional lack of variety in the menu a little odd.

'Tamagoyaki and potato salad, *again*?' I'd muttered one day.

'What are you on about?' my mother had snapped. 'We had hamburger steaks yesterday.'

At the time, I could only remember us having hamburger steaks a few days ago. I thought this was strange, but there was eating to be done, so I gobbled down the meal—only for the tamagoyaki and potato salad to appear again the next day. You can see why I might mutter '*again*?' again. And when I did, my mother narrowed her eyes again.

'What are you on about? We had hamburger steaks yesterday.'

At this point, even an elementary school kid with nothing but food on his brain started to notice that the problem wasn't limited to the dishes on the table. When I turned my attention to the conversation around the dinner table, it turned out my father and brothers were talking about the same thing as the day before. Something about how Westerners were obsessed with picking on other countries for what they ate, and what difference did it make if we ate a bit of whale or tuna every now and then? Now, maybe I only noticed because the topic involved food, but they talked about the same thing the day after that, and the day after, too. The exact same exchange. The weirdest thing was that they were even repeating themselves word for word.

Then I realized that it wasn't just my family. My teachers and friends at school were all saying and doing the same things as the day before.

'Alright, everyone, listen up,' said our square-faced teacher, eyeing us sternly through her black-rimmed spectacles. 'No going near the shrine on the hill behind the school, okay?'

'Why's that, Miss?' asked Oda, who at the time was my rival

for biggest-dunce-in-the-class. 'Is it haunted or something?' he added quizzically.

'How very unenlightened of you, Oda.'

'What's an "onion light" mean?'

'It means you're a very silly boy. No, there's something much worse than your average ghost at the shrine.'

'What, like a monster?'

'There's no such thing as monsters, Oda. You've been watching too much anime. No, some naughty kids have been going there and doing very naughty things. So, no going to the shrine on the hill. Otherwise you might see something you shouldn't.'

'What kind of naughty things?'

'Well, that's… erm… I… See, there was a girl from another school who went there to play, and she saw two older kids playing a funny game. The girl had taken her trousers off, and she was trying to make the boy do the same.'

'Why did she try to make him take his trousers off?'

'Well, it was all part of the game. I'm sure I don't have to tell you what happened next.'

'They swapped trousers?'

Just to be clear, Oda wasn't trying to crack a joke. He was asking because he really didn't know. In fact, I'd say that fewer than half the pupils in the class were precocious enough to decipher the teacher's cryptic allusion. Even I had assumed they were just swapping trousers, as ridiculous as that seems now. Anyway, I digress, but the point is that this conversation was repeated verbatim in class the next morning.

'Alright, everyone, listen up,' said the teacher, her nostrils flaring like those of some beast scrambling after its prey—exactly as they had the day before. 'No going near the shrine on the hill behind the school, okay?'

'Why's that, Miss?' Oda's voice sounded just as dopey as it had yesterday, too. 'Is it haunted or something?'

'How very unenlightened of you, Oda.'

'What's an "onion light" mean?'

'It means you're a very silly boy. No, there's something much worse than your average ghost at the shrine.'

'What, like a monster?'

'There's no such thing as monsters, Oda. You've been watching too much anime. No, some naughty kids have been going there and doing very naughty things. So, no going to the shrine on the hill. Otherwise you might see something you shouldn't.'

'What kind of very naughty things?'

'Well, that's… erm… I… See, there was a girl from another school who went there to play, and she saw two older kids playing a funny game. The girl had taken her trousers off, and she was trying to make the boy do the same.'

'Why did she try to make him take his trousers off?'

'Well, it was all part of the game. I'm sure I don't have to tell you what happened next.'

'They swapped trousers?'

This exchange happened in first period the next day, and the day after that, too—always starting with the teacher telling us not to go to the shrine on the hill and ending with Oda's line about swapping trousers. And this wasn't the only thing that kept recurring. In fact, everything that had happened the previous day—from the menu at breakfast to our teacher's every word; from the specific details of the break-time dodgeball match to who got in a fight with whom, and who started crying, and who stepped in dog poo on the way home; from the menu at dinner to the programmes on TV—it was all exactly the same, day after day.

And then all of a sudden the repetition stopped, and the real 'tomorrow' arrived. No more tamagoyaki and potato salad for dinner, no more angry criticism of the views of Westerners on whale and tuna, and no more mention of trouser-swapping, except as something funny that the idiotic Oda had said the previous day.

As you've probably worked out, the same day was repeating itself over and over. Not only this, but I appeared to be the only one aware of what was happening. Like so many wind-up toys, everyone else would go around doing and saying exactly the same things as the day before—as though it were the most natural thing in the world and this was simply an ordinary day like any other. They had no idea they were acting out the same scenes over and over, like on a videotape caught in a loop. I was the only one who knew.

My secret name for this phenomenon is the Trap. Basically, once I fall into the Trap, I'm condemned to repeat the same day over and over until I climb back out of it. Like a scratched record where the needle keeps skipping back and playing the same passage over and over.

I never know when the Trap is going to spring into action next. As far as I can tell, there's no fixed pattern for how often it occurs. It might be as often as a dozen times in one month, or only once in eight weeks.

But when it comes to the duration of each 'loop', and the total period for which I'm stuck in the Trap, there are clear rules. Each loop lasts one full day, from midnight to midnight—twenty-four hours, in other words. And the Trap always lasts for a total of nine days. Of course, that's just my subjective experience of the situation, and in reality only one day has gone by—so strictly speaking, it would be more correct to say the day lasts for nine loops. It can also get confusing to refer mentally to 'yesterday' or 'tomorrow' while I'm in the Trap, so instead I tend to think in terms of the 'first loop', 'second loop' and so on.

As a general rule, once I'm in the Trap, everybody else's words and actions are identical from one loop to the next. I say 'as a general rule' because they can also be deliberately made to do something else entirely. Of course, the person making them do so is none other than yours truly.

Once the Trap is activated, the only person who can *intentionally* follow a different course of action to the previous loop is me, because I'm the only one aware that time is caught in a loop. If I speak differently to someone from one loop to the next, they can't help but respond differently. If I don't complain that we're having tamagoyaki and potato salad again, the end result will be that Mother *won't have said* her usual annoying line about how we had hamburger steaks the day before. This ability to alter the 'end result' is where my 'condition' really comes into its own. In other words, I can deliberately alter the course of reality.

The benefits of this first became clear to me one evening when I was watching a baseball game with my father and brothers. It was the Yomiuri Giants versus their biggest rivals, the Hanshin Tigers, and the Giants ended up winning by a devastating margin. The match had been billed as a pitcher's duel, but in the bottom of the fifth inning the Giants managed to score an astonishing and record-breaking nine consecutive home runs, from the leadoff hitter right through to the pitcher batting ninth, after which they just had to hold on for the win. My father, a Giants fan, was wild with joy; Yoshio, who hated their guts, was writhing around on the floor in agony; Fujitaka, who supported the Lotte Marines, sat there trimming his nose hair and yawning. It was a pretty lively evening.

Seeing as I didn't have a team myself, I just sat there scratching my head and went to bed as usual. But when I woke up the next morning, I discovered that this dramatic day had fallen into the Trap.

Just like in the previous loop, the baseball game started. My father sat there excitedly with his beer and edamame. Despite still being in middle school at the time, Yoshio swiped a mouthful of his beer. Fujitaka was cleaning his ears with a cotton bud. In other words, everyone was having a fun enough evening in front of the television, except me—I was bored stiff. How could I not be? I already knew the result. Nine-zero to the Giants, a runaway victory. With the added bonus of a record-breaking nine consecutive home runs.

Before I knew it, I had blurted it out.

'The Giants have got this one sewn up.'

My father loved the enthusiasm. Yoshio was infuriated.

'What are you on about?' he said. 'The game's barely started.'

Then it got started, and the score was nine-zero. The mixture of elation and despair in the living room was roughly the same as in the previous loop, except this time Fujitaka just yawned, without trimming his nose hair. My comment had subtly altered reality.

In the next loop, I got a little mischievous.

'Hey, you know what?' I said as my father and brothers were getting ready to watch the game. 'I feel like something crazy's going to happen in the fifth.' They had a good laugh at my expense, telling me to quit the Nostradamus act, but it played out just as I'd predicted.

Still, they didn't seem that blown away. I decided to take things up a notch. In the next loop, I very clearly predicted that in the second half of the fifth inning the Giants would knock out a series of home runs. When they went ahead and scored their nine homers, Father was too busy whooping with joy to notice how right I'd been, but Yoshio sat there staring slightly suspiciously at me. Fujitaka must have been slightly taken aback, too, because this time he failed to trim his nose hair *or* yawn.

In the next loop I got a little cocky and announced that I'd cast a spell on the Giants so that every single one of them would hit a home run. This was greeted with jeers of derision, but then the fifth inning came around and they all went quiet. There was something subdued about even Father's celebrations this time, while my brothers were just staring at me like I was some kind of freak. That I found a little nerve-wracking.

Realizing I'd taken things a bit too far, I spent the sixth, seventh and eighth loops simply watching the game in silence. Then, in the ninth loop, I suggested to my father that we make a bet. If the Giants managed the win with a shutout, he'd give me some extra pocket money that week. Then Yoshio, apparently feeling I needed to aim a little higher, made the following generous and somewhat rash remark.

'Idiot. If they manage a shutout, you can have every single one of my manga.'

The result, of course, was that I found myself with a cash windfall and Yoshio's entire manga collection. Now, if this was still the third loop, say, or the fifth, reality would have reverted to its original state and I would have had to do the whole thing all over again if I wanted to score the pocket money and manga, but because this was the ninth loop, this became the 'definitive version' of the day's events.

Basically, there are always nine loops in the Trap, and the first loop is the 'original' version of the day in question. After that comes the second, third, fourth, fifth, sixth, seventh, eighth and final loop. Whatever I do in the second to eighth loops, reality always reverts to its original state, but whatever happens in the final loop becomes, for everyone else, the only version—and for me, the 'definitive version'—of the events of the day in question.

Of course, my actions during the final loop may cause the day's events to differ significantly from their original version. On the other hand, if I so choose, I can ensure that the final or definitive loop matches the original completely. This is what I mean when I talk about deliberately altering the course of reality.

By now you've probably worked out how I was able to pass the entrance exams for a school as exclusive as the Kaisei Academy. That's right. If there's one area where the Trap really shines, it's school tests. And, in a complete stroke of luck, the Trap happened to activate on the day of the entrance exam. All I had to do was take the exam once, learn what questions came up, then memorize the answers afterwards. I got a total of eight chances to practise, too. There was no way I was failing that test.

A little unnecessarily, I scored full marks in every subject. This was partly to err on the side of caution, since I didn't know the exact pass mark, but mainly just because I wanted to show off. My results caused a bit of a stir. The Kaisei entrance exam was famed for being one of the hardest in the country. No wonder people seemed to think my results heralded the arrival of a genius the likes of which the school had never seen—and might never see again.

But remember: the Trap is a 'condition' I'm subject to, not an 'ability' I possess. If it was an 'ability', I'd be able to enter the Trap whenever I felt like it. And if I wanted to really become a renowned genius, I could have made that happen. But it's a 'condition', and I never know when it'll affect me next. I can't just decide to enter the Trap whenever we have our end-of-term tests, and even if I get lucky and the Trap happens to align with one of them, the tests are usually spread over several days.

As a result, my reputation at the school has taken a nosedive: I've gone from 'greatest genius ever seen' to 'complete blockhead'. The disparity between my entrance exam results and those in my first end-of-term tests was so severe that it was even suggested I'd engaged in some sort of foul play. The school carried out a witch hunt among the teachers on the assumption that one of them must have leaked the question paper. Now that I think about it, the whole ruse was pretty thoughtless of me.

It wasn't just the entrance exam. All the way through elementary and middle school, my results kept lurching between two extremes: exceedingly impressive and embarrassingly awful. Needless to say, the former I owed to the Trap. My report cards often featured comments like: *Has ability, but effort seems to vary—Should aim for greater consistency.*

The benefits of the Trap aren't limited to tests, either. As I explained, with loops number two to eight, it doesn't matter what I do during the course of the day: everything goes back to how it was the following morning. It's a bit like hitting the 'reset' button on a video game: basically, I can do whatever I like. So, for example, when there was a girl in my class I was sort of into, I decided I'd 'interview' her over and over again. Over the course of eight loops, I asked her anything and everything. I found out her date of birth, who was in her family, her interests, even the story of the first time she fell in love. Then, in the last loop, I offered to give her a psychic reading. Girls love that kind of thing—so when I could apparently see into the depths of her soul, she was completely bowled over. Sure, I was only telling her things I'd asked in advance, but because of the 'reset', she didn't remember a thing.

In my middle-school years, I used this trick to win the affection of quite a few different girls. Over time, though, it all got a little depressing. The main problem was that these dalliances never lasted. It was all well and good getting a girl's attention with my 'psychic' routine, but afterwards they tended to lose interest pretty quickly. I don't blame them, either. Even when a girl went out of her way to try to develop feelings, she'd soon realize that the object of them—me, in other words—had precious little to offer after the initial excitement.

It was the same with tests. When I aced an end-of-term test because it happened to coincide with the Trap, it wasn't like I owed the result to my own ability. It was cheating, really—a sort of fraud. The result was that I could score a hundred per cent and still only feel the shallowest kind of satisfaction. At first I'd thought of my 'condition' as a source of amusement, but over time I began to realize that the truth was more depressing.

Still, even now, I never hesitate to exploit my condition when the situation requires it— as demonstrated by my stunning performance in the Kaisei entrance exam. I'd been expecting to fail the test, thus ensuring my mother's transformation into one of those terrifying demons you see in a Noh play, so when the Trap happened to activate on the day in question, I was delirious with joy. It's all pretty pathetic, really.

All this probably explains why people are always telling me I seem old for my years, or teasing me by calling me 'Gramps'. I approach life with a sort of philosophical resignation, as though I'm convinced that in the long run, nothing really means anything. At the same time, it's not like I have the drive to try to get by without the Trap. I'm sort of stuck, really.

On top of all that, as I mentioned, the Trap can sometimes happen upwards of ten times in a single month. If I had to guess, I'd say the average is around three or four times. In each Trap, I go through eight loops before I get to the 'definitive version' of the day. In other words, on a subjective level, I experience eight whole days that no one else does. Add up all that extra time, and a month lasts about twice as long for me as it does for everyone else. In other words, my mind experiences about twice as much time as my body. By now you'll have realized why those comments about me having a mental age in the thirties weren't just rhetorical.

The truth is that if I don't have *some* fun with the Trap, then it's basically just a torture device. Repeating the same day eight times can get pretty mind-numbing. It doesn't really matter whether the events of the day in question are pleasant or not; the torture lies in the repetition itself. Which is why, rather than simply repeating the events of the original loop, I tend to tinker with them slightly in the second loop. And rather than simply repeating myself in the second loop, I do some more tinkering in the third. And the fourth, and so on. Then it all gets very depressing, so that in the final loop I often end up doing exactly what I did in the original loop and making that the definitive version of the day. And every time that happens, I feel a strange mix of frustration and emptiness, and ask myself what on earth any of it means.

This is probably why people are always saying I have the aura of some jaded old man. It's true that, if I had a choice, I'd probably just retire from life and spend my days sitting on my veranda and dozing, occasionally rousing myself to pick fleas from my cat. I mean, if my days are going to repeat themselves, I might as well spend them all doing the same thing.

But I'm still in my first year of high school. Retirement isn't the done thing at my age. All I can do is bumble onwards, caught somewhere between resignation and pure apathy.

The one area in which the Trap seems like it might be a universal force for good is when it comes to preventing accidents. Provided, of course, that I happen to fall into a loop on the day of the accident in question. Earlier I mentioned someone stepping in dog poo on the way home from school. Well, that person was me, and my realization that I seemed to be stepping in it in the same place every day coincided with my realization that the food and conversation at dinner were also repeating themselves. But because at that point I hadn't yet fully grasped the rules of the Trap—for example, how many loops it would take for the 'real' tomorrow to arrive, or the fact that the last loop would become the definitive version of the day—my brand-new trainers ended up stuck with the same yellowish and apparently indelible stain I'd inflicted on them originally.

These days, though, I have a pretty solid understanding of the rules. So, if I were to have some kind of serious accident and the Trap happened to activate on the same day, I'd be able to alter my destiny and save myself. If I get hit by a truck, all I have to do is stay away from wherever that happened on all the subsequent loops, and I'll make it through the day in one piece. Of course, this doesn't just apply to me—the same principle means I can save other people, too.

The thing is, I haven't actually had many chances to take advantage of this aspect of the Trap so far. Since the dog-poo incident, my life hasn't exactly been filled with drama. Neither have those of the people around me. It seems I'm just not destined to witness anything that exciting.

Of course, one glance at a newspaper is enough to confirm that plenty of accidents and crimes happen every day. There was a period where, whenever the newspaper on the day of the Trap revealed that some tragedy had occurred, I'd feel a sudden sense of duty. I'd tell myself that maybe the reason I'd been born with my 'condition' was that I had some divine calling to help those around me and make the world a better place.

But the world soon brought me down to size. To take just the example of traffic accidents, there would often be more than one of them reported in the newspaper, in which case I ran into the problem of which to prioritize. When they occurred at disparate locations within a short space of time, preventing all of them was physically impossible.

Still, if it meant I could save just one person, surely that was better than simply sitting around twiddling my thumbs. But the problem then became: how do I choose? At first I decided to focus on fatal accidents, but then it struck me that the ones where someone ended up in a coma were, in a sense, even more tragic. Once that sort of confusion had set in, I began losing all sense of what was right. It wasn't just traffic accidents that featured in the newspaper, either. What about people getting lost at sea or in the mountains? Or burning to death in a fire? Gas explosions? Typhoons, earthquakes, other natural disasters? Murders, even? Some things seemed so far out of my control that it seemed ridiculous to even try.

In the end, after a great deal of agonized soul-searching, I simply gave up. There were limits to what I could achieve on my own. Instead, I decided to prevent only accidents that involved me or people I knew, or which I happened to witness directly.

In short, the Trap wasn't quite the universal force for good I'd imagined it to be. It'd be more accurate to call it a force for *my own* good. Whenever I found myself gazing at a newspaper article on a Trap day, I'd remind myself of this and wait for the guilt of not saving lives to subside—drawing on whatever fatalism or agnosticism I could muster to convince myself that whatever happened in the world was always going to happen, and for reasons beyond human understanding. And so my 'jaded old man' persona became only more pronounced over time.

The conclusion my 'condition' has led me to is this: that our existence is predicated entirely on our own self-interest.

I know that sounds like a very convenient excuse. But then of course it does—in fact, that very fact is compelling evidence for my claim. Much as it pains me, I have no choice but to declare that the only person I'm capable of saving, in the end, is myself. Maybe, at a push, my family and friends—but even then I'd still essentially be putting my own interests first.

By good fortune—if I can call it that—as I mentioned above, I don't seem destined to witness many serious accidents, and in my sixteen years on this planet, neither I nor anyone I know has been involved in one personally. As a result, it would be fair to say I've never succeeded in making effective use of the Trap to achieve anything. Yes, I used it to get into my high school, but the drawbacks of that are beginning to look like they might outweigh the benefits.

Maybe my real mistake lay in thinking anything positive would ever come of this troublesome 'condition'. Like I said, it's not an ability, but just that: a condition. A disorder I have to live with for the rest of my life. There's no reason why it should ever be remotely helpful to anyone.

Just live with it, and forget about trying to use it for good. That was my philosophy. Until, that is, the New Year's holidays of my first year of high school.

3

THE CHARACTERS ASSEMBLE

'Happy New Year!'

Ryuichi Tsuchiya, my grandfather's personal assistant and driver, bobbed his head at us, the friendly smile on his face seeming to hang in the air for a moment afterwards.

'Happy New Year,' said my mother, returning the greeting with a series of bows bordering on the obsequious, especially given that Ryuichi was about the same age as her sons. She seemed to bow a little deeper every time we visited my grandfather's mansion for the New Year. 'Thank you for everything you did last year, and all the best for the year ahead.'

'To you, too. It's been—'

'Really, all the very best indeed. Ah, I almost forgot.' Her voice dropped as she produced a decorative paper envelope and practically forced it into Ryuichi's hands. Apparently she was giving him the otoshidama money usually bestowed on children at this time of year. 'It's not much, but I'd like you to have this.'

'Oh, I can't possibly—' Ryuichi replied, even as his hands looked for somewhere to put the envelope. He appeared to be struggling with the fact that the clothes he was wearing had no pockets. 'You really shouldn't have…'

'Really, it's nothing at all. A trifle,' she insisted, but I wouldn't have been surprised if the amount of money she was handing him was far more than she ever gave her actual sons. 'Now, where's…?'

'Ah. Mrs Kanagae?' said Ryuichi, apparently grasping just from the way my mother was peering at the house that she was looking for her youngest sister. This sharpness, despite his young age, was probably why my grandfather had made him his right-hand man. 'Already arrived. With the young ladies.' He glanced surreptitiously at me and my two brothers, standing behind Mother. 'By the way, your husband—is he…?'

'Right. Yes. He's, erm…' Flustered, Mother began gesticulating wildly with her arms. One of them collided with Fujitaka, who was standing just behind her, though she didn't even seem to notice him flinch in pain. 'Yes, he, er… said he was feeling a little under the weather.' She chuckled awkwardly. 'Honestly, I don't know what to do with him sometimes.'

'Ah. So he's… ill?'

'Oh, I wouldn't go that far. He's fine. There's barely anything wrong with him. Really. It's probably just his age.' She gave another forced-sounding chuckle.

'What an unfortunate coincidence,' said Ryuichi, wincing slightly at my mother's shrill laughter. 'Your sister's husband is also unable to attend this year, as it happens.'

'Really? Hitoshi's not here, either?' Mother gazed off into space for a moment, as if trying to quickly work out whether this was good or bad news, as far as she was concerned. 'Why's that? Is he unwell, too, or what?'

'Well, erm…' began Ryuichi, but at this point Fujitaka suddenly broke in with a laugh.

'I think I know why.'

Outraged by the fact that her son, who she seemed to view as her own property, would dare to hide even the slightest snippet of gossip from her, Mother narrowed her eyes fiercely at Fujitaka.

'What, know something we don't? Go on, then—out with it!'

'How about going inside first of all, Madam?' offered Ryuichi, who seemed anxious about the direction the conversation was taking. 'The Chairman and President are waiting.'

'Alright, then. But…' Mother gave Ryuichi a fresh once-over with her eyes. He was clad in a loose-fitting black tracksuit, on top of which he wore a dark blue chanchanko jacket. It was a pretty amusing getup, all told—and also faintly absurd for someone to wear while politely greeting his boss's family. 'He won't let us in unless we dress up like that, will he? It's ridiculous… I mean, *really*… Is there no other way?'

'I'm very sorry. I'm under strict instructions from the Chairman not to let anyone in until they've agreed to change clothes.'

'My word. I mean, I know Father has his whims, but still…' For all her complaining, Mother had still taken care to turn up in a casual outfit she could easily change out of. 'Fine, then.'

'Thank you. This way, please,' said Ryuichi, gesturing towards the old house that stood apart from the main mansion. 'Emi will see to you in there.'

'Right, then, you three,' said Mother, fixing me and my brothers with an imperious glare, as if to compensate for all the toadying she'd done to Ryuichi. 'Hurry up and get changed. No dawdling, you hear!'

With these harsh words—as if our 'dawdling' was somehow to blame for all her problems—she disappeared into the old house. Meanwhile, Ryuichi led us into the annex that stood across the courtyard from the old house, and which served as the men's changing room.

'Sheesh,' sighed Yoshio as he pulled on the yellow tracksuit that he found waiting for him. 'The same lame outfits, year after year. Ryuichi, don't you think we should be wearing something a little, I dunno, *fancier* for the New Year?'

'You may have a point,' said Ryuichi, apparently unsure if he should fully concur. He nodded vaguely. 'For the gentlemen it's one thing, but for the ladies…'

'Exactly. I mean, we only meet up like this once a year. I'm sure they'd prefer to look a little more glamorous while they're at it, right? Instead, just look at this…' Yoshio gave a dramatic sigh as he pulled on his blue chanchanko. 'I just don't see why we have to sit around celebrating in clothes that, frankly, I'd be embarrassed to be seen nipping out to the convenience store in. I mean, I'm not some penniless student any more… *And* it means I don't get to see Runa in a kimono…'

With that last comment, a strange tension seemed to suddenly fill the changing room. This was getting interesting. Runa was the second daughter of Aunt Haruna—in other words, our cousin. I'd long known that Yoshio was infatuated with her—he seemed unable to hide it—but the charged atmosphere in the room indicated that Fujitaka, without ever having expressed his feelings in so many words, was also not immune to her charms. It wasn't just Fujitaka, either. Ryuichi,

33

of all people, must also have fallen under her spell, because he'd joined Fujitaka in staring somewhat menacingly at Yoshio.

'You're lucky—at least your tracksuit's yellow,' I said, in an attempt to lighten the mood and avoid being embroiled in this bizarre standoff. 'Mine's red. A red tracksuit and a chanchanko. It's so... decadent.'

My branch of the family—the Oba family, that is—had only started joining my grandfather, Reijiro Fuchigami, for his New Year's celebrations a few years ago. Before that, we'd been estranged from him for various reasons. It wasn't just the Oba family, either. The family into which his third daughter, Haruna, had married, the Kanagae family, had also distanced themselves from him completely. Like us, they had only begun attending these New Year's gatherings in the past few years.

At this point I should probably explain a little about my grandfather and his company, the Edge Restaurant Group. Originally, Reijiro and his wife, Fukae, had run a small restaurant serving Western-style cuisine on the outskirts of the city of Atsuki. It seems he was quite the talented cook; at the same time, he was a pleasure-seeker with a weakness for the three cardinal sins of any husband—drinking, gambling and philandering. When it came to gambling, in particular, there was a period during which he would happily squander the restaurant's entire monthly earnings in a single evening, causing my grandmother all sorts of grief.

They had three daughters. My mother, Kamiji, was the eldest. After that came Kotono, followed by Haruna. As children, all three of them resented their father for the hardship and poverty he brought on the family. However much he angrily insisted that they do so, they could hardly be expected to respect a father who couldn't afford to buy them proper clothes and diverted the money that was supposed to pay for their food into his gambling. On top of that, he never missed an opportunity to demand that one of them marry a man who would be happy to be adopted into the family in order to carry on the Fuchigami name. In other words, they were expected not just to put up with years of hardship, but also to become the successors to a family which had nothing to offer them but a name and mountains of debt. Who could blame them for desperately wanting to escape a house like that—a *father* like that—as soon as they possibly could?

My mother, Kamiji, was a model daughter in one area only: her grades. Fending off her father's spiteful insistence that high school was a waste of time and she'd be better off helping him at the restaurant, she graduated top of her class and received a scholarship to study at Atsuki National University.

The truth of the matter was that academic success was my mother's only escape route. Running away from home would probably only have meant swapping one form of misery for another. If she wanted a decent job, or a husband she could depend on, first she needed to get herself to university: that seems to have been the thought that kept her going.

As if in support of this determination to escape, my grandmother died from a stroke just before my mother graduated. Once the funeral was out of the way, my mother never returned to the family home, instead marrying a man her age she'd met at university. That man was my father, Michiya Oba. My mother didn't even invite her two younger sisters to the wedding, never mind her father. It was her way of showing that she intended to permanently sever all ties with the Fuchigami family.

Meanwhile, her sisters panicked. Not only had their mother—their ally, at least up to a point—died on them, but their older sister had run away, leaving them to handle the burden that was Reijiro on their own.

They must have been furious. Haruna, the youngest, had only scraped her way into high school—albeit a girls' school with a less-than-demanding entrance exam. Whether she'd initially intended to follow her older sister's example and land a university scholarship is unclear, but at this point she abruptly dropped out of school—and moved in with her young teacher. That teacher, Hitoshi Kanagae, was now her husband. Perhaps the farsighted Haruna had decided this would make for a more reliable future than shacking up with some penniless boy her own age. They only held an official wedding ceremony once their first child, Mai, was born. Of course, once again, Reijiro was not invited.

So it was that Kotono, the middle daughter, found herself living alone with Reijiro. Her sisters had well and truly hung her out to dry. Kotono was nineteen at the time, and after graduating from middle school had spent the previous three years working at her father's restaurant instead of pursuing her education. As the second daughter, she'd always assumed she would at least be spared having to succeed her father as head of the family. Compared to her sisters, she'd never been a particularly capable daughter.

Kotono had always been the most good-natured of the three, but when it dawned on her that Kamiji and Haruna had abandoned her to the task of handling their impossible father, she became moody, and her behaviour grew increasingly erratic. It even reached the point where she had to go and see a psychiatrist.

Meanwhile, Reijiro had fallen into a depression following his wife's early demise. You might have thought that, finally liberated from her nagging, he would have begun indulging in his vices to his heart's content, but in fact the opposite happened: he lost his appetite for hedonism entirely. I don't know—maybe that's men for you. Two of his daughters had lost patience with him and eloped with their lovers, while the one who remained had descended into despair and neurosis. He felt deserted on all sides. By the time he realized that he had only himself to blame for his unhappy lot, the damage was already done.

Reijiro sold off all his assets and announced to Kotono that they were going on a 'trip', though in reality this simply meant drifting back to his hometown. They departed abruptly, at night, in an attempt to give his creditors the slip. Overwhelmed by despair, it seems his thoughts then turned to suicide. There followed a brief period of relative luxury during which, in order to atone for the way he'd treated Kotono, he spent the proceeds of his firesale on taking her out for delicious meals and buying her beautiful clothes—after which he planned to throw himself into the ocean.

But at this point fate took an unexpected turn. In an effort to use up every last yen he had left before he died, Reijiro struck on the idea of betting on a horse race. Of course, having lost his gambling spirit, he wasn't even trying to win. He just wanted to use up his money. And so he placed a series of high-odds bets that flew in the face of the day's tips.

The thing was, Reijiro's bets came good. Every single one of them. Instead of using up his money, he'd managed to multiply it by several factors of ten. He almost fainted. What on earth was going on? All those years of desperately trying to win big at the races, only to fail miserably every time—and now this?

Reijiro decided this was the devil whispering in his ear, telling him there was still plenty of fun to be had in life. That he should devote his winnings to some wild indulgence— something that would well and truly ruin him.

Acting on impulse, he decided that this time he'd try the stock market. Of course, now he was actively trying to throw his money down the drain, so he traded as idiotically as he could, buying up as many seemingly worthless stocks as he could lay his hands on. But irony continued to have its way with him. He had barely concluded the transaction when the stocks in question shot up in value, leaving Reijiro in possession of what could only be described as a fortune.

After discussing the matter with Kotono, who had mellowed again somewhat in response to her father's sudden outpour- ing of affection, Reijiro decided they would return to Atsuki. He used the proceeds from his stocks to pay off all his debts, after which he and Kotono opened a restaurant serving inter- national cuisine. The cook that had lain dormant inside him was finally roused. With Kotono's help, he managed to avoid falling into his old dissolute ways, instead devoting himself to his work.

Reijiro developed dish after spectacular dish, filling his menu with mouth-watering and tastefully presented meals that proved especially popular among young female cus- tomers. Day after day, they flooded through the restaurant's doors. Eventually, after years of hard work, they relocated from the tiny, out-of-the-way premises Reijiro had rented in a mixed-use tower block to a fancy brick building on a major thoroughfare.

After that, things practically took care of themselves. Additional branches of the restaurant began springing up left, right and centre until, with thirty-seven of them located all around the country, Reijiro found himself the head of a major corporation. This dramatic transformation had taken place in the past ten years.

These developments were enough to make my mother and Aunt Haruna more than a little nervous. Reijiro, now eighty-two, had taken a step back from the frontline of the business to become chairman of the Edge Restaurant Group. His assets, whether reckoned in terms of the company itself or his property holdings, were nothing short of staggering. And upon his demise, it seemed they would pass entirely into the hands of Aunt Kotono, now the company's president.

Of course, in the absence of a will, civil law would provide for Reijiro's fortune to be shared equally between his three children. But the chances of that happening were beginning to look laughably slim. It seemed that, over the past decade, Reijiro had developed a habit of rewriting his will at the beginning of each year. There was no way of knowing whether he indeed intended to leave Aunt Kotono everything, but the fact was that both Mother and Aunt Haruna had deliberately severed all ties with him. It seemed quite plausible that they would never see a single yen.

And so, each in their own desperate way, the two of them had begun manoeuvring to regain my grandfather's affection. At first, he had put up a stiff resistance to this charm offensive—after all, where had they been when he and Kotono needed them most? But over time his attitude softened—a change of heart that could only be explained by the fact that Aunt Kotono was childless.

Having devoted almost all her time to helping her father expand his business, Aunt Kotono had never married. Naturally, this left an enormous question mark hanging over the matter of Grandfather's successor. What would happen once both he and Aunt Kotono had passed away? Aunt Kotono was still only forty-eight and in fine health, and it seemed unlikely she'd be leaving us anytime soon, but the question of who would succeed her was still one that needed answering as soon as possible.

Mother and Aunt Haruna both seized on this as their line of attack. Mother insisted that with her three sons, Grandfather was spoilt for choice; Aunt Haruna, unperturbed, pointed out that Aunt Kotono could easily adopt the husband of one of her two daughters as her heir. The greed-fuelled mudslinging began.

Even coming from his own daughters, my grandfather must have found this grasping behaviour quite distasteful. For a while he refused even to allow them to visit. When they turned up on his doorstep, cooing and imploring, he simply sent them packing.

A few years ago, he finally relented and agreed to an annual visit on the occasion of the New Year. However, he had a rather peculiar demand. Before entering his home, we would each be required to change into the outfit he assigned us, remaining in it for the entire duration of our stay. If Mother or Aunt Haruna refused, we would be prohibited from taking even one step inside the mansion. The outfit in question was, of course, the combination of coloured tracksuit and chanchanko jacket I mentioned earlier.

'*You* get to wear blue,' I said to Fujitaka now, tugging dejectedly at the cuffs of my own red tracksuit. 'At least that goes nicely with the chanchanko.' I placed my wallet and watch, together with the clothes I'd arrived in, in the basket provided. There was no rule against bringing in personal possessions, but I wasn't going to be needing my wallet, and anyway the tracksuits didn't have pockets. Taking off my watch, meanwhile, was a habit of mine whenever I changed into more comfortable clothes. 'I'm the only one who has to walk around in this red monstrosity.'

As you'll have noticed, we didn't get to choose the colour of our tracksuit. This, too, was in line with my grandfather's instructions. He himself wore brown. His assistant, Ryuichi, wore black, as did Kotono's own assistant, Emi, while his three daughters (and their spouses, when they attended) all wore green.

'Actually, Kyutaro, some people would say red's quite a dapper colour,' said Yoshio, as if graciously dispensing some hard-won nugget of wisdom. 'And people wear it for their six-tieth birthdays, don't they? Perfect for an old fogey like you. Meanwhile, I have to wear yellow. Yellow. Can you believe it? I mean, it'd be one thing on a woman, but as a guy…'

'I'd have thought you'd be happy. I mean, it's the same colour as Runa,' I said—before immediately regretting it. After carefully steering us onto the topic of the tracksuits, in an attempt to relieve the growing tension around the subject of our cousin, I'd managed to reopen the exact same can of worms. 'Erm, what I mean is… whatever the colour, a tracksuit isn't exactly the most, erm…'

'You know what?' said Fujitaka, ignoring my stutter-ing attempt to smooth things over. 'Sometimes I wonder if Grandfather's actually going senile...'

'Wait, what?' said Yoshio. He looked alarmed—and also a little uncertain whether we should be discussing a topic like this in front of Ryuichi. 'What are you on about?'

'Yeah,' said Fujitaka, still speaking in a low and slightly irritated murmur, as if more for his own benefit than ours. 'I reckon he's gone all fuzzy in the head, and now he can't tell his own grandchildren apart.' He wasn't even looking at any of us, and his eyes had glazed over slightly. 'You know, Yoshio, when I bumped into him in town once, he thought I was you.'

'Seriously? That really happened?' asked Yoshio. Like our father (in his prime, at least) he was the trusting type. He'd stopped glancing suspiciously at Ryuichi and now made no effort to hide his interest. 'So you're saying... he's gone senile and can't tell us apart, which is why he's making us wear dif-ferent coloured tracksuits?'

'Oh, I don't think that's likely,' said Ryuichi bluntly, with an expression of painful obligation. He was tucking the envelope of money my mother had just given him into the inner pocket of the suit he had changed out of earlier, which lay folded in the basket assigned to him. 'I mean, if that *were* the reason, why would he have several people wearing the same colour?'

'Well, presumably he can still tell boys and girls apart, at least. The only ones wearing the same colour are Fujitaka and Mai, who're both in blue, and me and Runa, who are both in yellow. There's no overlap within either gender, is there?'

'What about the young ladies?' In this context, when Ryuichi said 'young ladies', he meant my mother and her sisters. When he was addressing them directly, of course, he called them 'Madam'. Ryuichi thought about these things. 'They're all in green.'

'Yeah, because it's only his grandchildren he can't tell apart. But if he just made us wear the tracksuits, it'd be too obvious what he was up to, and everyone would realize he'd gone senile. So to avoid giving the game away'—Yoshio seemed to be gaining confidence in his own idea as he spoke, and now clapped his hands together dramatically—'he makes everyone wear them—even you and Emi. It's only Kiyoko who gets to wear that smock of hers instead.'

Kiyoko was the maid at the Fuchigami mansion. Apparently she was the niece of my deceased grandmother, and had no living relatives. About a decade ago, my grandfather had practically taken her in off the street.

'Sounds like a load of nonsense to me.' Unexpectedly enough, it was Fujitaka who decided to take the cocksure Yoshio down a peg. 'I mean, what happens when he forgets which colour is who? And if he *can* remember that much, surely he can remember our faces, too.'

'Well… colours are probably easier to remember than faces…' said Yoshio, before abandoning this counter-argument with a shake of the head. 'Anyway, you're the one who brought this up.'

'I didn't say anything about the tracksuits being different colours. I just said I thought Grandfather might be going senile.'

'What, so you were just making conversation? Well, anyway,' continued Yoshio, his thoughts already elsewhere, 'you know why Uncle Hitoshi's not coming this year, don't you? You do, I can tell. Go on, spill the beans.'

But by this point Ryuichi had led us out of the annex and back to the main building, where the conversation was put on ice. We walked through the foyer, as spacious as that of a high-class ryokan, and into the reception room that acted as a sort of antechamber to the main banquet hall. We found Mother waiting—dressed, of course, in her chanchanko and green tracksuit, so that she looked like some world-weary housewife who had wandered in from a nearby housing estate. She looked past Ryuichi, fixing me and my brothers with a glare that said: *What took you so long!*

Even the reception room was cavernous. You could probably have fit about thirty tatami mats on the floor. Aunt Haruna and her elder daughter, Mai, were sitting on the sofa. Runa, the younger daughter, was standing by the window.

'Happy New Year,' came the voice of Emi Tomori, Aunt Kotono's personal assistant. With a neutral smile in which it was impossible to detect either friendliness or hostility, she lowered her head in our direction, then pushed a small trolley towards us from which she began serving drinks. She seemed to have stepped into this role while Kiyoko, the actual maid, was busy preparing for dinner in the banquet hall.

Emi was wearing the same black tracksuit as Ryuichi. She must have decided there was little point in trying to doll herself up in an outfit like that, as there wasn't a dab of makeup on her face. Its absence only accentuated her good looks.

Having never met Emi outside of these annual visits to my grandfather's house, I had no idea what she was like in her ordinary life—and of course had never seen her in anything except a black tracksuit and chanchanko. Maybe she was a sort of social chameleon, adjusting her personality to whomever she happened to be interacting with at a given time. With people like us, from whom her job required that she maintain a certain distance, she adopted a poker-faced neutrality that made labels like 'friendly' or 'beautiful' seem irrelevant. But it was entirely possible that in the company of, say, her lover, she metamorphosed into a beauty beyond compare, like some magnificent flower suddenly coming into bloom. The peculiar aura she possessed encouraged this sort of speculation.

Once he had taken a glass of whiskey-and-water from Emi, Yoshio made a beeline for Runa and began chatting away to her. Fujitaka, after some hesitation, decided to sit down on a different sofa. Ryuichi, apparently having something to attend to, made his way off to the banquet hall—glancing over at Runa himself as he did so.

'Oh dear,' said Aunt Haruna, glancing first at me and my brothers and then sidelong at my mother. Whenever we met, the same lethargic and slightly insouciant smile seemed to play about her lips. 'No Michiya this year, then? Is he okay?'

Mother's eyes immediately narrowed, as if to declare loud and clear that her husband very much *wasn't* okay. Remaining composed wasn't her strong suit. 'I was going to ask the same about Hitoshi. Where is he, then? Caught a cold or something?'

'Oh, you know…'

'I *don't* know, actually. Is he ill, then? Or did something come up?'

'No, he's just…'

'Just what? Come on, Haruna.' A harsh edge had already come into Mother's voice. 'Tell us the details. It's only natural for us to want to know.'

'Oh, it's nothing serious.' As usual, Aunt Haruna was doing a much better job of containing herself. She smiled wearily, as if to suggest that she might be crying on the inside but she wasn't going to show it.

'Urgh, come on. Drop the act.' By this point Mother seemed barely able to stop herself from launching into a full-blown rant. Out of some small consideration for those watching, she limited herself to a derisive snort. 'You can be so *odd*, Haruna. Is it actually something really serious? I bet it is. It is, isn't it?'

'It's really nothing.'

At this, Mother's face turned bright red. She knew she was being made a fool of. But she must have realized that opening her mouth again would only unleash a torrent of abuse, because in the end she simply stood there in furious silence.

A bristling tension had filled the reception room—one that made the earlier awkwardness between my brothers and Ryuichi concerning Runa seem like child's play. This was a full-blown family feud, one in which the mutual hatred was plain to see. After all, whichever of the two sisters managed to secure the inheritance was likely to have the upper hand forever.

When Aunt Haruna had eloped with the man who was now her husband, moving to his apartment from Grandfather's house, my mother had apparently seen the whole thing as something of a joke. *The kid's out of her mind*, she'd thought. *Running off with the teacher from a third-rate girls' school? It was obvious how that would end. Meanwhile, the husband she had found was the absolute cream of the crop.*

It was true that my father, Michiya Oba, was the sort of elite white-collar worker that anyone in my mother's position would have been proud to snare. He'd been hired straight out of university by a large local trading company, where he'd cut his teeth in the planning department before moving into sales. There he'd used his forceful personality to achieve impressive negotiating breakthroughs, chalking up success after success as he climbed the ladder. When he made Director of Sales in his forties, my mother practically leapt for joy. She really *did* know how to pick them. Father was bound for the top, and the higher he rose, the cushier her life would get. Of course, all this was only natural. She was made of different stuff to her sisters. *She* had been destined for happiness. This was only what she deserved. And so her feeling of superiority over Haruna only deepened.

In a sense, my father was the perfect match for an unabashed social climber like my mother. He had an ingrained habit of treating life as one big game, cruising through it with an almost childlike nonchalance. Of course, he was also far more ambitious than the average person, but I think what really made it so easy for him to sail upwards in life was that, to him, none of it was actually *real*. (Incidentally, of his three sons, it seemed to be Yoshio who most clearly took after my father in this respect. These days, he worked for a software development company. After a period in the doldrums as a system operations manager, he'd been switched to sales, where he seemed to have finally found his calling.)

But life has a habit of tripping you up. Father's next ambition had been to make executive. Of course, neither he nor my mother had any doubt this would soon become a reality. In fact, he'd already been unofficially told the role was his—no wonder, then, that he and Mother felt like they were on top of the world. Father even had a new suit made. But it turned out the two of them had been a little too complacent. They had underestimated the sheer cruelty of which large organizations are capable.

Last autumn, Father had discovered that rather than being promoted, he had been relegated to the position of Product Inventory Administrator, a role he'd never even heard of, and which turned out to be entirely devoid of any real responsibility. With the economic headwinds gathering, it seemed he had fallen victim to the company's downsizing strategy. He was still technically a manager, but he had practically nothing to do. His pay plummeted to the level of a regular employee.

The change that came over my father can only be described as tragic. He used to touch alcohol only when he was out schmoozing with his clients; now he was drinking heavily on a daily basis. He'd also begun weeping desperately, like a child, in front of his own sons. *How can they treat me like this? After everything I did for them!*—that kind of thing. My father had devoted himself body and soul to the company, and its betrayal rocked the very foundations of his existence. It wasn't just his family he cried in front of, either—once the drink was in him, he'd happily start wailing away in front of strangers. It had got so bad that my mother, unable to bear the sorry sight of him, had taken him to see a psychiatrist. The diagnosis had been emotional incontinence—the inability to control one's emotions following an extreme shock. For now, Father had simply taken leave, but it was surely only a matter of time until he quit his job. In other words, the company's downsizing strategy was going exactly as planned.

And so Father's 'golden age' had come to an end. Now that he'd entered his dark night of the soul, it was Fujitaka, rather than Yoshio, that he began to resemble. Or, more accurately, it seemed Fujitaka had inherited a certain innate negativity that my father had previously never allowed to surface. Fujitaka, by the way, was yet to enter the working world—he was enrolled at a postgraduate school where he was researching quantum physics.

Yoshio, meanwhile, had inherited the more upbeat side of his personality—to the extent that, even as Father faced ruin, he seemed to think it was impossible for the same thing ever to happen to him. If my father's life had gone off the rails, Yoshio reasoned, he only had his own ineptitude to blame. As his younger brother, I found the detachment with which he seemed to view the situation a little troubling.

In any case, my father had suffered a dramatic loss of face. Mother had lost her source of pride—and the basis for much of the superiority she felt over Aunt Haruna. No wonder, then, that she fell into a panic. The only way for her to maintain her dignity now, she decided, would be to ensure that one of her sons became Kotono's adoptive heir and the eventual owner of the Edge Restaurant Group. If one of Haruna's daughters was made the heir instead, all her younger sister's long-held grievances would simmer to the surface; she'd be sure to torment Mother with her new-found superiority for the rest of her life.

The previous New Year's gatherings had, for my mother, essentially been a sort of semi-playful attempt to win back Grandfather's affection so that he might deign to give us some tiny portion of his estate. This time, though, the stakes were on another level entirely. Whatever it took, she meant to ensure that the old man took a liking to at least one of her sons. Having decided that my father's alcohol-fuelled weeping would only hinder her cause, she had foisted him onto her mother-in-law for the New Year instead.

Now, having eagerly arrived at the Fuchigami mansion, she had learnt that her sister had chosen this year of all years to arrive, like her, without a husband in tow. Naturally she was burning with suspicion. She seemed to be frantically imagining what might be going on behind the scenes and trying to calculate whether or not she could turn it to her advantage. And yet here was Aunt Haruna nonchalantly batting away her questions. It must have been infuriating.

'What can I get you, Kyutaro?'

All of a sudden, Emi had arrived in front of me with the trolley. I should point out that she was only calling me this because she had no idea that the correct pronunciation of my name was Hisataro. The others called me Kyutaro so casually that she must have assumed it was my actual name.

'Tea, please.'

'Will iced oolong do?'

'I'd prefer hot green tea, if possible.'

'Oh, come on, Kyu-chan,' interrupted Runa all of a sudden, handing Emi her depleted glass and gesturing for another whiskey on the rocks. 'What are you, a monk? It's the New Year. A drink or two isn't going to kill you, is it? Go on, knock one back.'

'Yeah. What are you doing?' Clinging to Runa like the proverbial crap to a goldfish, Yoshio was, it seemed, already in high spirits—and delighted to have found something to agree with her about. 'Get some drink in you. Hey, Emi-chan, I'll have another whiskey, too.'

50

'Hang on, Yoshio. Did you just call her Emi-*chan*?' Runa's earrings swung wildly as she turned to glare at Yoshio. They were a pale ochre in colour, long and thin and cylindrical, like a tiny stick of asparagus or one of those official seals people carry around to approve documents. Forced into the tracksuits, the other women seemed to lose their appetite for personal adornment and always left their accessories in the changing room—and yet Runa made it a rule to always keep them on, together with her rings and watch. 'She's Emi to you, or Ms Tomori. Isn't that right, Emi?'

'Oh, come on,' said Yoshio. 'Give me a break, Runa-chan.'

'Oi,' she snapped back. 'Runa-chan me again and I'll floor you. I hate to have to spell this out for you, but I'm a year older than you. Show a little respect, alright?'

Glare as she might with her almond-shaped eyes, though, Yoshio was undeterred. 'Oh, come *on*. You're so cute when you're mad.'

Runa worked as a promotional model at corporate events. She had a beautiful oval face, and, when she got angry, I always found the contrast with her usual smile pretty terrifying. Yoshio was probably the only person insane enough to do what he was doing now, which was to lean in and pinch one of her puffed-up cheeks.

Runa batted away his hand in irritation but showed no sign of leaving our little group. That made sense. My mother and Aunt Haruna were still glaring silently at each other like a pair of statues, Fujitaka was sitting cross-legged on the other sofa and staring off into space like some ascetic in training, and Mai was facing away from us with her headphones on. They were each about as uplifting to look at as a puddle of mud.

Runa seemed to have decided that, no matter how irritating Yoshio was, she was better off staying here and chatting to Emi, me and him.

Though her knee was bouncing away to her music, Mai kept glancing over as if she wanted to join our conversation. But whenever I or someone else tried to catch her gaze, she would immediately turn away again. Her whole body seemed to be sulkily saying, *Sure, leave me out. It's not like I'd say anything interesting.*

Mai wasn't unattractive, by any means, but she lacked Runa's effortless charm, as a result of which she seemed unable to escape a certain feeling of inferiority in relation to her younger sister. This wasn't helped by the fact that everyone else couldn't help comparing her to Runa, and then felt like they had to walk on eggshells around her, which of course only exacerbated the situation.

'By the way,' said Yoshio, abruptly lowering his voice. When Runa leant in to listen, he made to sniff her hair—and immediately had his foot stamped on. The guy had some nerve. 'Where's Uncle Hitoshi, then? Why isn't he coming?'

'I could ask you the same about Uncle Michiya. Where is he?'

'Oh, he's not doing too well right now.'

Yoshio began nonchalantly describing the circumstances that had led to our father being mercilessly demoted and his subsequent descent into a state of more or less complete despair—all as if it were the funniest thing in the world. At least he was speaking quietly enough that my mother and the others wouldn't be able to hear.

'So, yeah,' he concluded, 'he's not in a good way at the moment. Starts blubbering away like a baby at the slightest thing.'

'Wow,' replied Runa. 'What a coincidence.'

'What do you mean?'

'My dad's gone a bit off the rails, too,' said Runa, her tone just as nonchalant as Yoshio's. 'Still, I guess that's what you get for trying it on with a high schooler.'

'Wow. A high schooler?' Yoshio sounded oddly envious. My suspicions were confirmed when he went on: 'Nice. She must have been, what, eighteen? I'm getting excited just thinking about it.'

'The hell are you on about? This is serious. It started with all these rumours among the pupils. Then the PTA got wind of what was going on, and it all kicked off. The board of education even got involved. The headteacher looked terrible for not finding out about it earlier. Which meant *he* lost it completely, which obviously wasn't good for Dad. Dismissal for unprofessional conduct, they called it.'

'You mean he got the sack?'

'Yeah. No severance, either.'

'Ouch. Sounds like a bummer.'

'It's been chaos. That's why Mum's so on edge right now. She reckons our only chance is to persuade Aunt Kotono to adopt me or Mai, so we can take over the company.'

In other words, bizarrely enough, the breadwinners of both the Oba and Kanagae households had managed to lose their jobs at the same time. Sure, in Father's case, he was still technically employed, but for all intents and purposes they had suffered the same fall from grace. This did not bode well. It looked like the feud between Mother and Aunt Kotono, already one of undisguised animosity, was about to grow even fiercer. Something told me we'd struggle to make it through this New Year's gathering without some sort of crisis.

Uncle Hitoshi really had put his foot in it, though. The girl had been in her last year of high school: in other words, the same age as Aunt Haruna when she'd first moved in with him. Was this history repeating itself? By staking her happiness, thirty years ago, on a man like Hitoshi, had Aunt Haruna simply been sowing the seeds of her own eventual downfall?

Just as I was growing pensive, Ryuichi came back into the reception room. 'Everything's ready, if you'd all care to come through.'

We all filed into the banquet hall. I'd heard my grandfather invited all his executives and branch managers here for meetings, and the tatami-matted hall was correspondingly enormous—so enormous, in fact, that it seemed a little ridiculous for the mere ten or so of us.

'Right then, everyone. Happy New Year!'

The bespectacled, middle-aged woman modestly bowing to each of us in turn was the current president of the Edge Group, Aunt Kotono. She looked so utterly serene that it was hard to believe she was even related to my mother—whose brow was so tightly furrowed that I half-expected it to start squeaking—or to Aunt Haruna, who had resorted to her usual supercilious smile, in an attempt to hide her inner turmoil. I suppose we really are products of our environment.

'Ms Fuchigami,' said Emi, arriving with a weighty-looking copper vase she'd wrapped with a ribbon. In it was a bunch of moth orchids. Their round white petals, which reminded me of the flour wrappers used to make gyoza, were lined up in neat rows, as if bowing their heads in our direction. They were one of Aunt Kotono's favourite flowers. 'I'm sorry. I forgot to give you these earlier…'

'Ah, Emi. Moth orchids again? They're beautiful.'

'Shall I take them up to your room for you?'

'Oh, no, there's no need. Just set them down somewhere and I'll take them myself later. Now, could you take a seat, please? Ah, that reminds me. Kyutaro?' I was about to sit down next to Yoshio when Aunt Kotono beckoned me over and handed me an envelope. 'A little something for you.' My otoshidama money, it looked like.

'Lucky Kyutaro! I'm jealous…' said Runa, who had just sat down but now rose again, eyeing me with genuine envy. 'Can I have my otoshidama too, please, Auntie?'

'Me too, please!' came the voice of Yoshio, blindly following Runa's example.

'Oh dear,' said Aunt Kotono, chuckling in amusement. The part of the high-society dame seemed to come to her naturally—to the clear chagrin of my mother and Aunt Haruna. 'You're all in, erm, gainful employment, if I'm not mistaken? A little too old for otoshidama, wouldn't you say?'

'Fujitaka's still a student. And if Kyutaro gets one, then logically speaking shouldn't he, too? And if *he* gets one, then it would be weird for his other younger brother not to—*ouch!*'

Mother interrupted Yoshio's entreaty with a deft slap to the back of the head, then gave me a meaningful smile. 'Kyutaro, say thank you to your auntie properly.'

She seemed to have interpreted Aunt Kotono's decision to single me out for otoshidama money as evidence that we were in her good books. Still, I wished *she* at least would get my name right. After all, she was the one who gave it to me.

'Thank you very much, Aunt Kotono.'

'That's what we like to see,' she replied, 'good old-fashioned politeness. Makes me glad I gave it to you.'

Having apparently concluded that this praise for her son put her in pole position, Mother shot Aunt Haruna a spiteful glare, as if to say: *What do you make of that, then?* Aunt Haruna, never one to back down, gazed back at her with a sarcastic, ennui-laden smile that seemed to reply: *Remember—it's Father who has the final say, not her.* There was such furious energy in the looks they were exchanging that they might have generated some sort of electromagnetic field. Just being around them was exhausting.

Then, just when the fraught atmosphere seemed like it might finally be calming, the shoji screen slid open and in walked my grandfather, Reijiro Fuchigami. The wrinkles etched into his face, like so many knife marks in a block of clay, contributed to a sort of permanent scowl that must have been the product of his many years of toiling away in the kitchen. His round, sunken eyes glowered at the assembled group. When Aunt Kotono called out 'Happy New Year!' we all awkwardly followed suit.

'Before we begin, I have something to say,' he announced in his raspy, high-pitched voice as he lowered himself onto the cushion at the head of the table. A brief silence ensued—one which confused me until I realized that Kiyoko had just entered the room and he was waiting for her to sit down. Grandfather could be oddly particular about such things. Unlike the rest of us, Kiyoko was dressed not in a tracksuit, but her regular maid's smock. Everyone watched her with bated breath. Once she had safely taken her place at the side of the room, Grandfather cleared the phlegm in his throat and abruptly got to the heart of the matter. 'Yes, that's right—it's about my successor.'

4

THE OMINOUS ATMOSPHERE DEEPENS

As had become the yearly tradition, both the Oba and the Kanagae families were to spend the night—the night of the New Year's dinner on the 1st of January, that is—at my grandfather's mansion before returning home the next day.

The mansion was a blend of the Japanese and Western styles. The main building was a modern two-storey structure that had been added at a later date, though it featured Japanese-style rooms such as the tatami-floored banquet hall. My mother and brothers, as well as the Kanagaes, had all been assigned their own rooms within this main building.

Meanwhile, the original house was an old, wooden structure which, perhaps because it was now connected to the main building by a roofed walkway, had an oddly asymmetrical appearance. Its interior consisted of a kitchen and a storage room, and ordinarily no one slept there.

However, it also had a small attic. Six tatami mats in size, with a single naked light bulb dangling from the ceiling, the room was entirely out of keeping with the stately appearance of the mansion as a whole. An exposed beam ran overhead, and the slanted ceiling felt more like a wall pressing in from the side. A tiny window was set into its middle.

It wasn't what you'd call spacious. Depending on your emotional or physical state, it might even have triggered some sort of acute claustrophobia. Still, I liked it. A psychologist would probably have had something to say about the narrowness of the space appealing to my yearning for a return to the womb. In any case, whenever we stayed at the Fuchigami mansion, this was my room.

After retrieving a futon from one of the closets downstairs, I laid it on the floor and immediately curled up on it. The alarm clock I'd also found in the closet told me it was just after eleven o'clock. I'd had quite a bit to drink, and yet sleep was taking a long time to come. If anything, my alcohol-induced queasiness was what was keeping me awake.

Lying there spread-eagled on my back, I reflected on the first day of the year. As I'd half-expected, the dinner had soon taken quite a chaotic turn. This was due to the bombshell of an announcement Grandfather had made concerning who was to be adopted by Kotono and become his heir and successor.

'Before we begin, I have something to say. Yes, that's right— it's about my successor.'

As soon as the words were out of his mouth, a collective gulp seemed to echo around the banquet hall.

'As you all know, Kotono's adoptive heir will automatically take control of the Edge Group. Consequently, it is of the utmost importance that any potential heir is indeed *willing* to do so.'

'My sons are *very* willing!' blurted Mother, apparently deciding to throw herself on Grandfather's mercy right from the off.

'All three of them. Fujitaka's studies aren't going to get in the way of anything, and Yoshio can quit his silly job any time. Kyutaro's keen, too, as long as you don't mind waiting for him to finish university.'

After this, I expected Aunt Haruna to launch into a passionate counter-attack in favour of her own daughters, but she remained silent. The smile playing about her lips could almost be described as insouciant. *Slow and steady wins the race,* she seemed to be mockingly telling my mother.

'Let me finish, would you?' said my grandfather reprovingly, glaring with open disdain at Mother as if to say: *Stop wagging your tail at me like a little dog!* 'I will be consulting the individuals concerned directly. I don't need *you* explaining things to me.'

My mother bit her lip, mortified. She'd jumped the gun, and she knew it. As Aunt Haruna watched her, her airy smile seemed to twitch ever so briefly into a grimace of pure scorn.

Time really does things to a person, I found myself thinking all of a sudden. Whenever I'd heard the story about how Mother, armed only with her academic ability, had managed to escape the Fuchigami home by attending university and bagging herself a young man with a promising future, she'd always come across as the patient and farsighted type. By contrast, Aunt Haruna, who had settled for her class teacher at school—in other words, basically the closest eligible adult to hand—had seemed erratic and impulsive.

Looking at them now, though, they seemed to have swapped roles. Mother's every emotion seemed to get the better of her; her impulse was to try to twist situations to her advantage by sheer force. Meanwhile, Aunt Haruna seemed to have the composure to assess the circumstances carefully before taking action. Of the two of them, it was clear that she had become the real schemer. When exactly had this reversal taken place?

'While we're on the subject,' continued Grandfather, rolling up the sleeves of his brown tracksuit to reveal forearms that were surprisingly fleshy for an eighty-two-year-old—the air in the room *was* getting a little warm—'Kotono has informed me that she feels unable to choose an heir. Consequently, she wishes to hand all responsibility for the decision over to me. Isn't that right, Kotono?'

Aunt Kotono nodded without breaking out of her serene smile. 'Truth be told, I actually asked Father if he wouldn't rather adopt someone himself. I mean, if the point is to establish his successor, then it boils down to the same thing. Anyway, Father—how about we continue the discussion over dinner? It's such a wonderful spread that it seems a shame to sit here just looking at it!'

'True, true. Let's tuck in, then.' When they saw just how meekly my grandfather went along with Aunt Kotono's suggestion, my mother and Aunt Haruna seemed ready to self-combust with jealousy.

'Kyutaro,' he called. At this rate I was going to start thinking that *was* my real name before long.

'Yes, Grandfather?'

'Mind leading us in a toast?'

'Me?'

'You have a certain way with words.'

'Is that so…?'

Quick, do as he says, hissed my mother over the shoulders of Fujitaka and Yoshio. Yoshio, sitting at my side, began enthusiastically slopping beer into my glass. As they say: oh, brother.

'Well, then, with your permission.' I raised my glass. 'To the happiness of the entire family!'

Every inch of the table in front of us was piled with the osechi food that Kiyoko had prepared. She appeared to have gone for a modern take on the traditional New Year's cuisine, and standard dishes like soy-simmered sardines and boiled black soybeans rubbed shoulders with things like Japanese-style meatloaf and smoked salmon. It was a literal smorgasbord of temptation—and yet we were all so apprehensive about Grandfather's next words that our chopsticks remained motionless. Even the happy-go-lucky Yoshio barely touched his food. As if to compensate, everyone began nervously gulping down their drinks.

'As I was saying, Kotono has entrusted me with the task of choosing who she adopts,' said Grandfather, sipping on his sake cup as he surveyed us all once more. 'Kamiji, Haruna— my decision to begin inviting you and your families to these New Year's gatherings was, in part, guided by the need to determine who that might be.'

My mother and Haruna looked up, their eyes practically glowing with excitement. After all their efforts to persuade Grandfather to choose one of their offspring as his successor, here was confirmation that they hadn't simply been beating their heads against a brick wall. The old man really did have one of their children in mind.

'In fact, I've been taking the liberty of naming my successor once a year—without, I must admit, ever asking the individual in question whether they actually wanted the job. Some of you may know this already, but in recent years I've got into the habit of rewriting my will on the 1st of January. Then, on the 2nd, I have my lawyer, Mr Munakata, come and collect it.'

'You mean to say,' broke in Mother—once again unable to control herself; she really wasn't very good at learning from her mistakes—'you've been putting someone's name down every year?'

'Well, yes, that's what I said.'

'Right. And... I don't suppose you'd be able to tell us who exactly they were?'

'Why, what's it to you?'

'It would just be, er, good to know.'

'Fine. The will I'm writing tonight makes my previous choices invalid, so I may as well reveal them. The first year, it was Runa.'

The collective exclamation of disbelief that filled the banquet hall was so loud that for a moment I worried the ceiling might cave in. My mother's piercing squeal of dismay was particularly noticeable.

'The next year, it was Runa again.'

At this point Runa, who had just taken a sip of her sake, sprayed it out again like a spouting whale before making a series of low, spluttering sounds.

'The next year it was Ryuichi.'

Mother and Aunt Haruna let out two shrieks that, combined, sounded a bit like a cat being trampled by an elephant. Mother's expression darkened and contorted, her eyes goggling so much that they seemed in danger of popping right out of their sockets like a pair of ping-pong balls. 'Wh-wh-why? F-f-father, wh-why would you...?'

'Control yourselves, you two,' said Grandfather. 'You look like a couple of monkeys in heat.'

'But why Ryuichi?' asked Mother. 'He doesn't have a drop of Fuchigami blood in his veins!'

'Why do think it's called *adopting* an heir? The whole point is that they don't have to be related.'

'What, so you're just going to skip over Fujitaka and Yoshio and hand the company over to some… *man* we don't know the first thing about?'

'Watch your tongue, child. That's my assistant you're badmouthing.'

'But… but…' Mother squirmed, apparently torn between the risk of angering her father even further and the difficulty of keeping her emotions bottled up a single moment longer. Tears of frustration showed in her eyes. 'This really is too much, Father. Too much to bear. I simply can't…'

'Ryuichi's a capable individual. He'd make a very decent successor. Anyway, didn't you ever wonder why I kept inviting him and Emi to these gatherings?'

'Emi? Wait… *she's* in the running too?'

At first Mother simply stared disbelievingly at Ryuichi and Emi, but before long she was fixing them with a murderous glare. Ryuichi appeared to be the particular focus of her wrath, presumably because of the excessive otoshidama money she'd given him earlier. She'd hoped that bestowing a lavish gift like that on Grandfather's assistant would somehow give her the edge in the ongoing battle for his affection—and now it turned out that assistant was one of her rivals. 'Ryuichi… but you… I don't believe it…'

Ryuichi, uncertain how to respond, was glancing between Grandfather and my mother. His expression seemed to imply that this was not the first he'd heard about being a potential successor to the Edge Restaurant Group.

'So it was Runa for the first two years and then Ryuichi?'

Aunt Haruna seemed to have recovered from the shock more quickly than my mother and had resumed her confident, sarcastic smile, as if to say that this was all rather tedious but she'd at least hear Grandfather out. 'Who came after that, then?'

'After that? Fujitaka. Then last year it was Emi.'

'Father, can I ask something?' Mother suddenly seemed a lot calmer, as if relieved that Grandfather had finally mentioned at least one of her son's names. 'What are the, er, criteria for these choices?'

'Isn't it obvious? I pick whoever I liked best that year.'

'So, when it was Runa two years in a row, that was just because you... liked her?' Mother seemed to be trying to ascertain how, exactly, Runa had managed to get herself into Grandfather's good books five years ago. 'What was it about her that you, er, liked so much?'

'Shouldn't you be asking what it was about *Fujitaka* that I liked?' said Grandfather, sighing as he directed an ominous glare at my mumbling mother. 'Anyway, let me be clear: there *are* no criteria. It simply depends how I'm feeling.'

For some reason, my grandfather chose this moment to let out a peculiar and somewhat deranged-sounding peal of laughter. He seemed half drunk with power; his control over the situation was absolute.

'That's right! How I'm feeling. What, think I'm being ridiculous? Well, let me tell you: I *am* being ridiculous. Deciding a thing like this on a whim—why, it's absurd. And I intend to be as absurd as I please. Got anything to say about that, eh? *A-ha-ha-ha!*'

While we all sat there flabbergasted, Grandfather abruptly resumed a serious expression, sipped on his sake, and tucked into his food. As though worried that we'd lack the strength to keep up if we just kept swigging down our drinks, we all followed his lead and began munching away in silence.

'Now,' he went on. 'I'll be writing a new will this year, too. And, Kamiji, before you have another one of your outbursts, let me be very clear: I still have no idea who I'll pick. I'm writing the will tonight, you hear—tonight! Which brings me to what I really wanted to tell you all: this will be the last time I do this. Yes, you heard me. I won't be rewriting the will in future years. Consequently, whoever I pick tonight will be my final choice.'

Mother and Aunt Haruna were glancing surreptitiously at each other. It was clear from their faces that they had each concluded that the winner of their little contest would be whoever managed to most endear themselves to Grandfather before he sat down to write his will later that night.

'Now, as I was saying earlier, I can't decide on my successor until I know whether the individual in question is actually *willing*. After all, this is my final decision. It's no good me choosing someone if they don't even want to run a restaurant chain. Fujitaka, you're up first.'

Fujitaka looked up, bewildered. He clearly hadn't expected to be put on the spot like this. 'Sorry?'

'Well? Are you willing to become Kotono's heir and my successor?'

'Erm—yes!' yelped Fujitaka. I glanced over and saw that Mother had just pinched him on the back. 'I mean, in theory!'

'Right. Yoshio?'

'Leave it to me, Grandfather,' replied Yoshio with a confident chuckle. 'I'll raise the company to even greater heights. Never mind Japan—I'll set our sights on the entire globe! I'm a hell of a—sorry, er, a very capable—businessman.'

'I see. Kyutaro?'

I was about to politely turn down the offer when I became aware of the terrifying look Mother was giving me over Fujitaka and Yoshio's shoulders. If I dropped out of the running now, there was no telling what sort of abuse she'd heap on me later. And so, out of concern for my own mental wellbeing, I found myself embarking on the kind of weaselly response you might expect from some second-rate politician.

'Well, erm, provided it were not, so to speak, a solo endeavour, but rather something undertaken with the cooperation of all those present, I would certainly not be averse to the possibility of devoting myself in some capacity to the task at hand, this being merely my current position with regards to—'

'I have literally no idea what you're talking about,' said Grandfather. 'Are you interested or not?'

'It is certainly my position that I would not be uninterested.'

'Right, got it.' I wasn't sure he had. 'Next, Mai.'

'If Aunt Kotono adopted me as her daughter,' said Mai, sulkily twirling her hair without even looking at Grandfather, 'would that mean she gets to pick my husband?'

'Oh, goodness, no,' said Aunt Kotono—initially startled, then inexplicably giggling. 'What, you think I'd trap you in some marriage of convenience? Heavens, this isn't one of your manga stories, Mai! You can marry whoever you please.'

'Indeed, indeed,' said Grandfather. 'Though, of course, it'd be helpful if you chose someone with a head for business. Like... I don't know... Ryuichi. Now, Runa.'

'Sure, I'd give it a shot,' said Runa simply. '"Chairwoman" has a nice ring to it. I'd be, like, the ultimate career girl.'

'*Career girl?*' replied Grandfather. 'I thought nobody said that any more.'

'Sorry, yeah, don't know where I got that from. Kyutaro, probably.'

'And now for Emi.'

'I'm sorry, Mr Chairman, but I really must decline,' replied Emi without the slightest hesitation. She almost sounded like she was admonishing my grandfather. 'I know the tendency these days is not to get too hung up on bloodlines and such, but I really do feel your successor should be one of your grandchildren.'

'Hear, hear!' put in my mother, as if this were the perfect moment for another interruption. It really wasn't. She seemed to be physically incapable of remaining silent. 'Father, if you don't mind, I think it's a little naive to assume that some *outsider* would make a good successor just because you know them to be capable. After all, there's no telling who they might end up marrying! They could end up bringing some other outsider into the family. Barging in like they own the place. And I'd be especially wary of young women these days. They're hopeless when it comes to judging a potential partner—all they care about is what happens in the bedroom, without a thought for what comes after! Before you know it, they've fallen under the sway of some smooth-talking yakuza scumbag. After all your efforts to make the Fuchigami family into the precious institution it is today, do you really want two degenerates taking over? Put a pair of sex-crazed good-for-nothings like that in control and this family will go to the dogs, you can be sure of it. And by then it'll be too late for anyone to do anything about it!'

Just then, I happened to look at Emi—at the precise moment when her usual neutral expression yielded, very briefly, to something else entirely. A word like 'hostility' wouldn't quite do it justice. She seemed to be literally seething with rage at this insinuation that she was some sort of cerebrally challenged nymphomaniac. Her large round eyes grew even larger and rounder as she glared at my mother—who must have noticed the laser-beam of fury being focused in her direction, because she gulped and fell silent.

'Mr Chairman.' All of a sudden, there was no sign of the anger that, just a moment ago, had silenced even my mother. Emi had resumed her neutral, impenetrable expression—but the intention behind what she said next was crystal clear. 'Sorry, but I've changed my mind. Now that I think about it, it *would* be a little old-fashioned to insist on bloodlines and so on, wouldn't it? If you think I have what it takes, then I'd be honoured to be included in your list of candidates.'

'Very well,' said my grandfather with evident satisfaction, before shooting a derisive glance at my mother, whose arms were now trembling uncontrollably. 'As for Ryuichi, I've already confirmed that he would be willing to take on the role.'

Ryuichi appeared unfazed by the black look my mother turned on him. In fact, he was staring back with something approaching defiance, as if to say: *You can glower at me all you like—I'm not giving you back your little present.* I'd always thought of him as the mild, good-natured type and nothing more, but the fact that he had earned my grandfather's confidence suggested that there was more to him than met the eye.

'Right. Looks like you're all willing, then. No objections? Good. In that case, I'll write my final will tonight and have Mr Munakata collect it tomorrow, for his safekeeping until my death.'

'In other words,' broke in Aunt Haruna, in a displeased tone that contrasted oddly with the smile still plastered on her face, 'we'll have no way of finding out who you've officially chosen until you pass away?'

'Of course not. I can't have you finding out early. I mean, what would be the fun in that?' Grandfather let out another shrill cackle, this time reminiscent of a chicken having its neck wrung. 'Anticipation is half the pleasure in life, Haruna. Oh, and whoever I choose, no hard feelings among the rest of you, alright?'

'Sorry, can I just ask something?' piped up Fujitaka, his expression serious for once. My mother's enthusiasm seemed to be rubbing off on him. 'Just a hypothetical question, obviously. If, after your death, your heir were to die in an accident or something, what would happen then?'

'That would be up to Kotono. Once I'm out of the picture, all such decisions will lie with her.'

'What if she dies, too? Who gets to decide then?'

For a New Year's dinner, Fujitaka wasn't choosing the most auspicious of conversation topics. Still, the situation he was describing wasn't outside the realm of possibility.

'In that case, there'll be nothing for it: the Fuchigami family will be deemed to have died out. The fate of my company and the estate will be decided by my lawyer and the top executives. If Kotono dies with no heir, Kiyoko will receive a certain portion of the estate, and the rest will probably be donated to charity.

As for the company, the executives will proceed as they see fit. Meaning, of course, that the company would pass out of the hands of the Fuchigami family entirely.'

There was another hair-raising wail of despair from Mother and Aunt Haruna.

'Erm,' said Mother. 'Father, I'm sorry to be so direct. But about the, erm... the distribution of the estate. You don't mean to say that—'

'If Kotono's alive, she gets two-fifths. Her adopted child gets another two-fifths, and the remaining fifth goes to Kiyoko. That part of the will is the same every year.'

Kiyoko was smoothing a loose strand of her grey hair, a composed look on her face. Clearly this wasn't the first she'd heard of this—though Mother was in no state to notice.

'W-what if both Kotono and Kiyoko are dead?'

'I just told you. It all goes to charity. Pay attention, child!'

'B-b-but... hang on a moment, Father. W-w-what about... us? You can't... possibly...'

'I can't what? You and Haruna both married out of the family, remember.'

'But we're your daughters! Your own flesh and blood! And you're not leaving us a single yen? Nothing—not even for your own grandchildren? Father, *why*?'

'Your memory of the past few decades seems a little hazy.' Grandfather gave an unsettling, dry chuckle, though his eyes weren't smiling. 'So let me refresh it for you. You two both ran off and married someone without my permission, and then you didn't invite me to the wedding or even notify me by letter of the birth of my own grandchildren. Well, fine. That was your choice, and I took it to mean that you'd each stand on your own feet from now on—and that when the time came, you'd be happy to be buried at the Oba family grave, or the Kanagae family grave. Good for you. An impressive display of resolve. You'd severed all ties with the Fuchigami family. And no one forced you into it, either. You both did so of your own free will, and what a fine thing that is. But tell me, where's that resolve of yours now, eh?'

An abrupt silence fell over the banquet hall. Grandfather still hadn't forgiven my mother and Aunt Haruna: this fact began to press down on the shoulders of everyone present like a millstone. The pair had abandoned him when he was still reeling from the loss of his wife, leaving him and Aunt Kotono to fend for themselves—and he hadn't forgotten.

Of course, Mother and Aunt Haruna had had their reasons for doing so. They hadn't abandoned their family simply because they felt like it. Surely, they might have argued, the blame lay with the man who, instead of showing an ounce of fatherly responsibility, spent most of his time gambling and the rest of it tyrannizing his family? But they appeared to have lost the will even to mount such a defence. The anger in Mother's eyes had given way to a sort of dazed expression, and even Aunt Haruna seemed incapable of adopting her usual nonchalant and knowing smile. The sheer force of Grandfather's grudge seemed to have left them completely paralysed.

At the same time, it was possible that the *real* grudge was Aunt Kotono's. She was the only one among us who was still smiling, as she had been from the start. In all fairness, there wasn't a trace of malice in her expression. But maybe her smile was like the pellucid surface of a lake which only appears that way because there's so much filth settled at its bottom.

71

After all, Aunt Kotono must have felt nothing but bitterness towards her sisters. Their abrupt departure had cast her into an abyss of despair and near-insanity. It was possible that my grandfather was simply the mirror by which that grudge was being reflected.

At least now the gravity of the situation was clear to Mother and Aunt Haruna. If the will Grandfather wrote tonight did not specify one of their children as his successor, not a single yen of the Fuchigami fortune would find its way into their hands. With their respective breadwinners on the ropes and their financial situation looking increasingly shaky, that was a result they wanted to avoid at all costs.

But what should they actually *do*? The question was written so clearly on both their faces that it was almost comical. What would win them Grandfather's favour? How could they get one of their own children to the top of his list?

As if guided by some magnetic force, the eyes of the covetous sisters landed on Runa. Grandfather had picked her as his favourite two years in a row, after all. What had she done, at the New Year's gatherings of four and five years ago, to get herself in his good books? Eager to know the answer, they were openly gawping at her.

Noticing their attention, Runa gave a snort of displeasure. 'Can I just make one thing clear? The times when Grandfather chose me, I didn't do anything special to win his affection. Isn't that right, Grandfather? You didn't choose me as your successor because I was particularly helpful or anything, did you?'

'She's right,' said Grandfather, 'I didn't. Whether or not someone manages to get on my good side is irrelevant. In fact,

72

they can annoy the hell out of me and they still might end up being the one I choose.'

Mother looked at him for a moment, as if she wanted to ask: *Well then, what on earth* are *you basing your decision on?* Eventually, though, she simply sought refuge in her sake cup, recklessly draining its contents. Aunt Haruna also seemed to have concluded that at this point her fate was out of her hands and, with a woeful grimace, began guzzling her own drink with similar abandon. Ironically enough, this meant that the atmosphere at the dinner finally began to liven up. And that I ended up drinking—or being made to drink—far more than usual.

I must have fallen asleep while ruminating on the evening's events. I awoke to see pale sunlight streaming through the window. The alarm clock told me it was just after eight o'clock in the morning.

Starting the second day of the year with a hangover wasn't ideal, but at least I was in no rush to get up. We were heading home that day, but normally we only set off in the evening. Before returning to my slumber, I decided to visit the bathroom downstairs.

I made my way down the stairs that led from the landing outside the attic room. The steps were so steep that when you climbed up them your nose practically brushed against them, and when you descended them you had to lean backwards to avoid losing your balance.

To get to the toilet, I had to turn right at the bottom of the long, steep staircase and pass through the storage room. As I was about to do so, I heard voices from the kitchen on my left. It seemed someone was visiting the old house at this early hour.

'I couldn't find the red origami paper,' came the grumbling voice of my grandfather. Peering into the kitchen from the corridor, I saw that he was talking to Aunt Kotono and Kiyoko. 'I don't know why. I'm sure it was there before. It's the only colour that was missing.'

'Then, what did you do?' asked Aunt Kotono, putting a hand to one cheek as if to express her dismay. 'Last night, I mean.'

'I didn't do anything. I mean, I didn't make them. I'll do it tonight instead.' He turned to Kiyoko. 'Sorry, but could you nip out and buy some new origami paper? From that stationery shop around the corner.'

'But, Sir,' began Kiyoko apologetically, 'all the shops will be closed for the first three days of the year.'

'Ah. So they will.'

'What about using a different colour?'

'No, never mind. I'll just have to do it another day.'

As I snuck off to the toilet, I couldn't shake the feeling that I'd just overheard something I shouldn't have. For one thing, I'd had no idea my formidable grandfather had a passion for origami, of all things. Whatever floated his boat, I told myself. If he wanted to spend his nights excitedly folding pieces of paper, then who was I to stop him? Still, something about the way he'd been fussing over that red paper had come across as, well, slightly unhinged.

Back in the attic, I curled up under my futon cover and, shielding my eyes from the morning sun, slept until almost noon.

When I awoke, I went downstairs. The old house was deserted. As I was ambling along the walkway that led to the main building, I bumped into Emi. Of course, we were both wearing the same tracksuit and chanchanko as the day before.

'Good morning,' I said, bowing deeply as I recalled the rather shameful developments of the previous evening. 'I'm very sorry for the way my mother behaved yesterday. Please forgive us.'

Having meant to pass me with a polite nod, Emi was now obliged to stop short. 'Not at all,' she replied, looking troubled. 'I acted rather childishly myself. Telling the Chairman I'd do it, after all, just because I was a little worked up—how ridiculous!' She sighed and finally allowed herself a smile. 'Still, I can't take it back now.'

'Indeed. Grandfather said he was going to write the will last night, didn't he?'

'If he chose me last year, I doubt he'll do the same this year. Still, it does make me nervous.'

'I imagine. And he did choose Runa twice in a row, after all.'

'Oh dear.' For once, Emi looked genuinely worried. The usual neutral mask had given way to a wince of despair. Rearranged in this way, her features were strangely beautiful. 'I wonder what I'll do if he *does* choose me.'

'It's a one-in-seven chance. I don't think you need to worry yourself too much about it.'

'Yes, but what bothers me is that we won't know until the Chairman passes away. I feel like I'd rather die first myself!'

'Being adopted by my aunt is that off-putting, is it? Ah— sorry. I'm sure you have your reasons.'

'Well, for one thing, wouldn't you be upset if your grandfather chose me over you as his successor?'

'Not at all. Actually, I wanted to decline his offer yesterday. I only agreed to it because my mother was glaring at me like that. If anything, I'd be grateful if you took the job instead.'

'Are you joking? If I did, your mother might actually kill me.'

'Alright then, how about this?' There was something so stirring about the worried look on Emi's face that I found myself saying something I really hadn't anticipated. 'If he does pick you, then you'll just have to marry me. That should quell any murderous intentions of my mother's.'

'Oh, I'm sure that's exactly what your mother has in mind. Yes, if the successor is a woman, she'll waste no time in trying to marry her sons off to her.'

'I'm not talking about my mother's games, Emi.' I found myself getting oddly worked up. Maybe I was just hurt by the way she seemed to be twisting my words. 'This is personal.'

A distant look came over Emi, as if she were carefully considering what to say. 'You know, if this were anyone else, I'd tell them to stop messing around. But coming from you, it really doesn't sound like you're joking.'

'Well, of course it doesn't, because I'm not.'

'And if I'm not chosen as the heir? What happens to this idea of yours then?'

'Nothing. Because I'm in love with you.'

Emi looked as though she didn't know whether to burst out laughing or frown. '…Thank you. You know, I like a gentleman. A nice, straight-talking gentleman. In other words, someone like you, Kyutaro. But marriage is quite another matter. Do you mind if I have a little think about it?'

'Certainly. Oh, and while you're at it, do you think you could call me Hisataro?'

'Hisataro?'

'That's how my name's supposed to be pronounced.'

Emi covered her mouth in surprise. 'I am *so* sorry. I've always—'

'My family have insisted on "Kyutaro" for so long that even they seem to have forgotten it's not my real name. It's only natural for you not to have known.'

'Right. Well, Hisataro… I'll have a good think about what you said. See you later.'

I felt slightly brushed aside, but that was only to be expected. Emi was hardly going to pay much notice to the ramblings of some high schooler. At the same time, she couldn't afford to be too brutal with a member of her boss's family. It had probably been a struggle for her just to extract herself safely from the conversation.

Once she'd gone on her way, I made my way to the dining room in the main building. Its adjoining kitchen was much larger and better fitted than the one in the old house. This was where my grandfather and Aunt Kotono normally ate.

There was no one else in the dining room. Two meals were still set out on the table: one at the head of the table, and one at the end where I usually sat. The others must have already eaten. When we stayed at the Fuchigami mansion, our meals were generally a casual affair, and we each had to wash our own dishes. This was for the very sensible reason that, with us all getting up at different times, Kiyoko could hardly be expected to do the washing up after each of us. I looked at the clock and saw that it was a few minutes after noon.

I was sitting there shovelling down a bowl of cold rice in silence when my grandfather walked in. Needless to say, he was wearing his brown tracksuit.

77

'Oh. Eating on your own, eh?'

'Have you not eaten yet, either, Grandfather?'

'No. I only just got up.' This puzzled me, as I'd seen him in the old house at around eight o'clock that morning. He must have gone back to bed after that conversation with Aunt Kotono and Kiyoko. 'Anyway, I'm just grateful to have a bit of peace and quiet while I eat.'

'I guess it's all been quite hectic.'

'Hectic isn't the word.'

'Has Mother started behaving herself yet?'

'She still hasn't given up. Last night she kept pestering me. Asking me over and over who I was going to pick as my successor.'

'I'm sorry.'

'It's not *your* fault. It's funny, though: Kamiji's running around like a headless chicken, but Haruna has been oddly calm about the whole thing.'

I thought the reason for this was obvious. Mother's only route to victory was for me or one of my brothers to be made heir, while Aunt Haruna could always resort to other tactics. For example, if Grandfather did choose one of us over Runa or Mai, she could always just marry one of her daughters into our family. My mother might oppose the match, but Aunt Haruna could easily force the matter by getting her daughter to seduce the successor and establish their relationship as a fact. The same tactic would probably work on Ryuichi, if he were chosen. In other words, for Aunt Haruna, the only really disastrous outcome would be if Grandfather chose Emi. Of course, if he *did* choose a woman, Mother could always (as Emi had so eloquently pointed out a moment ago) try to marry off

78

one of her sons to the heir, but the chances of that working seemed a lot lower. Between gloomy Fujitaka, frivolous Yoshio and underaged me, we weren't exactly the most appealing trio of potential suitors.

Grandfather had barely touched his food when he produced a large bottle of sake from somewhere and plonked it down on the table. 'I need a stiff drink. How about it, Kyutaro—fancy joining me?'

'I'm very flattered, but I don't think I should.'

'Oh, come on…'

'Grandfather, I'm sure you know this already, but I'm still in high school.'

'Don't be such a killjoy. It's the New Year. Ah, that reminds me…'

'Yes?'

'Kotono tells me you're staying in the attic. In the old house.'

'That's right.'

'We can drink there, then.'

'Erm, why would we do that?'

'Because if we stay here, there's no telling when Kotono or Kiyoko might show up.' Grandfather scrabbled around, gathering various snacks to go with the sake, then urged me to my feet. 'See, after my little tumble, they've been on my case about the drinking.'

Grandfather dropped his voice as we entered the corridor. I followed suit, speaking in a whisper.

'Your… little tumble? What happened?'

'Well, everything went all dark for a moment,' replied Grandfather, checking nobody was around as he led me in the direction of the old house. 'And then I just sort of toppled over. Apparently I was out for a few minutes.'

'Were you… okay?'

'Of course I was. Must have been a little tired, is all. Kotono kicked up a huge fuss about it, mind. All this nonsense about how my symptoms seemed similar to someone she knew who collapsed from a subarachnoid something-or-other. Kept telling me to go and see a neurologist. She's unbearable, really.'

Just then, something darted past the corner of my vision. A yellow afterimage lingered on my retina. Someone's tracksuit, maybe? When I turned to look, the corridor was empty.

'Still,' I said, gathering myself, 'are you really sure you should be drinking?'

'Shush, you're beginning to sound just like Kotono. I'll be fine.'

When we reached the attic, Grandfather planted himself on the futon I'd left out, filled one of the ceramic cups he'd brought, and began glugging down the sake.

'You know, this stuff is like fuel to me. My body wouldn't know what to do without it. Come on, drink up.'

When I reluctantly did as he said, I found that the cold sake trickled down my throat with alarming ease. Suddenly convinced I was less of a lightweight than I'd thought, I began trying to keep up with the old man—little knowing how much I would come to regret it.

'Brings back memories, this room,' said Grandfather.

'It does?'

'Before we built the main building we used to live in this old house. You know, back when we weren't quite as well off. We were happy just to have a house of our own, though. It was the sort of life I could never have dreamt of back in the day, when it seemed like throwing myself in the ocean might be the only solution. And back then, this is where I slept every night.'

'Grandfather, I had no idea. I've been sleeping here every time we come to stay, without ever realizing how important it is to you…'

'Don't be silly. You know, you have a habit of reading too much into things. It's odd in someone your age. You don't take after Kamiji, that's for sure. Not one bit. If she had only half your sensitivity…'

'Grandfather…' The fact that the mere mention of my mother had reminded me of Grandfather's will was, in a way, symbolic. 'Should you really be sitting up here like this? Didn't you say your lawyer was coming today?'

'Ah yes. Mr Munakata. He arrived earlier.'

'He's already here?'

'Yes. Got here just after I woke up. I meant to contact him last night and tell him not to bother, but it slipped my mind completely. Never mind. Anyway, I didn't want to send him home empty-handed, so I've asked him to look through some other paperwork for me this afternoon.'

'Sorry, I'm not sure I follow. What about the, erm, will? Weren't you going to write it last night?'

'Yes, but I didn't.'

'You… didn't write it?'

'I couldn't quite decide who to make my successor. So—no will.'

'Oh. And that's… okay, is it?'

'Of course it's okay. I've instructed Mr Munakata not to dispose of the old will until I've handed him the new one. I

81

told him I don't feel like writing it today, either, and I'll let him know when I have.'

Grandfather was in a merry mood. Was he just happy to be drinking, away from Aunt Kotono and Kiyoko's prying eyes? A look of mischievous delight had stolen across his features, as if he couldn't believe what a wonderful hiding place we'd stumbled upon.

I got up to go to the bathroom. Just as I reached the door, I heard a faint sound, like the distant crash of thunder. Later, it struck me that this had probably been the sound of someone rushing down the stairs. But when I opened the door and looked down them, I saw no one.

When I returned to the attic, I remembered what Grandfather had been saying about not having written the will yet, and decided this might be a good opportunity to make my request.

'So when *are* you going to write the will, then?'

'Hmm. Tomorrow, maybe the day after. Why?'

'I'd like to be removed from consideration, please.'

'You mean you don't want Kotono to adopt you?'

'That's right.'

'Why? You don't fancy becoming my successor?'

'It's just that, if I did, I'm sure I'd only end up squandering everything you and Aunt Kotono have so carefully built together. I don't really have the brains for business, Grandfather.'

'Listen, if that happens, it happens. Nothing lasts forever, Kyutaro. One day, Edge will go belly-up. It's simply a matter of when.'

'You think so?'

'Of course. In a hundred years' time, pretty much every business around will be toast.'

'Emi wants to drop out of the running, too. She told me earlier. She only put herself forward because Mother got under her skin like that.'

'Oh, come on, Kyutaro, enough of that. Just because someone's in the running doesn't mean I'll pick them. You should loosen up a little.'

It seemed Grandfather had no intention of removing either Emi or me from consideration. Instead, as if to distract me, he just kept pouring out the sake. Before I knew it, I'd drunk far more than I should have.

At some point, I must have passed out. When I came to, I was lying on top of the futon. The attic was gloomy, with only the last vestiges of daylight coming through the window. No sign of my grandfather, either. Just the empty bottle of sake lying on the floor.

All of a sudden, I had the horrible sensation that something was crawling in my chest. I rushed to the toilet, where I vomited until it felt as though I'd evacuated not only the contents of my stomach but also most of my internal organs.

Strangely, though, the vomiting only made me feel worse. Lacking the energy to climb back up to the attic, I went and collapsed on a chair in the kitchen. Just as I was feeling so dizzy that the objects in the room were losing their outlines, in walked Yoshio. He had changed out of his tracksuit and back into his regular clothes. *Hey, what are you doing? We're leaving,* I heard him say. Was it that time already? I tried to get up, struggling against the weakness in my knees, then managed to trip over my own feet. *What are you...? Hey, you stink of booze. You been at it again?*

Grinning, he held out one of the baskets from the annex. It had my clothes in it. He must have brought it here just for me. After a lengthy battle with my clothes, I managed to get changed and stagger out to the car, Yoshio lending me a shoulder in support.

At the entrance to the main building we passed an unfamiliar middle-aged man in a grey suit. He was busy with the shoehorn and appeared to be on the point of leaving himself. Just as it dawned on me that this must be Grandfather's lawyer, Kiyoko arrived to see him out. *Mr Munakata, thank you very much for coming.* It seemed he'd been busy until this late hour with that paperwork Grandfather had mentioned. Quite the industrious start to the new year, then. Was the look of irritation on his face his default expression, I wondered vaguely, or was he angry that instead of being entrusted with the will as agreed, he'd spent the day trawling through a pile of unrelated documents?

I stood there in a daze and watched him drive off. Then Yoshio bundled me into the back of his car, where I found Mother waiting. She was scowling, probably because she could smell the alcohol on me. Fujitaka was in the passenger seat. The last thing I remembered clearly was Yoshio climbing in on the driver's side.

I couldn't even tell you how long it took us to drive off. Before I knew it, my entire body had been sucked into the swamp-like depths of a profound sleep.

5

THE MURDER HAPPENS

I remembered waking up once in the night. I didn't know what time exactly, but it was pitch-dark. My throat was parched. I got up briefly from my futon with the idea of drinking some water, before being overcome by sleepiness again. In the end I felt myself sliding back under the covers and back into sleep.

Then I woke up properly. Pale sunlight was streaming through the small window. My alarm clock told me it was just after eight o'clock in the morning. I was in the attic of the old house at the Fuchigami residence. At first, nothing about this struck me as odd.

It was only when I was halfway down the stairs to the toilet that I finally thought: *Hang on. What day is it?* It should have been the 3rd of January. Making yesterday the 2nd. And on the evening of the 2nd, I had gone home with my family. Hadn't I? Yes, now it was coming back to me. Yoshio bundling me into the car. I'd fallen asleep after that and had no recollection of us arriving home. But the 2nd of January had, I felt certain, come to an end.

That being the case, I should have woken up not at the Fuchigami residence, but at my family home. And yet here I was, back in the old house. Not only that, but instead of the normal clothes I'd changed into when we were leaving, I was back in the red tracksuit. Which could only mean one thing…

'I couldn't find the red origami paper.' As I'd begun to half-expect by the time I arrived at the bottom of the stairs, I heard my grandfather's voice coming from the kitchen. 'I don't know why. I'm sure it was there before. It's the only colour that was missing.'

'Then, what did you do?' This, of course, was Aunt Kotono. Even the way she was standing, hand on cheek and head cocked to the side, was the same as yesterday—or should I say, the original loop. 'Last night, I mean.'

'I didn't do anything. I mean, I didn't make them. I'll do it tonight instead.' It was like rewatching a TV programme I'd taped. Wait, didn't he look at Kiyoko at this point? Ah, there we go. He was looking at Kiyoko. 'Sorry, but could you nip out and buy some new origami paper? From that stationery shop around the corner.'

'But, Sir, all the shops will be closed for the first three days of the year.'

'Ah. So they will.'

'What about using a different colour?'

'No, never mind. I'll just have to do it another day.'

I slipped back up to the attic. There was no doubting it: my 'condition' had activated, and I had fallen into the Trap. Including the current loop, the 2nd of January was about to repeat itself eight times.

It didn't take me long to realize what was likely to happen next. If I went back to sleep now, then went to the dining room in the main building at around noon, I'd bump into

Grandfather again and end up having to keep him company while he drank himself silly.

Anything but that, I thought, as the memory of my copious vomiting in the previous loop came bleakly back to me. It was an ordeal I'd rather be spared in the remaining eight versions of the day.

So, what to do? I had two choices. I could hide here until the evening, when Yoshio would come and find me. But that would mean spending the whole day on an empty stomach. If I wanted to avoid that, I would have to get up for breakfast now, instead of going back to sleep.

After thinking it over, I decided to get up. I waited until nine o'clock, then left the attic. By that time there was no one in the kitchen downstairs. I went out to the walkway that led to the main building.

In the original loop, this had been where I had bumped into Emi. But that had been at around noon. Her appearance on the walkway had been 'established' as an event that took place at that time. So, at this time of the day, I met neither her nor anyone else on my way to the main building.

I felt a slight pang of disappointment. If I repeated my present course of action in the remaining seven loops, that conversation I'd had with Emi would ultimately be deemed never to have happened. The exchange would be wiped entirely from her memory. Not that the disappearance of a conversation that trivial from the annals of history would make much difference in the wider scheme of things, but still, it felt like a shame. After all, I'd been telling the truth when I confessed my feelings to her. No matter how inconsequential the exchange might have been—and even though Emi would probably have soon forgotten all about it, even without the Trap's assistance—it would be a memory that I, at least, would treasure.

Still, I wasn't sure I wanted to endure another round of drinking and vomiting. I did wonder if there wasn't some way of recreating only the meeting with Emi, and not the part where I bumped into Grandfather, but experience had shown me that the Trap usually attempted to replicate the original loop as faithfully as possible. It was as though there was some sort of guiding force that sought to prevent the permutations that took place within each loop from ever straying too far from the 'original' version. If I really didn't want Grandfather to catch me, the most reliable strategy would be to stay away from the main building at around noon. It would be all well and good retreating to the old house after I'd finished the conversation with Emi, but on the off chance that Grandfather still found me, I'd be certain to end up being forced into drinking with him, just like in the original loop. No, the thing to do was to play it safe. And unfortunately that meant sacrificing the pleasure of my brief conversation with Emi entirely.

I decided to go to the main building and eat the breakfast that was waiting in the dining room. Even though I knew he wouldn't be here for a few hours, I couldn't quite shake the feeling that my grandfather was going to appear at any moment. I bolted down my food and made my way back out of the dining room. Phew. Now all I had to do was avoid the main building until evening.

But what was I going to do until then? My attic would be the perfect spot for catching some shuteye, but it might get a little stifling if I spent the whole day there. In any case, there was no guaranteeing that Grandfather wouldn't appear in the old house at some point. According to the timetable established in the original loop, he would be back in bed now, after briefly rising earlier. Then, at around noon, he would speak to Mr Munakata, his lawyer who was visiting for the day, before going down to the dining room, which he'd find empty—unlike in the original loop, when I'd been sitting there. It was all too possible that, dismayed by the prospect of eating alone, he might then make his way to the old house in search of company. The very fact that he'd made me join him in the original loop was evidence that he saw me as someone he could talk freely to. If I holed up in the attic and then Grandfather came looking for me, I'd have nowhere to run.

At the same time, if I stayed in the banquet hall or the library, the chances of Grandfather finding me would be even higher. What I really wanted was to avoid bumping into him all day. If I did, he would inevitably force me into a drinking session, as he had in the original loop.

Having considered my options, I went out into the courtyard and from there into the annex. This was the small building we had used as a changing room to get into our tracksuits. It had originally been built to serve as guest accommodation, making it the perfect location for a nap. I opened the door and peeked inside. The tatami-floored room was deserted.

Grinning to myself with glee, I opened the closet, meaning to retrieve one of the futon sets from inside. Just then, I glimpsed someone in the courtyard. They were coming towards the annex. Fearing it might be Grandfather, I panicked and dived into the closet. I had only just pulled the sliding door closed when I heard the door to the annex open.

Sitting there in the darkness with my cheek pushed up against the futon, scarcely daring to breathe, I heard voices. A man and a woman. The man's voice was too young for Grandfather, which was a relief, but at this point it was too late for me to emerge from the closet. Instead, I silently slid its door open a crack and peeped into the room.

'Not here,' came a coquettish voice. Runa. 'What if someone walks in?'

'What, at this time in the morning? No chance.' My jaw dropped as I recognized the man's voice. It was Fujitaka.

'No, we shouldn't. Not here.'

It was beginning to feel a little stuffy in the closet. I couldn't see much through the crack in the door, but it was pretty clear what sort of situation was unfolding. For all her protests, Runa didn't sound entirely displeased. There was a lot of fumbling and gasping and heavy breathing. As I say, I couldn't see exactly what was going on, but the closet was practically reverberating with the comically sloppy smacking of lips.

'Seriously, we shouldn't. Not here. Not… here!'

'Oh, come on…'

'No. That's all you're getting for now. Anyway, that's not what we came in here for. We came in here to talk!'

I heard Fujitaka tut in response.

'Don't sulk,' continued Runa. 'There's a public holiday coming up—I'll come round to your apartment then. Bet you've got loads of laundry lying around.'

'Well, alright then. But tell me, what was all that with Yoshio? He was acting pretty chummy with you.'

'Ooh, is someone jealous?'

'Why wouldn't I be? The guy's a smooth talker.'

'Well, I don't like smooth talkers.' I heard what sounded like an enormous suction cup being removed with great effort from a tiled surface. Another kiss. 'Now, pull your trousers up. There's a good boy.'

'Alright, alright. Hey…'

'Hm?'

'I was wondering why I couldn't hear them. Where are your…?'

'What? Oh. I lost one somewhere, so I thought I'd go without the other one, too.' Being unable to see the pair clearly, I had no idea what they were talking about. 'Anyway. We have more important things to discuss.'

'What do you mean?' replied Fujitaka. 'What could be more important'—Runa giggled naughtily as if in response to his touch—'than this?'

'Isn't it obvious? I'm talking about Grandfather's will. The future of the company.'

'But… hasn't that ship already sailed?' Fujitaka's manner had abruptly switched from one of mischievous glee to a sort of bored grouchiness. I hate to say it, but now he sounded a lot more like the Fujitaka I knew. 'We can't do anything about it, and anyway he's already made his decision, hasn't he? All we can do now is sit tight and wait for today's announcement. Right?'

'That's the thing. He *hasn't* decided.'

'What do you mean?'

'He hasn't written the will.'

I couldn't help but feel slightly impressed that Runa already knew this. In the original loop (the 'first' 2nd of January), Grandfather had only revealed this to me in the afternoon.

Meanwhile, in this second loop (the 'second' 2nd of January), it was only morning and Runa already knew. Where had she obtained this information? I'd written my cousin off as a happy-go-lucky flirt, but it seemed there was more to her than met the eye.

Then it occurred to me that Fujitaka had said something odd. That was it—the part about sitting tight and waiting for 'today's announcement'. Given the context, this had to mean an announcement of who Grandfather had chosen as his successor. But hadn't he declared at the New Year's dinner that the contents of the will would only be revealed upon his death? Yes, I was sure that was what he'd said. In which case… what was Fujitaka talking about?

'Seriously? He hasn't written it?'

'Apparently he just can't make his mind up.'

'That's weird. I mean, he made it sound like he was just going to pick someone on a whim.'

What I found a lot weirder was the way these two were talking to each other—like some happily married couple. Judging from the syrupy tone of Runa's voice, Fujitaka had won her heart completely. This floored me. I'd always thought of him as congenitally gloomy and not much else. When, and how, had he pulled this off?

'Anyway, this is our chance.'

'Our chance? To do what?'

'To get Grandfather to change his mind.'

'To… change his mind?'

'That's right, Fu-chan. All we have to do is tell him we're getting married and that we'd like to be the ones to carry on his family name.'

Fu-chan? *That* was her pet name for him? I mean, come on…
Fu-chan. I had to press my face into the futon to stop myself
from bursting out laughing.

'It'll work out best for everyone. If we take on the Fuchigami
name together, my mum and Aunt Kamiji will finally be able
to bury the hatchet.'

'But wasn't Grandfather saying he might make Ryuichi his
successor? Or that assistant of Kotono's?'

'Silly. He was only saying that to keep Mum and Aunt Kamiji
on their toes. You know, warning them that they shouldn't take
anything for granted. He probably just wanted to vent his old
grievance more than anything. When it comes to down to it,
not even Grandfather would pick some *outsider* over his own
flesh and blood. I mean, that's just human nature, isn't it?'

'I guess you might have a point.'

'Of course I do! He's just using Ryuichi and that Emi woman.
Making them think, ooh, I might get to run the company one
day—then when he's finished playing with them, he'll toss
them to one side. If anything, we should feel sorry for them.
Blood's thicker than water, whatever people say.'

'You reckon?'

'Definitely. That's why we need to get a move on. We'll get
the old man to change his mind before he writes the will. Not
just for our sake, but for everyone else's.'

'Right. Yeah. Let's do it!' Fujitaka seemed to have come
around to her idea. After his initial half-hearted mumblings
of agreement, he suddenly sounded full of conviction. He was
in such high spirits that by the time they left, he was the one
hurrying Runa out of the door. If they did get married, Runa
was going to have him right under her thumb.

I waited until I was sure they'd gone, then crawled out of the closet. I was wide awake—and a little too stimulated by what I'd just heard to even think about taking my planned nap. However old and jaded I might be mentally, I was physically very much still a sixteen-year-old, and all that excitement had been a little overwhelming. A warm fug seemed to linger in the room. I decided to open the window and let some air in.

From the window, I could see the courtyard as well as the walkway that linked the main building to the old house. The air that rushed in was so cold that I immediately shut the window again, but I carried on gazing outside.

In the end, I sat by the window for some time, my knees tucked under my arms as I daydreamed. Then, all of a sudden, a figure cut across my field of vision. I rubbed my eyes and looked back outside. It was Grandfather. He was making his way along the walkway, glancing around furtively as he approached the old house. Dangling from one hand was the large bottle of sake. In other words, although Grandfather had been unable to invite me to join him, this minor alteration had not prevented the basic 'schedule' of the original loop—in which he went back to bed until noon, met his lawyer and then hid in the attic to drink—from following its established course.

Grandfather disappeared into the old house. Now he'd walk through the kitchen and up to the attic, from which he wouldn't emerge for some time. Did that mean it was safe for me to return to the main building? As I was pondering this, two more figures appeared in the walkway.

It was Fujitaka and Runa. Presumably they were following Grandfather with the intention of talking him round to their idea, as they had just discussed. They must have been feeling confident, because they were both grinning cheerfully as they slipped into the old house.

I continued gazing out at the walkway. There was nothing to stop me returning to the main building and lounging about in the banquet hall or reception room. But I was curious to see how the pair's proposal would go down with Grandfather. The time it took for them to reappear, and their expressions when they did, would hopefully give me a decent idea of what had transpired.

After a while—I wasn't sure exactly how long, because there was no clock in the annex and I wasn't wearing my wristwatch, but it can't have been more than five or ten minutes—a figure emerged from the old house.

It was Runa. She was on her own. She hurried along the walkway, glancing about anxiously, before disappearing into the main building. There was no sign of Fujitaka.

After a while, Runa reappeared. I'd been curious to see her expression, but my attention was drawn instead to the object in her hands. It was a vase filled with flowers whose round white petals looked like gyoza wrappers. The moth orchids. They must be the ones Emi had given Aunt Kotono as a present yesterday (on the 1st of January, that is). I hadn't seen them since the New Year's dinner, but Aunt Kotono had mentioned that she was going to put them in her room. So, what was Runa doing with them? The only explanation I could think of was that Grandfather had told her to bring them—but why would he do that?

Not long after entering the old house, Runa re-emerged and returned to the main building. This time, she wasn't holding anything.

A few minutes later, Fujitaka appeared and also made his way back to the main building. He, too, was empty-handed.

Scratching my head in confusion, I got to my feet. As I left the annex and headed for the main building, I tried to make sense of what I'd just seen.

When I'd been drinking with Grandfather in the original loop, I'd had the impression that someone was eavesdropping on the stairs. That, I now realized, must have been Fujitaka and Runa. They'd come to the attic to see Grandfather, but had to postpone their plan when they realized that I was already there with him. But now, in the second loop, I was absent, and Grandfather alone, meaning they'd been able to talk to him.

The question was, how had he responded to their proposal? And what connection could there possibly be between their attempt to persuade him and Aunt Kotono's moth orchids? The quickest way to find out would be to ask Grandfather directly, but if I went to the attic now, he'd rope me into drinking with him again. I decided to wait for him to return to the main building instead.

I must have been getting hungry again, because my feet led me to the dining room. I found Yoshio and Mai sitting at the table eating a late breakfast. There was no one else around.

'Hey, Kyutaro,' said Yoshio, deftly collecting a grain of rice that had stuck to his lip with his tongue. 'How's the hangover?'

Ah. It was true that on the 1st of January—the real 'yesterday', in other words—I'd had plenty to drink, too.

'I'm fine,' I replied, before pouring myself some tea and taking a sip.

'So, me and Mai were just having a little chat,' he said, nodding enthusiastically in Mai's direction. This ability to include absolutely anyone in a conversation, regardless of personality type, was one of Yoshio's more redeeming qualities. 'Who do you think Grandfather's going to pick? In that new will of his, I mean.'

Mai showed no sign of saying anything, so I went ahead. 'I have no idea.'

'Well, that's helpful. Come on, aren't you curious?'

'Of course I am.'

'Do you reckon he's writing it now?'

'Now? I thought he'd already written it.'

'I heard he hasn't yet. Can't make his mind up, apparently.'

'But…' I said, taken aback. It seemed it wasn't just Runa and Fujitaka I'd underestimated. 'How did you find that out?'

'Oh, I didn't find anything out. We heard it from Runa. Didn't we, Mai?'

Mai was pulling a strange face, as if she was simultaneously happy and mortified that Yoshio was trying to include her. In the end, perhaps afraid that responding too warmly would make her look desperate for affection, she simply shrugged.

I was confused. I'd assumed that the only person to whom Runa had confided her top-secret information—namely, that Grandfather hadn't yet written his will—had been Fujitaka, but it seemed I was wrong. Not only had she also told Yoshio and Mai, but it looked like she'd done so even *before* telling her secret lover.

Yoshio opened his mouth to say something else, but he was cut off by a bizarre and deafening sound. It began as a sort of low-pitched, almost feral howl, before rising into a wailing screech, like nails being dragged across a chalkboard.

We all rushed into the corridor to see what had happened. A figure in a green tracksuit came scrambling towards us on all fours before keeling over like a bowling pin. It was Aunt Haruna. Her hair was a mess, and she was panting hoarsely. It seemed the feral howl we'd just heard had been the sound of her screaming.

'Mum? Wh-what's wrong?' In her alarm, Mai's usual mask of indifference had fallen away, leaving only an expression of pure panic, like that of a toddler whose ice cream has just fallen off its cone. 'Did something happen?'

'Arghhh. Ergh.' Aunt Haruna was simply gasping at us, as if unable to form words. All that screaming must have ruined her voice. 'G-g-g. Gr.'

'Mum, just tell us what happened, okay? What's wrong?'

The usual sarcastic smile was nowhere to be seen. Aunt Haruna's mouth and eyes had each turned as round as a full moon. Shaking her, Mai looked like she might burst into tears, too.

'Come on, Mum! Tell us what happened!'

Drawn by the commotion, Ryuichi, Emi, Mother, Aunt Kotono and Kiyoko had arrived. But Aunt Haruna still hadn't formed a single word. Instead, she kept wildly waving her arms in the direction from which she'd come. In other words, the walkway that led to the old house.

Finally, a thought flashed through my mind. Could something have happened to Grandfather? I ran towards the walkway. Yoshio followed me, the others trooping after him.

I made my way through the kitchen and up the stairs. They were so steep I ran out of breath. A few steps before the top, I froze. I had spotted a small, cylindrical object wedged in one of the thin grooves that ran along the lip of each stair. It was shaped like one of the seals people carry around for approving documents, or a miniature stick of lip balm, and its pale ochre colour made it almost invisible against the wooden steps. My eyes had landed on it purely by chance. Without thinking, I grabbed it and continued up the stairs, opening the door to the attic.

My grandfather, Reijiro Fuchigami, was sprawled face down on the futon. His left arm was trapped under his belly; his right hand grasped at the tatami mat. Just beyond his reach lay a large sake bottle. It must have been almost empty even before it fell over, because the spilt contents formed only a small dark patch on the tatami.

The few white hairs Grandfather had left, a sort of candyfloss-like swirl at the back of his head, were spattered a dark red. Lying in front of his face, hiding it from view, was a copper vase. Its former contents, a bunch of out-of-season moth orchids, were strewn across the tatami. Without thinking, I glanced behind me. I was looking for Fujitaka and Runa. They appeared to have been the last ones to join the group, and were peering into the room from halfway up the stairs.

He's been hit with the vase. That was the thought that crossed my mind, and presumably everyone else's. But no one—not Mother, not Fujitaka, not Yoshio, not Aunt Kotono, not Kiyoko, not Aunt Haruna, not Mai, not Runa—moved an inch. Even Ryuichi and Emi seemed to have frozen in the face of this momentous event. Everyone just stood there, jostling around the cramped doorway, barely able to breathe.

Eventually, after who knows how long, I found myself stepping forward into the room. This was my bedroom whenever we stayed at the mansion—a fact that seemed to have instilled a strange sense of duty in me. In any case, no one stopped me as I went to kneel at my grandfather's side.

I took his wrist. It felt like a cut of ham that had been left out too long. There was no pulse. So he *was* dead. That much had been obvious from the moment we saw him lying there, but the confirmation still came as a shock. Or rather, it filled me with a fresh sense of despair.

I turned to look at my family, who were still peering through the doorway. I had no idea what you were supposed to do or say at a time like this. I must have had a pretty idiotic look on my face, but nobody was laughing. Instead their expressions were blank, as though all the emotion had been scoured from them. Watching them, I began to feel like bursting into hysterical laughter. For one thing, with the exception of Kiyoko, they were all clad in the combination of brightly coloured tracksuit and sleeveless chanchanko jacket. Given the circumstances, there was something almost grotesquely hilarious about the sight.

It was Emi who recovered first. She seemed to have received the silent message I was trying to convey, because she abruptly turned and clattered off down the stairs—presumably to phone the police.

Her departure broke the spell. There was a sort of collective sigh. Then, as if this were the cue they'd been waiting for, my mother, Aunt Kotono and Aunt Haruna suddenly turned on the histrionics. *Father, Father! Oh no! How could this happen!* That sort of thing. Sobbing and wailing as if trying to make up for all the time they'd been dumbstruck.

'Mum, stop! You can't do that,' said Yoshio, restraining Mother as she tried to embrace my grandfather's body. 'You mustn't touch him!'

Runa, meanwhile, was berating her own mother. 'Don't touch anything, okay!' Her eyes were bloodshot with agitation; her usual nonchalance was nowhere to be seen. She had shouted so loudly that everyone else fell silent. 'We have to preserve the crime scene until the police get here!'

'What crime scene? What are you talking about?'

I couldn't even tell who shrieked these words—my mother or Aunt Haruna. In the close confines of the attic, all hell was breaking loose.

'Isn't it obvious?' said Yoshio urgently. Even at a time like this, there was a trace of excitement in his expression as he sensed an opportunity to come to Runa's assistance. And, just as inappropriately, I couldn't help but feel a wave of pity for poor Yoshio, who had no idea that his brother had long since stolen her heart. 'Look at him. Just look at him! He's been *murdered*!'

Murdered. That one word from Yoshio was enough to make everyone freeze again. *Murdered*, their fearful eyes said. *Murdered, really? But how… how could something like this happen to us, of all families? This can't be real. A murder, among upstanding citizens like us…?*

But I was shocked for a different reason. The question on my mind was the same—how could this have happened?—but in my case it wasn't just rhetorical. I really wanted to know *how*. Today, after all, was no ordinary day. Today was the 'second' 2nd of January.

In the previous and original version of the day, nothing as ghastly as a murder had happened. I knew this to be true. So how, in this second version of it, in which events were meant to transpire more or less as they had in the first, had something so unexpected managed to occur? It simply wasn't supposed to happen. It wasn't allowed to happen. And yet it had. The evidence was right in front of me. Grandfather was, without question, dead. What on earth was going on?

As these thoughts swirled through my head, my eyes briefly met Runa's. She didn't seem to register my gaze. She was too busy staring fearfully back down at Grandfather's body.

Even at a time like this, I couldn't help noticing that she wasn't wearing her earrings. When had she taken them off? And—given that she normally insisted on keeping them on, even when she was forced to wear the yellow tracksuit and chanchanko that made them look so out of place—*why* had she taken them off?

Then I remembered what I was still clutching in my hand. The small, ochre-coloured cylindrical object…

'Hey, Runa,' I said, holding the earring out towards her almost involuntarily. 'Here you go.'

I'll never forget how Runa looked just then. Every inch of skin on her face seemed to go taut, as if something was on the point of bursting out from within it—a strange grimace that seemed just as likely to culminate in a torrent of tears as an explosion of rage.

'I was in the annex just now,' I went on, so intimidated that I felt compelled to lie. 'I found it lying on the tatami.'

This seemed to come as a huge relief to Runa, because— Grandfather's corpse be damned—she suddenly looked like she was about to break into a smile. Her whole body had visibly relaxed.

'Oh. Thanks,' she said, snatching the earring from my hand.

She must have panicked because she'd assumed I'd found it on the attic floor. After all, this was a crime scene. The discovery of one of her possessions here, where it had no right to be, would only have cast suspicion on her.

In fact, the earring had been lying not inside the room, but on the stairs just outside it. At this point I felt a wave of confusion. The question on my mind was this: when, exactly, could Runa have dropped the earring?

I thought back to her conversation with Fujitaka, the one I'd overheard from the closet in the annex.

I was wondering why I couldn't hear them. Where are your…?

What? Oh. I lost one somewhere, so I thought I'd go without the other one, too.

It was clear now that the mysterious objects Runa had been talking about had, in fact, been her earrings. Fujitaka, alerted to their absence by the lack of their characteristic jingling noise, had asked her where they were. She'd replied that having lost one of them, she'd decided to take the other one out, too.

This made sense. But *when* could she have dropped her earring on the stairs? Though I hadn't been able to check the exact time, that exchange with Fujitaka had taken place after I'd eaten breakfast in the dining room at nine o'clock in the morning. I reckoned it must have been an hour or so later—at around ten o'clock, that is—that I'd overheard the conversation. In other words, Runa must have visited the old house before ten o'clock in the morning.

The sequence of events, as I'd perceived it, had been as follows:

1st January—the 'real' yesterday. Runa was definitely wearing her earrings for at least the entire duration of the New Year's dinner. I retired to the attic just after eleven o'clock.

2nd January—original loop.
2nd January—second loop.

Now, as numbers 2 and 3 are in fact the same day, only repeated, it makes sense to think of them happening in parallel. Runa could only have dropped the earring between eleven p.m. on the 1st of January and ten a.m. on the 2nd. Of course, it stood to reason that Runa also noticed the earring's absence within the original loop. I might not have been in the closet eavesdropping, but the exchange with Fujitaka—him asking her where the earrings were, and her explaining that she'd lost one of them, which was why she'd taken the other one out—would still have taken place.

In which case... When I arrived at what appeared to be the logical conclusion, a funny feeling came over me. This was because it seemed quite possible that the person I'd thought I'd heard on the stairs, listening in on my conversation with Grandfather, *hadn't* been Runa, after all. It *could* have been her, of course, but I felt sure she hadn't dropped the earring at that time. This was because it was already the afternoon of the original loop by the time I was drinking with my grandfather. And on the morning of that day, she'd already lost one of her earrings and taken the other one out. It seemed highly improbable that she'd managed to lose her earring a second time that afternoon.

Even if it were true that, in the original loop, she and Fujitaka had come to the attic to have their talk with Grandfather only to postpone their plan when they realized I was there, she couldn't have dropped her earring at that time. She must have done so much earlier. Of course, the same applied in the second loop: she must have dropped it before that conversation in the annex.

This raised another question. If Runa could only have dropped the earring between eleven p.m. on the 1st of January and ten a.m. on the 2nd, then why, exactly, had she been visiting the old house between those hours? No—not just the old house, but the attic, in particular? I'd been alone in my room that whole time, and Runa must have known that. Did that mean she wanted to see *me*, for some reason? It just didn't make sense.

Never mind. I decided to set that question to one side for the time being. There was a bigger issue here. More than anything else, Runa had seemed terrified that I was going to tell her I'd found the earring in the attic or on the stairs leading to it. After all, such a discovery might have suggested her involvement in our grandfather's death.

It was true that, right now, she was one of the two prime suspects. I'd seen her and Fujitaka follow Grandfather down the walkway and into the old house with my own eyes. Not only that, but shortly afterwards she had gone to fetch the vase of moth orchids from the main building—the same vase that appeared to have been used to deal a fatal blow to the back of Grandfather's head.

After Runa—and a short while later Fujitaka—had emerged and returned to the main building, I had given up my little 'stakeout' in the annex and made my way in the same direction. In other words, I had no way of being certain that no one had entered the old house after they had left it. In fact, Aunt Haruna must have done just that—after all, she had been the one to find Grandfather in the attic.

This made it impossible to be certain Runa and Fujitaka were the murderers. Maybe Aunt Haruna, the first person to discover the body, had committed the deed. Maybe all her hysterical screaming when she came rushing into the main building had been an act. Still, until I had an explanation as to why they'd taken the vase of orchids to the old house, Runa and Fujitaka remained the chief suspects...

While I was trying to untangle these confused thoughts, the police arrived. A forensic investigator and plain-clothes detective came up to the attic and asked us to go downstairs. Under the instructions of another police officer, we filed back into the main building.

We were told to wait in the reception room that adjoined the banquet hall. The detective turned to Emi, apparently deeming her the most reliable, and asked whether this was everyone. She glanced around at the various people sitting on the sofas and leaning against the walls, then nodded.

'Please don't leave this room until we instruct you to,' said the detective, before walking out of the reception room. Two uniformed officers stayed behind, planting themselves in the entrance. It almost felt like we were under guard.

In fact, we probably were. It was extremely likely that the murderer was among our ranks. And I didn't seem to be the only one to think this way. Mother, Aunt Kotono, Aunt Haruna, Fujitaka, Yoshio, Mai, Runa, Kiyoko, Ryuichi and Emi—they had all adopted an oddly stand-offish air, as though only barely resisting the urge to glare suspiciously at the faces around them.

Two of them, in particular, seemed particularly deserving of such suspicion—at least from my perspective. Runa and

Fujitaka had been all over each other in the annex, but now they were standing at opposite ends of the room and gazing in different directions. To someone who knew what they'd been up to earlier, this could only appear deliberate.

'Excuse me, ladies and gentlemen,' came a voice, bringing us back to our senses. I must have been lost in my thoughts for some time. It wasn't just me, either—everyone looked as startled, as if they'd been woken from a dream. 'If I could have your attention for a moment, please. I'm Inspector Hiratsuka of the Atsuki Police.' He looked to be around Fujitaka's age. 'Now, who discovered the body?'

Our gazes converged on a single target. Aunt Haruna, her expression filling with surprise and dismay, raised a hand. Under other circumstances, this would have been when she produced her knowing smile—as if to suggest that of *course* she knew something important, but she wasn't going to tell you that easily—but clearly she was in no frame of mind to do so.

'Right, then. Well, if you could just come with me.' He turned to the rest of us. 'We'll be interviewing you all, one by one, in a separate room. This might take some time, but I'd appreciate your cooperation with our investigation.'

After Aunt Haruna, they summoned Aunt Kotono, then Kiyoko, followed by Ryuichi, Emi, Mother, Mai, Runa, Fujitaka, Yoshio—and, last of all, myself. I'd assumed that'd be the end of it, but then they summoned Aunt Haruna again and made another run through the list. Then, just when I was thinking they really *had* finished, the questioning started all over again. In the end, it went on and on into the night.

Once the first round of interrogation had begun, the silence that had reigned in the reception room was suddenly broken.

Each returning family member began excitedly discussing what the detectives had asked, and how they had replied. It was as though the state of depressive shock into which we'd all sunk following the discovery of Grandfather's body had given way to its manic counterpart. At the same time, there were two people who weren't involved in—or were deliberately excluded from—this frantic exchange of information: Ryuichi and Emi, the two 'outsiders'. This despite the fact that even the usually taciturn Mai was suddenly rambling away to anyone who would listen. It seemed that an event of this magnitude was capable of creating an almost festive atmosphere among the family—even when the event in question was the murder of one of our relatives.

And yet, for all the excitement, I failed to gain any real clues from this explosion of gossip. Aunt Haruna had been looking for Grandfather because she wanted to talk to him privately about the will. Runa had told her she'd seen him go into the old house. When Haruna had gone there to look for him, she'd discovered his body in the attic. We all knew what had happened after that.

It seemed the only person to know anything more about what had happened—other than Runa and Fujitaka themselves, of course—was me. Still, I decided not to tell the detectives what I knew about the two of them. I was reluctant to snitch on my own brother, yes—but more importantly, even if I did, the loop would soon be reset, rendering the action completely meaningless. In the end, I simply stated that I'd got up just before nine, eaten breakfast and taken a nap in the annex. After that, I'd returned to the dining room in the main building, where we'd heard Aunt Haruna's terrible scream.

The detectives didn't seem particularly suspicious of my testimony, but nor did they appear to have swallowed it without question. They were the hard-to-read type. The only thing they seemed genuinely baffled by was the fact that we were all wearing tracksuits and chanchanko jackets. All I could tell them was that Grandfather had insisted on it, and I didn't know the reason why.

Under circumstances like this, the Oba and Kanagae families could hardly return home as planned. By this point in the original loop, we had set off home in Yoshio's car, but the unexpected murder had given rise to a discrepancy in that part of the day's schedule. While the Trap generally attempted to adhere as closely as possible to the events of the original loop, it seemed it was powerless in the face of an event of this magnitude. The only option was for us to spend another night at the Fuchigami residence.

Another round of questioning began. The excited chatter that had filled the reception room now gave way to exhaustion and an unsettling silence. Mother and Aunt Haruna, perhaps concerned that we might think they were secretly happy about Grandfather's death, had adopted the most solemn expressions they could muster. Meanwhile, as I waited for the detectives to summon me once more, I began to feel a strange unease. As if I'd forgotten something. Something important.

I didn't know why it was important, or whether it had anything to do with my grandfather's murder. All I knew was that it was important. I felt this conviction filling me, together with a restless anxiety. Not only that, but I couldn't shake the feeling that it had something to do with one of the people in the reception room. I racked and racked my brain, but nothing came to mind.

Kiyoko was currently being questioned. That left Mother, Aunt Kotono, Aunt Haruna, Fujitaka, Yoshio, Mai, Runa, Ryuichi, Emi—and me. Convinced it had something to do with one of them, I scanned their faces one by one, but came up with nothing. The more I struggled, the more convinced I became of the importance of whatever it was I'd forgotten, and the more anxious I grew. And yet my mind kept drawing a blank.

Then, before I knew it, the hands of the clock on the wall reached midnight.

6

THE MURDER HAPPENS AGAIN

The reception room where I'd been waiting for the next round of questioning gave way to complete darkness. I had just woken up. My throat was parched. As I lay there, torn between the urge to go and get some water and the desire to stay curled up under the covers, some remote corner of my mind eventually noticed that I was back in the attic. The loop had reset. The clock had reached midnight, the Trap had returned to its starting point, and now the 2nd of January was going to happen all over again. Despite my grogginess, I just about managed to process this fact. In the end, though, sleep won, and I was pulled back into the depths of my slumber.

When I woke up properly, pale sunlight was streaming through the window. My alarm clock told me it was just after eight o'clock. Panicking slightly, I jumped up from my futon and went downstairs, where I peered silently into the kitchen of the old house.

'I couldn't find the red origami paper,' I heard Grandfather say. 'I don't know why. I'm sure it was there before. It's the only colour that was missing.'

I felt a wave of silent relief. I was used to the rules of the Trap by now, but no one had ever died on me during a loop before. I'd had a nagging worry that Grandfather might not return to life, but it seemed there was no cause for concern.

Just like last time, Aunt Kotono queried what he'd done last night without the red origami paper, after which he asked Kiyoko to go and get some from the stationery shop, and Kiyoko told him that all the shops would be closed for the first three days of the year. There was no need for me to listen to the entire exchange. I went back up to the attic.

A few steps before the top, I froze. I had spotted a small, cylindrical object wedged in one of the thin grooves that ran along the lip of each stair. I grabbed it. It was, of course, Runa's earring.

It had been on the stairs in the original and second loop, so there was nothing inherently strange about me finding it here in this third version of the 2nd of January. In the second loop, I'd returned the earring to Runa after we'd discovered Grandfather's body, but of course the 'reset' meant it had found its way back to its original position.

What was less clear was why it was here so early in the morning. That could only mean that between eleven o'clock last night (the 1st of January) and eight o'clock this morning (the 2nd of January), Runa had snuck out of the main building, into the old house and made her way up the attic stairs. Why on earth would she do that? It was the same question that had bothered me during the previous loop. If she had wanted to see me about something, surely she could have done so at a less unseemly hour? It made no sense. I briefly entertained the idea that she had been sneaking into my room with something else in mind, but that really *was* pushing the limits of plausibility.

I sat back down on my futon, twiddling the earring in my fingers, then crossed my arms. I had plenty of thinking to do. The biggest question facing me was this: how had something that hadn't happened in the original loop managed to occur in the second?

As I explained earlier, the only person capable of deliberately deviating from the Trap's predetermined schedule is myself, for the simple reason that I'm the only one aware of the phenomenon in the first place. In other words, if something had occurred in the second loop when it hadn't in the original, it could only have been my doing. Which made me, in a sense, responsible for my grandfather's murder.

Of course, I hadn't carried out the grisly deed itself. But because my actions had deviated from those I had taken in the original loop, the day had veered away from its usual schedule. As a result, a sort of domino effect must have occurred, the ultimate outcome of which was that my grandfather, who was supposed to make it through the day very much alive, had been murdered. I could think of no other explanation.

The most obvious difference in my actions between the original and second loops concerned Grandfather's drinking session. In the original loop I'd kept him company, while in the second loop I'd deliberately avoided doing so. Could that discrepancy, through some complex chain of cause and effect, have been what had ultimately led to his murder?

The logical conclusion was that all I had to do to stop my grandfather being killed was to keep him company while he drank. Simple, really. But that would mean another seven loops, including this one, of binge-drinking and intense vomiting. I didn't have much faith in my ability to simply *act* drunk instead—or to turn Grandfather down every time he told me to finish my glass.

Of course, if it really was a question of saving the old man's life, I'd be more than willing to put myself through something like that. But wasn't there another way? I had another seven loops in which to fix things; surely it wouldn't hurt to try a variety of strategies. If one of them succeeded in saving Grandfather from his fate, I could simply repeat it for however many loops remained.

I waited until nine o'clock, then made my way to the main building. After finishing the breakfast that had been set out for me, I went into the courtyard and began looking for a suitable hiding spot. My gaze landed on the cluster of bushes by the annex. I crouched among them and waited.

I kept my eyes trained on the entrance to the annex. Before long, Runa and Fujitaka appeared and hurried furtively inside. All in accordance with the day's 'schedule'.

When I climbed out of the bushes, went over to the annex and knocked, I heard a gasp from inside. I opened the door. I'd half-expected it to be locked, but it swung right open. Sloppy work, Fujitaka, I thought. He could at least have bolted the door.

'My apologies,' I said, adopting the gravest face I could as I peered into the room. 'I do hope I'm not interrupting.'

Runa, for her part, looked relatively composed. She was sitting on the tatami floor with her legs folded over to one side and eyeing me calmly. Fujitaka, on the other hand, offered a more entertaining spectacle. He had frozen a few paces away from her, in front of the open closet he had apparently been intending to hide in. He had pulled his tracksuit bottoms down for the purposes of whatever shameful business he'd had in mind, and there was something almost mournful about the sight of him staring into the closet in his underpants.

'Fujitaka, there's something I'd like to discuss.'

'Yeah?' he said, clearing his throat as he finally turned to face me. When he glanced at Runa, herself the picture of serenity, he looked almost resentful, as though wondering how she could possibly be so calm. 'Alright then, Gramps, what is it?'

'I'd like you to hear this too, Runa,' I said, stopping her as she got up to leave. 'Please. It's important.'

'Why, what's it about?'

'Grandfather's will, obviously. Ah, before I forget,' I said, producing the earring I'd brought with me. 'I believe this is yours.'

Runa's expression tensed. She stared warily up at me. Then, as if carefully extracting something from a pool of sludge, she took the earring from my outstretched hand.

'Sorry to be so direct,' I said, 'but I see the two of you are, erm, on good terms, shall we say?'

'Well,' said Fujitaka, who seemed to have decided there was no point in trying to gloss things over and finally pulled his trousers up. 'Sure. You can think that, if you like.'

'So much so that Runa has been visiting your apartment on your days off and doing your laundry.' I was so eager to get the two of them up to speed that, before I knew it, I was playing all the cards in my hand. 'Oh, and calling you Fu-chan.'

At this Fujitaka burst out laughing. 'Wow. Someone's got us all figured out.' My one-two punch seemed to have had the paradoxical effect of making him relax, as if he realized there was no point in trying to hide anything. In fact, I'd never seen him smile so cheerfully. He didn't seem to find it unsettling in the slightest that I knew all these intimate details. 'It's true. I've been telling Mum I do my own cooking, but actually Runa has been coming around and doing it for me. Only on her days off, mind. Runa's quite old-fashioned like that. Makes a hell of a stew. Her nikujaga is out of this world.'

As Fujitaka happily gushed away, I couldn't help noticing that Runa's expression was still as rigid as it had been a few moments ago. It was as though the two of them had swapped the roles they'd adopted when I first walked into the room.

'I assume the two of you plan on getting married at some point?'

'Well, actually… I mean, it's not out of the question, but it's not something we've specifically… Anyway, I'm still a student.'

'How about you, Runa?' I asked, cutting to the chase. 'No plans to marry my brother here? And—oh, I don't know— maybe take on the Fuchigami name? You don't have anything like that in mind?'

'Wh-what?' Runa's features finally crumpled into a weak smile. It must have come as a bit of a shock to have her secret plans suddenly repeated to her verbatim. 'I… erm… I… I don't know, okay?' she said, so flustered that it seemed her only recourse was to act the total airhead for once. 'Like, I have no idea what you're even talking about.'

'What I'm trying is suggest is this: that you two being in a relationship might actually be in all of our interests.'

'Yeah?' Fujitaka leant towards me, clearly intrigued. 'When you say take on the Fuchigami name… You mean, like, we'd both become Aunt Kotono's adopted heirs?'

116

'Exactly. That way, our mother and Aunt Haruna won't have anything to fight over, will they? After all, their two children will have taken on the family name together. And once you give them a shared grandchild, it'll be plain sailing. A happy ending for everyone—you two included, of course.'

'But what makes you so convinced this'll work? I mean, Grandfather told us all he'd be the one to pick his successor. And he's already written their name in his will.'

'Actually, he hasn't.'

'What?'

'He hasn't written the will yet, because he can't decide. Isn't that right, Runa?'

'Seriously?' Fujitaka asked Runa. She gripped the earring in her hand, tossed it in the air, caught it and finally nodded.

'That's right. He hasn't written it yet. I was going to tell you, Fu-chan. That's why I asked you to come in here with me in the first place.'

'Oh. Right.'

'*And* I had the same idea about us getting married and taking on the Fuchigami name. Kyu-chan here beat me to the punch, that's all.'

'Wow,' said Fujitaka, in simple amazement. 'So you both came up with the same idea at the same time. What a coincidence!'

'Yeah,' said Runa, staring uncomfortably at me, 'pretty crazy.'

'I wonder, Runa,' I continued, keen to press my advantage before she could ask any awkward questions, 'if you weren't hoping to approach Grandfather before he writes the new will—you know, explain your plan and get him to change his mind? Like, I don't know, immediately after this conversation? Taking Fujitaka along with you, maybe?'

117

'That's right.' Whether because this seemed like a reasonable enough thing for me to have imagined, or simply because she'd become numb to my constant second-guessing of her plans, Runa didn't seem particularly surprised. 'I mean, talking to him now is our only hope, isn't it?'

'I wouldn't be so sure.'

'What? Why?'

'Firstly, even assuming you did speak to Grandfather, there's the question of whether he'd actually listen to you.'

'True, true,' said Fujitaka. He seemed riveted by the conversation. Clearly, the idea of taking on the Fuchigami name had kindled his interest—and his ambition. 'That'll be the hardest part. Even if we go about it all properly, you know what he's like—he might just refuse to listen. He's stubborn like that. If we try to change his mind when he's already made a decision, he'll probably just flip out instead.'

'Well, then,' said Runa, now looking at me with something more like expectation, 'what should we do?'

'The key is to convince Grandfather that everything is going just the way he wants it to. Which means we let him go ahead and write whoever he wants into the will.'

'But then we'll be too late, won't we?'

'No. Think about it. This will is only "final" because Grandfather decided it is. There'll be nothing to stop him changing it later if he has a change of heart.'

'Oh, right!' exclaimed Fujitaka. 'If he wants to, he can rewrite it as many times as he likes.'

'Exactly. So all we have to do is *make* him want to.'

'But... how?' Runa, increasingly intrigued, practically pushed Fujitaka out of the way as she leant towards me. Her nostrils were twitching. 'How do we make him want to rewrite his will?'

'Simple. First, you two get married, but you don't breathe a word about your plan to take on Grandfather's name. The point is to convince him that all you're intending to do is start your own family, quite apart from the Fuchigami line.' Fujitaka and Runa were both nodding along in synchronized fashion, like they were connected by some sort of mechanism. This was the first time they'd ever listened this enthusiastically to anything I had to say. 'Then you, er, get to work. You have a baby. You could even say you got married *because* of the baby, if you like. The main thing is the baby. Grandfather gets a great-grandchild. A little darling for him to fawn over. Probably much more than he ever did with us.'

By now they seemed to have caught my drift. Their faces had taken on a sort of heavenly glow, their expressions as solemn as if they were receiving some sort of divine revelation.

'You don't let Grandfather see his great-grandchild too often, but nor do you keep the two entirely apart. The aim is to make it so that he's always impatiently awaiting their next reunion. The timing will be crucial. If you can just get Grandfather to start wondering whether there isn't some way he could live with his great-grandchild more permanently, then you've won. It shouldn't take long for him to realize that the answer is simple. All he has to do is get Aunt Kotono to adopt you into the Fuchigami family, and you'll all be able to live together here at his mansion. And when he does, you can be sure that he'll rewrite that will.'

'Kyutaro,' said Fujitaka, deadly serious, 'you're a genius.'

'Thanks.' I bowed my head, but inside I felt a little sorry for them. My plan might have the convincing veneer of a flawless strategy, but in reality it was so riddled with uncertainty that it seemed extremely unlikely that any of it would go off as planned. Still, that was of no concern to me. All that mattered was making sure that, for the remainder of the day, Fujitaka and Runa went nowhere near the old house.

I was convinced that Grandfather's murderer had been Fujitaka or Runa, or both of them. After all, Runa had been the one to carry the vase of moth orchids—the murder weapon—from the main building to the old house, and Fujitaka had followed her about all day. The only natural conclusion was that the two of them were behind the deed.

It wasn't clear why they had killed my grandfather, or what precise chain of events had led to his demise. It seemed unlikely that either of them had actually been planning his murder, so presumably there had been some sort of emotional flare-up during the course of their discussion about the will. Which was why, as long as I kept my eye on them and made sure they didn't go near the old house, Grandfather would make it through the day in one piece.

'There's one problem, though,' said Runa. A moment ago she'd seemed on the point of clapping her hands in delight, but now her expression had clouded over. 'My mum. And Aunt Kamiji, too, I guess. I don't think either of them is going to be happy about me and Fu-chan getting married. In fact, I reckon they'll do everything they can to stop it.'

'That's why we have to do it as soon as possible. Make a baby, I mean.' Fujitaka looked like he was ready to set about it that very minute. In fact, if I hadn't been there, I'm pretty sure he would have tried. 'Once we have the baby, they'll have no choice but to accept the situation. So our best bet is to make one right away. We'll need one if we're going to change Grandfather's mind, too.'

He began pawing at Runa, but she shook him off and turned to me, as if seeking my opinion on the matter. 'If possible, I think it'd be best to win our mothers round to the idea, too,' I offered. 'Which means it'd be a good idea to get Yoshio and Mai on your side in advance. Make them see that, instead of running the risk of being left out of the inheritance completely, it makes more sense for our families to work together and share the estate. If we can get *them* on board, our mothers should at least be willing to listen.'

Runa nodded enthusiastically at this suggestion. Then, as if convinced there was no time to waste, she hurried Fujitaka and me out of the room, explaining that Mai would be eating in the dining room around now and that we could start by enlisting her help. (Of course, I knew we'd find Yoshio in there too, but I kept this to myself.)

As we were making our way from the annex to the main building, I spotted Grandfather in the walkway that led to the old house. He was carrying his bottle of sake, a gleeful expression on his face. It appeared that, in accordance with the day's schedule, he was about to embark on a solo drinking session, safely away from the prying eyes of Aunt Kotono and Kiyoko.

Walking ahead of me, Fujitaka and Runa were so wrapped up in their own conversation that they seemed not to have noticed Grandfather—which was a good thing. As long as I kept finding pretexts to stay close to these two until evening, I should be able to prevent their heinous deed from ever taking place. That would prove that my approach was an effective one—in other words, that Fujitaka and Runa were indeed the culprits. Then I could simply repeat this alteration of the schedule for the remaining six loops, the last of which would become the definitive version of the day's events. My operation to save my grandfather would be a complete success.

'Ah, perfect,' said Runa as we entered the dining room and found Yoshio and Mai eating breakfast. 'Just the pair we were looking for.'

'Ooh, Runa-chan,' said Yoshio, waving his chopsticks with his usual lack of inhibition. 'Didn't know you'd be so pleased to see me.' He beckoned at the seat next to him. 'Go on, sit with me.'

'Listen, you two,' said Runa, ignoring Yoshio's invitation and sitting down opposite the pair instead. Fujitaka, of course, took the seat at her side. 'Kyutaro had this… epiphany. A real stroke of genius.'

'He had a *what*?' asked Yoshio, apparently unable to comprehend the juxtaposition of my name with the word 'epiphany'.

'It's about Grandfather's will. Kyutaro thought of a way to fix the whole mess in one go. Basically…'

Runa gave a step-by-step explanation of the strategy I'd outlined moments ago. Despite having just identified me as its creator, she seemed to have already assimilated it as her own. Twirling the earring between her fingers—she had no pockets to put it in, and apparently no intention of wearing just the one—she described the scheme with a level of enthusiasm and conviction that put me, the actual mastermind, to shame.

But to Yoshio, all this must have been a bolt from the blue. 'What?!' he exclaimed, spluttering on his mouthful of rice. 'You can't be serious! So you've been getting it on with Fujitaka all this time? But… that's just not fair!' In his agitation, a grain of rice seemed to have travelled from his windpipe to his nasal cavity. He winced as he blew his nose into a tissue, then opened the tissue out, sighed and stared pathetically at its contents. 'What about my feelings? My poor heart… Hey, Fujitaka, talk about jumping the gun! Breaking the rules, that's what this is…'

But it turned out Yoshio's protests weren't our biggest concern. Those, at least, we could dismiss as a joke. The main problem was what happened next.

Mai pounded the table and jumped to her feet. We all froze. In her surprise, Runa dropped the earring onto the table.

'I—can't—stand—this! I just… *can't*!' exclaimed Mai, her shrieks interspersed with sobs. Like a toddler throwing a tantrum, she started grabbing bowls and plates from the table and flinging them onto the floor, so that the sound of shattering ceramics began to accompany her screams. 'It's—not—*fair*!'

'Wh-what's not fair, Mai?' asked Runa, half-rising to her feet in fright. She seemed to be torn between the impulse to back away for her own safety and the knowledge that it would probably be a good idea to lean over and pacify her sister. 'What's got into you? Oh, no—don't—alright, enough with the plates!'

'Screw the plates!' shouted Mai, before suddenly launching herself across the table at Runa. The table creaked; the dinnerware rattled loudly. 'You—you—you—'

'Stop it! Ow!' shrieked Runa, her own voice turning tearful as her sister grabbed her hair. A glass-shattering scream erupted from her throat. 'Stop it! That hurts! Ow! Ow!'

'You *bitch*!' yelled Mai, slapping her sister on the cheek and clawing at her like she meant to gouge out her eyeballs. There was something almost demonic about her rage. 'I *hate* you! I wish you'd jump off a cliff and die! Argh! Aaaaargh!'

'Ouch! That really hurts! Stop it! Ow! Ow!'

'Hey, cut it out!' Yoshio, who had finally made his way around the table, threw himself at Mai and put her in a full nelson. 'Just stop, okay?' he shouted as he dragged her away from Runa. 'The hell's got into you? Calm down!'

Meanwhile, Fujitaka was struggling to restrain Runa, who seemed to be gearing up for a counter-attack on her pinioned sister. Neither of them seemed like they were going to back down anytime soon. 'Runa!' he yelled. 'Calm down! Just... stop!'

'What on earth's going on in here?' Aunt Kotono, alerted by the din, came rushing into the dining room, followed by Kiyoko. Her expression was unusually severe. 'What's got into you all?'

But Runa was oblivious to this reprimand. 'You *idiot!*' she half sobbed, half shouted at her sister. 'You *moron!* You're *crazy!* I wish you were dead!'

'Runa, that's enough!' snapped Aunt Kotono. She almost never raised her voice like this. 'How can you talk to your little sister like that?'

'*She* started it! Came right at me a second ago. I didn't do anything. It's her fault. It's all her fault!'

'Honestly, how old are you two?' Aunt Kotono gave an exasperated wave of her hand, as if to suggest that they could fight however much they liked for all she cared—or maybe it was a signal for them to take their fight outside. 'And here I was, thinking you were two responsible adults. Kiyoko, sorry, but would you mind tidying this up?'

As Kiyoko set about clearing away the shattered tableware, Yoshio hurriedly snatched the dustpan and brush from her.

'No, no—we'll, er—we'll clean this up. We're, erm… really sorry for all the fuss.'

Somewhat belatedly, Ryuichi and Emi came rushing into the dining room, followed by Mother and Aunt Haruna. Grandfather was the only one who was absent. Holed away in the attic of the old house, he must not have heard all the commotion. When my mother, looking quite excited by all this drama, asked what on earth was going on, Yoshio made an unconvincing attempt to play it down.

'Nothing, Mum. Nothing at all. It's over now, anyway.'

Just as the atmosphere in the room seemed to be calming, Mai decided she wasn't quite finished. 'It's just not fair, Runa. Why do you get all the luck? Why are you the one everybody loves? Tell me, what's the big secret? What makes us so different?' Her words might have been addressed to Runa, but from the start Mai's tear-filled eyes had been focused on only one target: Fujitaka. And yet, in a sense, Mai wasn't really talking to anyone but herself. The whole thing was a sort of interior monologue. There was something unsettling, almost uncanny, about her complete withdrawal into her own world, her clear reluctance even to acknowledge the existence of an external reality. 'What makes us so different, eh?'

With these last, spluttered words, Mai tottered out of the dining room. When Aunt Haruna followed her into the corridor, anxiously asking where she was going, we heard her shriek, *'Leave me alone!'*

Meanwhile, Runa looked as if she'd just awoken from a spell. Had she finally worked out the reason for her sister's explosion of rage? She seemed conflicted, glancing between Fujitaka and the direction her sister had gone.

'In other words…' said Aunt Kotono, who seemed to have grasped the basic state of play, even if she wasn't aware of the detail—she was staring at Fujitaka with what seemed an irresponsible level of curiosity—'both the Kanagae girls are vying for your attention. Well, well—I didn't know you had it in you. When did you become such a charmer, eh?'

'Yeah, seriously,' grumbled Yoshio as he continued sweeping up the shattered china. He'd attempted a joking tone, but there was no hiding his shock. 'You mean to tell me both Runa *and* Mai have a crush on you? Weird. I'd have thought I was by the far the better catch, but what do I know, I guess…'

'Oh, your charms are lost on youngsters like them.'

Aunt Kotono smiled as she offered these words of comfort, though whether or not Yoshio was glad to hear them was another matter. Then she left the dining room, followed by Kiyoko. Ryuichi and Emi, having clearly decided this was not a conversation they should be present at, also bowed and retreated. Runa lingered for a moment, apparently absorbed in an attempt to gauge Fujitaka's feelings from his expression. Then, yielding to our mother's silent pressure, she too left the room.

'*What* is the meaning of this, then?' began Mother, rounding on my brothers. Now that it was just the Oba family in the room, she could really let rip. 'You have to be *kidding* me. Of all the people! Are you two wrong in the head or something? Haruna's idiotic daughters? One would be bad enough, but the *pair* of them?' When neither Fujitaka nor Yoshio denied her accusation, she only grew more incensed. 'You *idiots*! What do you think you're playing at? What are you, twelve? Losing your heads over a bit of eye candy. Where's your self-control? Your…

backbone! Letting a pair of airheaded bimbos have their way with you. It's pathetic! Open your eyes, boys, open your eyes!'

'But, Mum,' said Yoshio, 'if one of us marries Runa, it'll fix all our problems.'

Once Mother got started like this, it was only ever Yoshio who was capable of getting a word in edgeways. Fujitaka tended to clam up completely.

'Wh-what did you just say? No, I must have misheard you. You can't possibly…'

'Think about it.' With the triumphant air of someone who'd been concocting it for years, Yoshio launched into an explanation of the plan he'd heard from Runa for the first time a few minutes ago. 'If an Oba son marries a Kanagae daughter, it'll really smooth things out between our families. And once we give Grandfather a great-grandchild, he'll be so moved that he's bound to make the parents his successors. It's the perfect solution, don't you see?'

'Oh, come on. If all our problems could be fixed *that* easily, life would be a cinch.' Still, it seemed Mother might have begun to see the promise of Yoshio's idea (or, strictly speaking, my idea). Rather than letting an outsider like Ryuichi or Emi swoop in and claim the entire fortune, it might be better to strike a deal with her sister. 'Anyway, the point is that you should *think* before you let yourself get all smitten like that. Hey, Kyutaro, stop gaping at us like this has nothing to do with you.' It wasn't clear what had made her decide to start spluttering away at me instead. 'It'll be the same with you before long. When you get to this age, make sure you develop a better eye for women than these two! Is that clear? Otherwise you'll spend your whole life regretting your choices.'

I considered retorting *What, you mean like Dad?* but that only seemed likely to inflame a situation that was just beginning to calm down. Mother left the room, followed soon afterwards by Fujitaka. Judging from the direction he went in, he was pursuing Runa. I glanced at Yoshio, curious to see what his next move would be, but he simply shrugged, sat back down at the table and resumed his breakfast. I watched as he retrieved the piece of grilled fish that had been flung some distance from his plate during the commotion and began casually picking the flesh from it and chewing away.

As I watched him with a mixture of disgust and admiration, I realized something was missing from the table. Runa's earring. She had dropped it on the table earlier, in her astonishment at Mai's sudden fit of rage, and I didn't remember her picking it up afterwards. She'd hardly been in a state to do so. And yet it wasn't there. Where had the earring gone? Could Mai have knocked it onto the floor when she launched herself over the table at Runa? But no, it wasn't there, either. Yoshio watched in confusion as I crawled around the room looking for it, to no avail.

I had a bad feeling. I didn't know what exactly had triggered it, but my heart was starting to beat a little faster. Thinking some air might do me good, I left the stuffy interior of the mansion and made my way out to the courtyard. The cold air was bracing. Drawing the front of my chanchanko together, I began pacing around the courtyard.

I suddenly found myself wondering where Fujitaka and Runa had gone. My plan had been to follow them around all day, but in all the excitement in the dining room I'd let them get away.

Maybe they'd gone back to the annex. I wasn't expecting to find them when I peered through the window, so when I did spot them, it almost came as a letdown. Nothing untoward was happening in the annex. The two of them were engaged in some sort of serious discussion. Probably something to do with Mai.

In any case, this was a relief. As long as I monitored the entrance to the annex, I'd be able to keep abreast of the pair's movements. And as long as *they* kept their distance from the old house, Grandfather would safely avoid being murdered. Comforted by this thought, I was looking for a suitable hiding spot from which to monitor the entrance when I spotted someone in the walkway.

It was Mai. She was walking from the old house to the main building. There was something almost weightless about the way she walked, as if she were simply floating along, her eyes gazing vacantly into space.

What could she have been doing in the old house? That bad feeling began swelling up inside me again. After the fight in the dining room, she must have headed back to her own room. But then Aunt Haruna had gone chasing after her. Of course, she'd only meant to console her daughter, but Mai wouldn't have been in the mood. Maybe, in the end, she'd retreated to a less obvious hiding spot—the old house. If that was the case, then good for her.

The problem was that look on her face. She'd seemed just as distressed as she had been earlier. If anything, the pall of despair that surrounded her had only intensified. So why had she left the old house—the one hiding place where she would have been left in peace? It was also odd that she appeared not to have even noticed me, given that I was standing slap-bang in the middle of the courtyard.

Could something have happened? I stood there waiting uneasily for some sort of commotion to break out. But not a sound came from the mansion. All was shrouded in silence. I began to feel like maybe I'd been overthinking the situation.

Nothing was going to happen, I told myself. After all, in the previous loop, it had been around now that Aunt Haruna had started screaming after discovering Grandfather's body. And yet the house was entirely silent. Which could only mean that, just as I'd hoped, Grandfather's murder had been successfully averted…

But it was at this point that I noticed an error in my reasoning. In the *previous* loop, Aunt Haruna (who wanted to see Grandfather about the will) had only tried the old house because Runa had told her she'd seen him heading that way. It seemed highly likely that Runa had told her this to ensure she was the one to discover Grandfather's corpse. The first step in any murder investigation is to grill the person who finds the body. For Runa and Fujitaka, who were anxious to avoid this being them, the fact that Aunt Haruna happened to be looking for Grandfather had been a godsend. But in the *present* loop, Runa and Fujitaka hadn't killed Grandfather—not yet, at least. I knew, better than anyone, that they simply hadn't been in a position to. Which meant that Runa had no incentive to send Aunt Haruna in the direction of the old house—and in any case, Aunt Haruna would be so worried about Mai right now that her discussion with Grandfather could hardly have been foremost in her mind.

130

I went back into the main building, then out along the walkway to the old house. I passed through the empty kitchen and climbed the stairs.

I opened the door to the attic. There, sprawled face-down on the futon I'd left out that morning, was Grandfather. I checked his pulse. He was dead. Exactly as he had been in the previous loop.

This time, however, there was no sign of the vase of moth orchids. Instead, when I peered at the bottle of sake lying on the floor, I saw that its surface was coated with what looked like a mixture of grey hairs and blood. It seemed he'd been bludgeoned with it.

There was one other difference. Grandfather's pose was the same—his left arm tucked under his belly and his right hand grasping at the tatami. But this time, there was an object lying near that hand. A pale ochre cylinder. Runa's earring.

I raced down the stairs and back to the main building. Without even meaning to, I found myself heading for Emi's room. As I was about to knock, the door opened and there she stood. She stared at me wide-eyed, as if wondering what on earth I wanted.

'The police.' I barely managed to get the words out. 'Call the police.'

7

THE MURDER HAPPENS... AGAIN

Once the police arrived, the general commotion in the house followed a very similar course to the previous loop. In fact, up to the part where young Inspector Hiratsuka gathered everyone in the reception room and gave his instructions, it was almost identical. The only difference was that this time I was the one who had discovered Grandfather's body, rather than Aunt Haruna. That meant I was up first for questioning. Runa was last. After that, we faced the same seemingly end-less rounds of interrogation as last time. As I was waiting to be summoned once again, the clock struck midnight. I awoke abruptly in darkness. My throat was parched. This time, I knew immediately where I was: in my futon in the attic. The 2nd of January had, once again, been 'reset'.

As I was lying there, torn as usual between the need to go downstairs for some water and the desire to go back to sleep, I had a sudden thought. Whatever time it was right now, would Runa's earring already be lying on the stairs? As I mentioned earlier, she could only have dropped it there between eleven p.m. on the 1st of January and eight a.m. on the 2nd. I decided I'd get up and check the stairs. If the earring was there, I'd take note of the time. That way, I'd be able to narrow the night-time window within which Runa must have come to the old house.

It was all well and good for my brain to have these thoughts, but unfortunately my body was less compliant. I was too sleepy, my mind too fuzzy. Still, I had the distinct impression that I had, after all, summoned up my strength and got up from the futon. That I had left the room and checked the stairs. Hadn't I? But then why was I still lying curled up in my nice, warm futon? I must have been dreaming. I had the sensation of falling from some high place—and, as I hit the ground, awoke with a start. It was a bit like when you dream that you need to get up and eat breakfast and get ready for school, feel all the relief of having done so, and then realize you were actually still dreaming. Soon, even the shock of crashing into the ground subsided, and I was pulled, once again, into a deep sleep.

When I woke up properly, it was just after eight a.m. and pale sunlight was streaming through the window. All according to schedule. Immediately I remembered the earring and looked for it on my way down the stairs. There it was, wedged in the usual spot.

As I went down to the kitchen, toying with the earring in my hand, I heard the hale and hearty voice of my grandfather. 'I couldn't find the red origami paper. I don't know why. I'm sure it was there before.' And so on. Of course, I knew Aunt Kotono and Kiyoko were going to say and do exactly the same things as in the original loop, but I patiently listened to the end and waited for the three of them to leave the kitchen. Once they were out of sight, I went over to the main building and up to Mai's room.

In the last loop but one (the 'second' 2nd of January) it had been Runa and Fujitaka who killed Grandfather, but in the previous loop (the 'third' 2nd of January) it had been someone else. And I was sure that someone was Mai.

Her motive was unclear. Her shock at learning that her secret crush, Fujitaka, had long been smitten with Runa instead may well have been a contributing factor. Mai had a deep-seated complex in relation to her sister—a beautiful woman who worked as a promotional model at corporate events. When she'd learnt about Fujitaka, all that long-held jealousy and resentment had come explosively to the fore. Then, in a bid to escape her mother's unhelpful attempts to console her, Mai had sought refuge in the old house—where she had found her grandfather drinking on his own. As to what they might have talked about, I could only speculate. Perhaps Grandfather had made some insensitive comment that only exacerbated her feeling of inferiority. Something along the lines of: *Your sister's always had the edge on you in terms of looks, hasn't she?* An inno-cent if misguided remark, made with the intention of getting a laugh out of her. He could hardly have expected it to provoke his own murder. But after the Fujitaka incident, Mai was not in her right mind—and this must have driven her right over the edge. Seeing red, she had reached for the near-empty sake bottle and dashed it against Grandfather's head.

The presence of Runa's earring at Grandfather's side had probably been Mai's doing, too. Acting on the spur of the moment, she must have decided to frame her detested sister for her grandfather's murder. She'd only had the earring on her by chance. Maybe she'd grabbed it without thinking when she jumped over the table to launch herself at Runa. Then, caught up in her rage, she had unconsciously kept hold of it rather than throwing it away. It was only after killing Grandfather that she realized she still had it with her—and decided to use it to her advantage.

Just when I was thinking that I'd managed to consign Runa and Fujitaka's crime to oblivion, I'd been blindsided by a sneak attack. It seemed the consequences of the irregularity I'd introduced in the day's original schedule by avoiding Grandfather were more complex than I'd anticipated. A murder had occurred in the second loop: a bizarre occurrence, certainly, but not out of the question when I'd so significantly deviated from the original course of events. What was more unsettling, compared to my previous experiences of the Trap, was that I seemed to be unable to 'repair' the irregularity I'd introduced. As I explained earlier, the Trap seems to have some sort of guiding force that causes the day's events to adhere, as far as possible, to the pattern established in the original loop. With a little effort from me (in other words, keeping Runa and Fujitaka away from the old house), the day should have 'automatically' reverted to its usual schedule.

But that hadn't happened. Instead, the murder had simply reproduced itself. Based on previous experience, this shouldn't have been possible—but then nothing as dramatic as a murder had ever taken place during the Trap before. I was in unknown territory here. No wonder I was struggling to understand the discrepancy I'd introduced. As I said, its consequences appeared to be more complex than I had anticipated. But I had neither the brainpower nor the time to attain a thorough understanding of them. All I could do was keep trying to improvise a method by which to repair the 'anomaly' of my grandfather's murder. And if, despite my efforts, I found myself unable to carry out that repair successfully, the only way to save Grandfather would be to adhere to the day's original schedule and keep him company while he drank. But that would remain my last resort.

I knocked on Mai's door. There was no response, though I tried several times. She must be downstairs already. I made my way to the dining room and found her reheating a pot of miso soup on her own. When I walked in, she gave a perfunctory nod but remained silent. The day had barely started, but it seemed she was already in a sour mood. Even without her makeup, she wasn't unattractive. In fact, she had a quite elegant set of features. If anything, it was probably her moody personality that was preventing her from rivalling Runa in popularity. Of course, this was all a trifle rich coming from a little runt like me.

'Mai, could I have a word?' It was getting on for the time in the day when Yoshio would appear in the dining room. Speed was of the essence. 'There's something I'd like to ask you. Something important.'

'Oh yeah?' she replied languidly, as though convinced that whatever I considered important could only be some incredibly trivial matter. Her expression was a dead ringer for the one Aunt Haruna always wore. Give it a decade or two and maybe she would even take up her mother's mantle as a middle-aged master of the weary smile. 'Sounds a little dramatic for this time in the morning. Can't it wait?'

We didn't have time to dance around the issue. 'What are your feelings towards Fujitaka?' I began. 'Because to me, it looks a little bit like you're attracted to him.'

I'll never forget how Mai looked just then. The flush that started in her cheeks spread rapidly outwards, turning her entire face a rosy pink. And, if only for a brief moment, the cynical expression that was her armour against the world had fallen away, exposing the shy and vulnerable woman underneath. She was in no state to even ask how I could know something like that, or where I'd heard it. She was simply consumed by embarrassment. It was a reaction so straightforward that it took me slightly by surprise.

'I promise I'm not just being nosey,' I continued, anxious to get my point across while she was still in this unguarded state. 'It's a serious matter. So please, hear me out, and I—'

But before I could get any further, Yoshio came waltzing into the dining room.

'Mor-ning,' he said, drawing the word out longer than he needed to. This was terrible timing. He'd arrived much earlier than I'd been expecting. 'Ooh. You two look thick as thieves. What's the gossip?'

'Nothing,' I blurted. 'I mean, nothing to do with you, anyway.'

'Oh, come on, that's just rude.' Yoshio had been about to sit down at the table, but now, adopting a wounded expression, he strode over to us instead. This was not good. Not good at all. 'Wait, Kyutaro, you're not trying it on with Mai, are you? If you are, forget it. You're still in high school, mister. Try again when you're a big boy.'

'I'm doing nothing of the sort.'

'Then what *are* you doing?'

'It's, erm... well, a bit of a personal matter.'

'A personal matter. So you are trying it on with her, then? I can just imagine it. "Hey, how about it? I promise I'll more than make up for the age gap." Appealing to her maternal instincts. You dark horse.' On and on he went, letting his bizarre fantasies

137

get the better of him. My brother could be a real piece of work sometimes. 'Seriously, I never knew you were such a little lech.'

'I'm telling you, Yoshio, that is very much *not* what we were discussing. We were actually having a serious conversation. And frankly I'd appreciate it if you'd stop butting in.'

'Ooh, a *serious* conversation. Good for you. So it's not just physical, that's what you're saying? You're *serious* about her. *Kyu*taro the *cutie*-pie.'

Reluctant to waste any more time on this nonsense, I hurried Mai out into the courtyard. I half expected Yoshio to follow us, but when I glanced back I was relieved to see that he'd seated himself at the table, grinning all the while.

'Where are we going?' asked Mai, eyeing me with a resentment that was understandable given that I had dragged her out of the warm mansion and into the cold. 'Does this... I mean...' She sounded dubious. 'Does this have something to do with Fujitaka?'

'It does,' I replied, guiding her into the patch of bushes I'd hidden in last time, from which we could observe the entrance to the annex. 'Now, watch carefully, and you'll realize what it is I wanted to tell you. But, please—stay quiet. Whatever you see, try not to get too worked up.'

Mai was staring at me doubtfully, but then her expression froze. This, of course, was because Runa and Fujitaka had appeared, walking side by side and exchanging what could only be called amorous looks. They glanced around furtively, then slipped into the annex together. I sensed Mai's body begin to tremble, but as instructed she managed to remain silent.

'Mai, listen,' I began, choosing my words carefully. It would be counterproductive to provoke her jealousy any more than

I needed to. 'As you'll have guessed, Fujitaka and Runa are in an intimate relationship. But if that was all there was to this, I wouldn't have brought you here and made you see this. I'm not a sadist.'

'What are they…?' Mai didn't seem to have properly understood what I was telling her. Her eyes were practically burning with hatred. She looked almost high on her own rage. 'When did they start…?'

If I started trying to sate her curiosity, we'd be here all day. I decided to press on with what I had to say. 'What this comes down to is Grandfather's choice of successor. As I believe you're aware, he hasn't rewritten his will yet.'

'Oh, yeah,' replied Mai, her attention suddenly returning to me. It seemed that even for Mai, for whom a sort of affected indifference was normally a point of pride, the matter of the Fuchigami inheritance was an urgent one. 'He did say something like that.'

'Those two are planning to convince Grandfather to make them his heirs. In other words, they want to get married and take on the Fuchigami family name. They're going to tell him it's the only way to heal the rift between the Oba and Kanagae families—that it's the perfect solution for everyone involved.'

I gave Mai a rundown of everything Runa would be telling Fujitaka right at this moment. Fortunately, she seemed to believe me. Perhaps it seemed, to her, like just the sort of underhand thing her sister was capable of.

'Of course,' I continued, 'if they want to fall in love and get married, that's their choice. But it doesn't seem fair for that to affect the inheritance.' As for *why* it wasn't fair, I wasn't exactly sure, but I decided to press on before Mai could think too hard about what I was saying. 'If they pull a stunt like that, you'll hardly be able to give the marriage your blessing, will you? Given your secret feelings for Fujitaka, I mean.'

'Of course not!' Mai exclaimed, as though she'd suddenly discovered her fighting spirit. It looked like I wasn't going to have to come up with a reason why two people getting married counted as a 'stunt', either. 'They're mad if they think I'll let them get away with this. Trying to have their... their little happy ending all to themselves—shameless, that's what it is. Well, I'll show them. Yeah, I'm going to rain all over their stupid parade. Oh, but...' Her expression abruptly darkened. 'I wonder if I've really got it in me. Whatever I say to them, I bet Runa will find a way to wriggle out of it. I've never won an argument with her, you know. Not once, in my whole life...'

Maybe that was why Mai always seemed so gloomily on edge around her sister. 'You'll just have to strike first,' I replied. 'Show them that you already know exactly what they're up to. That'll give you the advantage.'

'But... how?'

'Listen, Runa has been going around to Fujitaka's apartment. Doing his laundry and cooking for him. He's particularly keen on her nikujaga stew, if you're interested. And she's planning on visiting him on the public holiday that's coming up. Oh, and her secret pet name for him is Fu-chan. All you have to do is reveal that you know all this, and they'll realize that you're not to be messed with.'

Of course, physical evidence would be even more convincing. I produced Runa's earring and handed it to Mai, explaining that if she claimed she'd picked it up after seeing Fujitaka drop it (a complete fabrication, of course), she'd be able to inflict quite the shock on her rival. As I handed her trump card after trump card, Mai eyed me warily, as if wondering how on earth I could know all this. Still, having apparently concluded that she might as well use the ammunition I'd provided, she was now simply glaring at the entrance to the annex, waiting for the pair to re-emerge.

'By the way,' I said, remembering something that had been weighing on my mind, 'it was Runa who told you Grandfather hadn't written his will yet, right?'

'Yeah.'

'When exactly *was* that?'

'When?' repeated Mai, as if baffled as to why this should matter. 'Yesterday. Last night, actually.'

'Last night?'

The night of the 1st of January, in other words. Something about this seemed odd to me. Grandfather had been planning to write his will after the New Year's dinner that evening. He'd declared as much in our presence. And yet he hadn't written it. How had Runa managed to discover this, and gain enough evidence to feel confident spreading the news to Fujitaka and Mai, all before the night was out?

'Did she tell you how she knew?'

'No. But she was all excited about it. I didn't believe her at first, but she seemed so sure of herself. Then again, she always does…'

'Who else was there?'

'Yoshio. Fujitaka-san was off somewhere.' She used the honorific suffix for Fujitaka, but casually omitted it for Yoshio. It made me wonder if I ever merited a *san* when I was out of earshot. 'Mum was there, too. And Aunt Kamiji. Ryuichi walked in at some point, too. I think that's everyone. Aunt Kotono and Kiyoko weren't there, and neither was Emi. Oh, and Grandfather wasn't there, either.'

'Where was this?'

'The banquet hall, obviously. We were drinking in there.'

I didn't know what time it had been when Grandfather decided not to write his will that night. At eleven o'clock, when I'd excused myself from the New Year's dinner and returned to my room in the old house, almost everyone—including Grandfather—had still been in the banquet hall, so it must have been later than that. If it was only after the dinner that he'd sat down to rack his brains over his successor, it could easily have been getting on for dawn by the time he'd decided to give up. 'You must have stayed up pretty late, then.'

'More like *you* went to bed too early.'

Eleven o'clock sounded like a perfectly reasonably time to go to sleep, but before I could protest, the door to the annex swung open. Fujitaka appeared—and, having fully embraced Runa's idea that all they had to do was talk to Grandfather and he'd make them his successors, was excitedly hurrying her out into the courtyard. All according to schedule.

'Grandfather's going to be in the old house today,' I whispered to Mai. 'So all you have to do is to stop them from going anywhere near it. Right then—you go get 'em, Mai.'

'H-hang on.' Mai sounded like she was getting cold feet. 'You're not coming with me?'

'No. They'd just use it against you. You know, saying you'd brought me along as your protector or something.' I felt a little guilty egging Mai on like this, but there was no turning back now. 'If you really want to be the one to steal Fujitaka's heart, you'll have to be brave. You can't back out now. You've got this, Mai. Show them what you're made of.'

By now you've probably worked out what my 'repair' strategy was, this time around. I wanted to stage a direct confrontation between Fujitaka and Runa on the one hand and Mai on the other. That way, I'd be able to keep any of them from going anywhere near the old house. As long as I managed to detain all three of my grandfather's would-be murderers in that way, he would be sure to make it through the day in one piece.

Of course, it was very unlikely Runa and Fujitaka would abandon their plan to get Grandfather on their side. But if they could just be persuaded to put it off until another day, that was all that mattered. Whether that happened or not depended entirely on Mai, and how much of her love for Fujitaka she'd manage to convert into the rage and venom required to obliterate her rival.

Personally, I rated her chances pretty highly. From the way she'd furiously launched herself over the table at Runa in the previous loop, it seemed her attachment to Fujitaka and her animosity towards her sister were both forces to be reckoned with.

And as I watched, Mai's surprise attack did seem to be getting off to an impressive start. After blocking the path of the pair who had just emerged from the annex, she began by waving the earring at a startled-looking Runa. Then, just as I'd suggested, she explained that she'd picked it up after seeing Fujitaka drop it, before slapping the earring into her sister's hand. After landing this devastating first blow, there was no stopping her. Judiciously dealing all the cards I'd given her— from 'Fu-chan' to the mention of nikujaga stew—she launched into a blistering and perfectly executed attack. In the face of the revelation that Mai not only knew about their relationship but was even familiar with its most intimate details, all Runa and Fujitaka could do was squirm.

Mai, meanwhile, seemed to be thoroughly enjoying herself. She seemed almost high on the experience—the first in her life, apparently—of putting her sister on the spot like this.

'Got some nerve, haven't you?! It's one thing hooking up behind my back. But to try and steal the company from under everyone's noses like this, I mean really… It's shameless, is what it is! Well, if you think I'm just going to stand here and watch, you've got another thing coming.'

At first, Runa could only listen in stunned silence as her normally submissive sister laid into her mercilessly. But her eyebrows, normally one of her most charming features, were bristling with anger, and now that her eyes had narrowed in rage she had begun to look oddly like my own mother. Given the family connection, maybe that wasn't such a surprise.

'Listen,' she eventually replied, 'it's not like I need your permission. You don't get to decide who I fall in love with. Or have sex with. Or do other things with, like—' Maybe it was the blood rushing to her head, but at this point Runa's counter-attack got a little racy. Out poured a stream of obscenities, all of them basically unprintable here without a lot of asterisks, the gist being that it was up to her whether she performed the acts in question. Watching Runa stand there in the middle of the courtyard screaming to all and sundry about her sexual proclivities was a pretty unsettling experience, but then I guess having her love life criticized by the sister she'd always looked down on had really touched a nerve. 'What, you think I care what you think? You, of all people? You must be crazy or something, Mai. Yeah, you heard me, crazy! Just because you'll never get to do anything like that. I mean, men don't even *look* at you, do they? What, has all that sexual frustration turned your brain to mush or something?'

'Fujitaka-san,' said Mai, turning to my brother, 'is this really the kind of woman you want to be with? I thought you were always saying you'd hate to end up with someone like your mum.' To my surprise, Mai had made the very point I'd been mentally urging her to—and managed to stay calm to boot. It seemed that the more frenzied and shrill her sister became, the easier she found it to observe her calmly and time her comments to perfection. 'I mean, just look at her now. I hate to say it, but she's a dead ringer for Aunt Kamiji. It's those angry eyes. The hysteria. Shrieking away like that about things nobody wants to hear. Come on—you really think you'd be happy married to *that*?'

Fujitaka had taken a step back and was watching the showdown between the sisters with a vaguely shellshocked expression. In the face of this sudden descent into angry vulgarity, it seemed cracks were beginning to show in his feelings for Runa—a fact that hadn't escaped Mai, who began to turn it to her advantage.

'Seriously,' she went on, 'are you going to let the promise of some nikujaga stew tempt you into the biggest mistake of your life? Anyway, nikujaga isn't hard. I bet you'll like mine even more.'

'It's not just my nikujaga!' exclaimed Runa. 'He doesn't just like me for my cooking. He likes me for all sorts of… other things I do for him! What, you think you can make him happy the way I do? What about—'

145

Mai chuckled as her sister began running through another list of actions that are unrepeatable here. 'What, you think being subservient to his every whim makes you some sort of catch? You make it sound like you want to be his slave. Listen, I like him, I really do. But if his love is conditional on me wearing underwear that sounds frankly impractical, or doing things that sound like they'd cause serious muscle pain, then count me out. That's not the kind of woman I want to be. Get this into your head: I want to be with him as his *equal*. Not his toy.'

It was a massacre. As the magnitude of Mai's victory sank in, Runa burst into tears, then began lashing out at Fujitaka.

'How can you let her do this? I thought you *loved* me! Remember when you told me how much you cared about me? How you'd always protect me? Well, now's the time. Tell her what she needs to hear. Go on, *say* something!'

But Fujitaka's discomfort had yielded to apathy. With a slightly affected shrug of the shoulders, he walked off and disappeared into the main building—without even a glance at either Runa or Mai. He must have realized that taking either side in the argument would only make him look like a clown. If he stuck up for Runa, he'd be a spineless lech trapped under the thumb of a hysterical woman. If he sided with Mai, he'd be a hopeless philanderer happy to swap one woman for another. Either way he'd end up a laughing stock. Better to cast them both aside and act like none of this had anything to do with him. In other words, Fujitaka had chosen to protect his own pride over that of the two sisters.

Despite being the orchestrator of this showdown, I found its tragic denouement a little hard to watch. Taken aback by

Fujitaka's rejection—not cold so much as glacial—Runa began blubbering like a baby. Mai, meanwhile, apparently high on the sheer elation of finally venting the feelings of inferiority and resentment she'd harboured for her sister over all these years, had an unsettling grin plastered on her face. There was a dangerous glint in her eyes: that of someone half drowning in the joy of discovering that hurting other people might just be the key to her own happiness.

Never had I been gladder to remind myself that, when the loop reset, all this would be undone and the memory of it obliterated. I wasn't sure I could bring myself to keep repeating this unsavoury tactic so that it became the 'definitive' version of the day's events. I decided right there and then that I'd try a different approach. Yes, devising a new way of preventing Grandfather's death would be a challenge, but that would still be preferable to a repeat of this distressing experience.

Runa, still crying her eyes out, disappeared into the main building. After all this, she would hardly have the energy for a visit to the old house; instead, she'd probably retreat to her room until she'd calmed down. Mai, meanwhile, seemed to have completely forgotten my presence (I had remained hidden in the bushes, watching the scene unfold) and disappeared into the same building without so much as a glance in my direction. What would *she* do next, I wondered. Throw some kind of celebration? Anything seemed possible.

Then, just as I was worrying that witnessing a scene like that might turn me into a misanthrope for life, I saw someone come hurrying down the walkway. It was Grandfather, clutching his large bottle of sake and making for the old house. Fine, I thought. All according to schedule.

But then I did a double take. Grandfather wasn't alone. At his side, glancing furtively about, was Yoshio. Yoshio, of all people. He was clasping various snacks to his chest, and the message written on both their faces was: *We're off for a secret drinking session in the attic!* They wore the knowing grins of two partners in crime.

What was going on? I was so bewildered that I couldn't even move. With me avoiding him all day, Grandfather was supposed to end up drinking on his own. How had Yoshio managed to insert himself into the situation? *That wasn't in the schedule!*

If, in the original loop, it had been the three of us— Grandfather, me and Yoshio—drinking in the attic, I might have understood. It would have been a simple case of me being subtracted from that equation. But that wasn't what had happened. It had only been me and Grandfather in the original loop, and in the second and third loops, when I'd removed myself from that situation, I had personally witnessed Grandfather heading into the old house alone.

Right now, though, I was witnessing the exact opposite. Grandfather was not alone. He was with Yoshio. How could something like this happen when it had never been part of the day's original schedule? The only answer, I decided, was that once again, by acting differently from in the previous loops, I had somehow set in motion a series of unforeseen consequences—one of which was this 'anomaly'.

The only specific trigger I could think of was the fact that Yoshio had overheard the beginning of my conversation with Mai. I'd explained that it had nothing to do with him and ushered Mai outside, after which I'd assumed he'd given up the chase. But had he? Yoshio was one of the nosiest people

I knew—and hardly the type to back down just because his little brother had insisted on it. What if, instead of returning upstairs after breakfast, he had taken up a position by one of the ground-floor windows and spied on us, hoping for a snatch of juicy gossip? And what if that window had been one of those closest to the walkway that led to the old house?

I didn't know how much of my conversation with Mai or her subsequent face-off with Runa he had heard. But even if, bored by the overly serious nature of the conversation, he had given up and decided to return to his room, he would still have bumped into Grandfather, clutching his bottle of sake, who would have quickly identified him as a suitable drinking companion. Yoshio, who had never heard a plan he didn't want in on, would have happily agreed. It wasn't like he had anything else to do. And so, like a dog merrily wagging its tail, he had followed Grandfather into the old house.

Whatever the details, I felt confident in the general accuracy of this hypothesis. Or rather, if I was honest, it was the only explanation I could think of for the discrepancy that had arisen in the day's schedule. Not that it mattered. Even if it turned out that I had successfully prevented Grandfather from dying, I couldn't bring myself to repeat this approach. If this version of the 2nd of January became definitive, a terrible and lasting rift would open up between Mai, Runa and Fujitaka—and I would be responsible. And if I was going to have to devise a brand-new strategy in the next loop anyway, a small discrepancy like Yoshio joining Grandfather was irrelevant.

But if that was the case, then why was I still standing out here in the cold? Maybe because I was getting one of my bad feelings again. For who knows how long, I simply stood there in the courtyard, staring at the walkway, my breath white in the air.

All of a sudden, Yoshio emerged from the old house. He was almost running, and stumbled slightly on his way back into the main building. I couldn't make out his expression from this angle. Was their drinking session already over? I waited for Grandfather to follow him, but there was no sign of him. Before long, Yoshio reappeared in the walkway.

When I saw what he was holding, I let out a low, stunned gasp. In Yoshio's arms were the flowers with petals shaped like gyoza wrappers. He was carrying the vase of moth orchids. Without even noticing my stupefied presence, my brother made his way back into the old house.

By the time I'd recovered from my state of shock and begun making my way towards the main building, Yoshio had already returned from the old house. I waited for Grandfather to return, but there was still no sign of him.

This can't be happening. I felt a wave of dizziness, as if the hangover I thought I'd shed had returned with a vengeance. No, this was far worse than a hangover. Could Yoshio really have… But no, that was ridiculous. For one thing, what on earth could be his motive? In fact, forget motives—was it even logically possible? However underhand my methods, I had managed to prevent Runa, Fujitaka and Mai from going anywhere near the old house. Consequently, Grandfather ought not to have been murdered by anyone. The entire incident had been consigned to the dustbin of history, as just one of the many possible versions of the past. It simply couldn't happen. It wasn't *allowed* to happen.

Still, I should probably check on him.

Then, just as I was urging my half-paralysed body back into the main building, I heard Aunt Haruna's scream. The blood-curdling feral howl.

This time, I didn't have to run to the attic to find out what had terrified her so. I already knew.

8

THE MURDER KEEPS HAPPENING

It was becoming painfully clear that I needed to rethink my approach entirely. At first, I'd assumed that all I needed to do was prevent Runa and Fujitaka from going near the old house. When I'd tried that, Mai had blindsided me—and when I'd attempted to restrict *her* movements, Yoshio had launched his own surprise attack.

A summary of the various individuals who had been with Grandfather in the attic—the scene of the crime—would look something like the following.

ORIGINAL LOOP: I drank with Grandfather. No harm came to him during this loop.

SECOND LOOP: Runa and Fujitaka, who had gone up to the attic in order to present themselves as his potential successors. Possible motive: the discussion regarding the inheritance went awry, eventually leading to some sort of emotional flare-up. Murder weapon: the vase of moth orchids that Emi had given Aunt Kotono as a present. Aunt Haruna had discovered the body.

THIRD LOOP: Mai. After learning about her sister's relation-ship with Fujitaka and flying into a rage, she may have gone up to the attic intending to hide until she'd calmed down— only to discover Grandfather sitting there drinking. Possible motive: Grandfather made some throwaway comment that happened to inflame Mai's already fragile emotional state. Murder weapon: the bottle of sake that Grandfather had been drinking. I had discovered the body.

FOURTH LOOP: Yoshio. Grandfather may have bumped into him and invited him to join him in the attic for a drink; or Yoshio, spotting the bottle in his hand, may have proposed the idea himself. Murder weapon and discovery of body identical to number 2.

If I wanted to prevent my grandfather's demise, it seemed it wasn't enough to restrict the movements of whoever had murdered him in the previous loop. A clear pattern had devel-oped whereby, even if I managed to prevent one murderer from approaching the old house, another would spring up in their place and successfully carry out the crime. As for *why* this should happen, I had no idea. Grandfather's murder was not an event that featured in the original loop, which meant there was no logical basis for its continued occurrence. And yet the reality was that it *was* occurring, like clockwork, every single time.

As I mentioned earlier, the root of the problem might lie in the fact that, from the second loop onwards, I had not kept Grandfather company while he drank. That certainly seemed plausible. In fact, it was the only real explanation I could think of. In other words, as long as I stayed by Grandfather's side and spent the afternoon drinking with him, the murder would not take place—assuming that, in some fit of passion, I didn't somehow become the 'substitute' murderer myself. Still, for the time being at least, this remained my plan of last resort.

While I'd been able to conceive of a motive for the killers in the second and third loops, I was completely stumped when it came to Yoshio. And yet he had opted for the exact same murder weapon as Runa and Fujitaka—the vase. Not only that, but just as in the second loop, it turned out he had told Aunt Haruna—who wanted to discuss the will with Grandfather— that he'd seen him heading for the old house, thereby ensuring that she would be the one to discover the body. In other words, the motive was a mystery, but the method was practically identical. It was downright bizarre. Of course, with the events of the second loop having long been 'reset', there was no way Yoshio could have somehow copied the approach taken by Runa and Fujitaka in committing the crime. The whole thing was an enigma.

I even had the rather outlandish idea that maybe Yoshio had not even killed Grandfather of his own will. That he had been driven to commit the crime by some force beyond human comprehension.

In any case, there was no escaping the fact that if I wanted to prevent the murder, my current method was useless. I needed to rethink my approach from the ground up. This was the conclusion I arrived at while I waited, once again, to be summoned for the next of my many interviews with the police. So, with that resolve burning in my chest, I sat and watched as the clock ticked towards twelve.

154

Midnight came, and the 2nd of January was reset. The fifth loop had begun. As usual, I woke in complete darkness, my throat parched. At this point I normally lay there thinking about whether to go to the kitchen for some water before eventually dropping off again, but this time I decided to seize the moment. Still half-asleep, I writhed around, pinching my thigh repeatedly. Then, once the pain had brought me back to consciousness, I got up from my futon. I didn't want to fall into the old trap of dreaming that I'd woken up when really I was still asleep, so I pinched my cheek for good measure. The pain felt pretty real to me. Right, I was awake. I stifled a yawn and stretched my sleepy muscles. My alarm clock told me that it was a few minutes past three in the morning.

I turned the light on, then began by checking the stairs. In the usual spot, by now so familiar, I found Runa's earring. So it was already here at this time of night. In other words, Runa had visited the old house at some point between eleven p.m. on the 1st of January and three a.m. on the morning of the 2nd. Unfortunately, it would be impossible to narrow this window any further. Three o'clock in the morning had already been established as the time at which I woke up upon each 'reset', and it was impossible for me to wake myself up any earlier. The moment the clock's hands reached midnight, I would find myself waking up in my futon at a few minutes past three.

Still, at least I'd managed to narrow the window to a mere four hours. Runa could have been here moments ago. As for the reason for this visit in the middle of the night, perhaps it was in some way connected to her being the first to learn that Grandfather had postponed writing his will. I decided, in any case, that this would be the initial focus of my investigation.

I turned the light off and, eyes still adjusting to the dark, made my way down to the kitchen. Of course, it was empty. Guided only by the half-light coming through the windows, I passed along the walkway and into the main building.

First I checked the banquet hall. When I had gone to bed at eleven p.m. on the 1st of January, the New Year's dinner had still been in full swing. Which meant it was very possible that even now, at three a.m. on the 2nd, my family would still be there, carousing into the wee hours. But I found the banquet hall pitch dark, deserted and deathly quiet. The reception room next door was the same.

Next I tried the dining room. This too was empty, though the light was on above the sink in the adjoining kitchen. Suddenly remembering my parched throat, I poured and drank a glass of water.

Where next? I had abruptly run out of steam. I'd been convinced that everyone would still be in the banquet hall, and that I'd be able to eavesdrop while some revealing exchange took place. For example, Runa announcing that Grandfather hadn't written his will yet. But it seemed they had all gone to bed.

I decided to go upstairs, though I didn't know exactly what for. Worried that anyone who caught me wandering around at this time of night would assume I had some shady motive, I deliberately steered clear of the wing where the women slept. As a result, I found myself walking in the direction of my grandfather's study.

I stopped short. Light was leaking from the cracks around the study door. It seemed Grandfather was still awake. For a moment I wondered if he might even be writing the will at this very moment. But no, that was impossible. By this time, Runa had already told everyone in the banquet hall that he'd put it off.

Still, I pressed my ear up against the door to listen. The door must not have been closed properly, because it swung open under the weight of my body.

I peered into the room. There, slumped over a writing desk the size of a small swimming pool, was Grandfather. For a moment I worried he might be dead—but then I was reassured to hear him snoring slightly. He looked as though he'd been in the middle of something when he'd dozed off. There was a blanket around his shoulders. Kiyoko or Aunt Kotono must have wrapped it around him when they found him like this.

I glanced at what was in front of him on the desk. I'd assumed he'd been busy with some sort of paperwork, but the truth was more surprising. Although, given how familiar a certain conversation had become over the past four days—or loops, rather—maybe I should have seen it coming.

Strewn in front of Grandfather were various sheets of origami paper. Ordinary-looking, handkerchief-sized sheets of origami paper. Two of them appeared to be work in progress, while one black sheet had already been folded into a crane.

When I'd overheard the conversation with Aunt Kotono and Kiyoko, I'd had my doubts, but it seemed the old guy really did like to stay up late at night making origami. Each to their own, of course, but knowing my grandfather's character, I couldn't help thinking there was something odd about this habit.

I scanned the desk and saw that, as expected, there was no red paper. The colour whose absence, he'd claimed, meant he couldn't make his origami at all. And yet here he was, having already completed one crane with the black paper. As I was gazing at the desk in confusion, I noticed something. Red wasn't the only colour that was missing. The origami paper scattered on the desk was much less varied than you would expect. I could only see three colours: black, blue and yellow. There wasn't even a scrap of paper in any other shade. Okay, we all have our favourite colours, and maybe Grandfather simply had his heart set on those three plus the missing red, but I couldn't shake the feeling that there was something more to it.

There was one other peculiar object on the desk—a sort of box. It appeared to have been hand-made, using white card, and was about the size of the boxes they give you at a cake shop. A round hole, roughly the size of the palm of someone's hand, had been cut into its upper surface. It looked a bit like a large-size box of tissues. I tried turning it upside down and shaking it, but there was nothing inside.

But my attention was soon distracted from the box. I had just noticed something else on the desk. A diary. Grandfather's fingers lay on the edge of its cover. Slowly, so as not to wake him, I slid it out from under them. It was for the year that had just started. Brand-new, of course, and fitted with a lock. When I flicked through it, my eyes were immediately drawn to the entry on the first double-page spread.

1st January. New Year's dinner. Kamiji and sons plus Haruna and daughters in attendance. No sign of either of their husbands. It's all going swimmingly. Ryuichi and Emi also here as usual. Kiyoko's osechi was delicious.

This was all the first page said. On the next was the following:

2nd January. Kotono and Kiyoko both pestering me to cut down on my drinking. I know they're worried, given that Fukae died from a stroke, but I haven't got much longer to live anyway and I wish they'd stop trying to ruin one of my few remaining pleasures. Had a good drink anyway. Feel wonderful.

Presumably this part referred to him staying up past midnight to drink at the New Year's dinner. Though this meant that technically the date *had* changed, it still seemed very pedantic of him to record what was essentially the same evening on a new page with the next day's date. I guess that was another side to the old man I hadn't known about.

I flicked over to the next page, expecting it to be blank, only to find another entry.

3rd January. Still can't decide. Everyone's staying over, but I've decided to postpone the will until at least the 4th. Shop's closed, so nothing doing.

Grandfather appeared to have written this part just before dozing off. The date of the entry had to be a mistake. Maybe he'd been confused by his own decision to record the events that took place after midnight on a new page. He may have intended to leave a gap before continuing but, in his drunken excitement, accidentally started another new page, even writing in the date to match.

Well, now I knew how Runa had been the first to discover that Grandfather had postponed writing his will. She must have secretly read the diary. Maybe she'd come here hoping to talk to him about the inheritance and happened to catch sight of it—Grandfather being away from his desk or, as he was now, fast asleep.

That all made sense. But there were aspects of the diary that confused me. For example, he'd written that he'd postponed writing the will until at least the fourth, but what did he mean by *Shop's closed, so nothing doing*? What sort of shop could he be talking about? There was something else, too—in the entry for the 1st of January, he'd written *It's all going swimmingly.* What did 'it' refer to? All I could guess was that it referred to some personal matter of Grandfather's—after all, very little was going 'swimmingly' when it came to the parlous state of the Oba and Kanagae families.

As I carefully slid the diary back under his hand, I had an idea. If the old man was in the habit of keeping a diary, maybe I could glean something from those he'd kept in previous years. For example, I asserted earlier that there was no plausible motive for Yoshio to have killed Grandfather in the fourth loop, but it was possible that there was actually some deep-seated antagonism between the two of them that I simply didn't know about. Grandfather's old diaries might shed some light on that sort of thing.

I set about searching his bookshelves. The diaries were surprisingly easy to find. What looked like almost two decades' worth of them were neatly arranged on one of the shelves, all lavishly bound and fitted with locks. Without hesitating, I swiped the diaries from the shelf. I decided to take them somewhere and read them. As for the locks, I would simply break them open. When the current loop ended, the diaries would 'repair' themselves without me having to lift a finger, and wherever they ended up, they'd find their way back to these shelves. It was at times like this that the 'reset' feature of the Trap really came into its own.

With the stack of diaries in my arms, I made my way back to the old house. I was about to go up to the attic when it struck me that, later that day, Grandfather would come here for his drinking session. I could always hide the diaries somewhere in my room, but I'd still have to retrieve them at some point. In the end, I went back out into the courtyard, my breath white in the frosty air, then headed to the annex. I hid the diaries in the closet there, then returned to the main building.

My plan now was to find a hiding spot in the dining room before Kiyoko started making breakfast, so that I'd be able to eavesdrop on the conversation around the table. I wasn't sure this would yield any particularly useful information, but if I wanted to develop a truly effective strategy, I needed a more detailed understanding of the overall situation on this 2nd of January. The dining room was the one place that everyone was sure to visit at least once, making it perfect for intelligence-gathering.

The only problem, it turned out, was that it had no decent hiding places. While I hurried around looking for one, it was getting on for six o'clock. The day was dawning. I heard the sound of slippers in the corridor. Seeing no other option, I crouched between the sideboard and the spare table. As hiding places went, it wasn't ideal. I was just about hidden from view, but the moment someone decided to sit at the spare table, the game would be up. With everyone eating at different times, that didn't seem too likely, but if anyone did find me I'd struggle to find an excuse—though of course I always had the 'reset' to fall back on.

The dining room light came on. I peered out from my hiding place and saw Kiyoko, wearing her usual smock. I was impressed to see her up so early the morning after the New Year's dinner. She briskly set about preparing breakfast for everyone. A while later, she was joined by Aunt Kotono, dressed of course in her green tracksuit, who helped her. When they'd finished, they began tucking in themselves.

'Tell me, Kiyoko,' I heard Aunt Kotono say. I thought about peeking out, then realized that I'd be directly visible from where she was sitting. I decided to stick to eavesdropping. 'What do you reckon?'

There was silence for a few seconds. Kiyoko seemed to be politely refraining from replying until she'd chewed and swallowed her mouthful of food. 'About the adoption, you mean, Madam?'

'Do you think my father meant it?'

'Meant what, may I ask?'

'That thing he said about announcing it this afternoon.'

'Hmm. Hard to say, isn't it? I certainly don't think he meant it as a joke, but… something tells me he'll just end up putting it off again. I mean, what with the shop being closed…'

'That does makes things difficult, doesn't it.'

All these references to the 'shop' were, frankly, starting to get annoying, but I decided to focus on something else my aunt had mentioned: the part about Grandfather making an announcement this afternoon. Of course, the announcement in question had to refer to his choice of successor. I'd been baffled when I'd heard Runa and Fujitaka discussing the same thing, but here was confirmation that Grandfather really *had* changed his mind about keeping his will a secret until his death. He must have raised the topic after I went to bed on the night of the New Year's dinner, when the others had stayed up drinking.

'Kiyoko, I want your honest opinion. Who do *you* think would make the best heir?'

'Do you mean best for yourself, Ms Fuchigami? Or best for the master of the house?'

'I don't think Father really cares, you know. The company only exists in the first place because he got lucky and came into all that money. I think as far as he's concerned, his successor can run it back into the ground if they like. In fact, I wouldn't be surprised if he almost wants the place to go belly-up while he's still around—you know, so he can tie up all the loose ends.'

'Well, then, I suppose it depends on you. But tell me, why aren't *you* the one making the decision?'

'Because I can't decide! The problem is, the ones I'd like to have as sons or daughters all seem like they'd be useless at running the company. And the ones who do seem to have a head for business are the ones I don't really fancy adopting. In the end, it feels like all I can do is leave it up to my father to choose.'

'If you don't mind me asking, who exactly are you thinking of?'

'Well, Emi would make a fine successor to Father. She's the sharpest of the bunch, that's for sure. A real professional. But see, that's exactly why, as a daughter, I don't know if I'd be able

163

to really love her deeply, or feel comfortable with her, if you see what I mean.'

'Well, if it's talent you're after, wouldn't Mr Tsuchiya be a good choice?'

'No, Ryuichi's no good. I know he comes across all shrewd and resourceful, but something tells me he's the type to panic when it comes to the crunch. One unexpected setback and he'll get all flustered and come running to Mummy in tears. That's just a hunch of mine, mind.'

'What, you think he's secretly a mama's boy? That *would* be an issue…'

'Like I say, it's just a hunch. But there's also the fact that he's smitten with Runa.'

'He is?'

'Apparently. And I mean, if *that's* his taste in women…'

'Right. Well, who do you think would make a good adopted child, then?'

'Mai, I reckon. You know, I see myself in her. That feeling of always being overshadowed by your younger sister. Of course, I'm sure she has her problems. But she's the one I can most *see* as my daughter.'

'Then why not adopt her? I mean, if it doesn't matter whether she's any good at business…'

'That's the problem. Father might think that way, but I certainly don't. The company is my life these days, Kiyoko.'

'Right. That *is* a problem.'

'Which is why I've left the decision to Father. Still…' I heard Aunt Kotono set her dish down on the table and let out a deep sigh. 'I didn't expect him to come up with an idea like that. I mean, of all the ways of going about it…'

164

'Well, the master does like to gamble.'

'You can't even call it gambling, what he's doing. At least with gambling there's a bit more to it. He just doesn't seem to be taking it seriously.'

'I hate to put it this way, but, erm…'

'What?'

'Well, people do say that old age is a sort of second childhood. I wonder if—'

But Kiyoko was cut off by someone walking in and saying good morning. I recognized the voice as Emi's.

'I'm very sorry, Ms Fuchigami,' she said. 'Here I am, staying in your family home, and I've gone and overslept.'

'Oh, shush. It's not even seven o'clock yet. We're the only ones up. You could have slept longer if you liked.'

There was no sarcasm in Aunt Kotono's voice, but I could see why Emi might be struggling to relax into the role of a mere guest, given that this was her boss's house. From the tone of her voice, it was clear she felt embarrassed not to have helped with breakfast.

Aunt Kotono and Kiyoko finished their breakfast and left the dining room, after which I could hear Emi quietly sitting and eating on her own. Then I heard another voice. It was Ryuichi.

'Ooh, someone's up early.'

'This isn't early,' replied Emi. 'Ms Fuchigami and Kiyoko have already eaten.'

'Really? What about the Chairman?'

'I haven't seen him yet.'

'Must still be in bed, then. Phew. I'd be a pretty lousy assistant if I slept later than my boss and sat around eating after he'd finished. Sorry, no offence.'

'None taken.'

'Right, then. Well, I think I might join you.'

I'd never heard Ryuichi speak in such a loose, familiar tone. If this was how he talked when it was just him and Emi, then maybe he wasn't quite as considerate as I'd assumed. I'd been surprised by Aunt Kotono's suggestion that he wasn't heir material, but I was beginning to feel strangely convinced.

'You hear?' he asked, his tone growing even more casual. He sounded like he was talking with his mouth full. 'He hasn't written the will yet.'

'Really, is that so?' Maybe it was just my imagination, but the chummier Ryuichi got, the more Emi seemed to stiffen. 'I wasn't aware.'

'Look at you, acting like it's got nothing to do with you.'

'Well, it's none of my business.'

'Oh, but it is, isn't it? I mean, you *are* one of the candidates for adoption, after all.'

'I'm planning on asking Ms Fuchigami for permission to withdraw.'

'Too late for that. I mean, the Chairman already asked if you were interested, and you said yes. That was your chance to turn it down, and you missed it.'

'Yes, I'm aware that was a little ill-advised of me.'

'You're overthinking this. I mean, you've got nothing to lose if he doesn't pick you—and everything to gain if he does.'

Emi gave no reply.

'Listen,' he went on. 'I've been meaning to say this for a while, but don't you think the two of us should try and… get on a little better?'

'What is that supposed to mean?'

'What do you think it means? The future of the Edge Restaurant Group may well rest on our shoulders, Emi. A closer relationship between us would be the most natural thing in the world.'

'I don't plan on letting anything rest on my shoulders. My job keeps me busy enough as it is.'

'Have I done something to upset you?' said Ryuichi with a forced chuckle, as though he was beginning to lose patience with Emi's reserved manner. 'You know, I think of you as an important... partner.'

'Sorry, what?'

'You're a capable woman. Just the kind of talent Edge needs. Don't you think? Meanwhile, I might be running the company before long. I know, nothing's been officially decided yet, but the odds have got to be in my favour. Still, I won't be able to do it all on my own. That's why I need you as a partner, Emi. Not just at work. I'm talking about our... private lives, too.'

'What exactly are you trying to say?'

'Isn't it obvious? If the President makes me the heir, I want you to be my wife. We'd be a team—both at work and in the home.'

I found myself wondering if what Ryuichi was really after was a sort of insurance policy. In other words, if he was picked as the successor, he would make Emi his wife—and in return, if she was chosen, he expected her to return the favour. Of course, if even slow-witted me had managed to work this out, then Emi would have seen it coming a mile off.

'Really. And what's the plan if the Chairman doesn't choose either of us?' she asked sardonically. 'Oh, I get it. If it's Runa, you'll try and make her your wife instead, will you?'

'You know, I wish you wouldn't second-guess people like this.' As Emi's tone lightened, Ryuichi's seemed to stiffen in response. 'That's *not* what I was implying.'

'Let me make one thing very clear, Ryuichi. My heart already belongs to another man.' I couldn't see Ryuichi's expression, but I heard nothing to suggest that he found this revelation particularly shocking. If anyone was shocked, of course, it was me. 'And I plan to marry him.'

'Come on, who are you kidding? You've never even mentioned a boyfriend before.' This was quite some logic: *I haven't heard about something, so it can't be true.* 'Not that you're an unattractive woman. Let me be very clear on that point. But you're a workaholic, Emi—when would you even have the time to date someone? There's no chance you're in that deep with someone. Admit it—you're just trying to throw me off the scent, aren't you?'

'Okay, so our relationship is in its early stages. But I've been in love with him for a long time. And just recently he told me he wanted me to seriously consider a future together. I haven't given him my reply yet, but I'm planning on accepting.'

'Wow. So… you're serious.' Ryuichi voice was trembling ever so slightly. It seemed she wasn't just his insurance policy, after all: he really had fallen for her. 'Well, I think you should break it off. Not that I know the first thing about him. But I do know you. An ordinary marriage like that will never be enough for you. I'd think twice about this, Emi.'

'Actually, I know it sounds a little old-fashioned, but that's what I've always dreamt of: having an ordinary marriage, becoming an ordinary housewife, being an ordinary mother. It's not like there's anything tying me to this job. So, please, would you stop trying to interfere? Now, I should be going.'

'You'll regret this.' Ryuichi's words sounded less like an expression of bitterness than an attempt persuade himself that he was right. 'I'm going to take over the company, Emi. Mark my words. There's no one else who can do it, and the Chairman knows it. Which is why I'm telling you: think twice. Hey, where are you—'

After Emi had left the room, I peered out to see Ryuichi staring vacantly into space with an expression that suggested he'd lost his appetite slightly. He must have been utterly convinced his plan would work—which was why Emi's rejection had come as such a shock. Still, he can't have been all that shaken, because by the time he'd polished off the food on his plate, I could hear him whistling away to himself. Maybe he'd remembered that there was always Runa.

No such recovery was on the cards for me, on the other hand. I was genuinely heartbroken. In fact, the shock was so great that, for a moment, my grandfather's murder seemed to pale into insignificance. I should have seen this coming. I'd been conceited enough to believe, without any real evidence, that I was the only one who saw Emi for the attractive woman she was, but no: the world was a big old place, and somewhere in it there was someone—a grown man, presumably—who had beaten me to the punch. I was out of luck.

The intimate conversation I'd had with Emi in the original loop had already been 'reset', and in my desperation to prevent Grandfather's murder, I'd been obliged to give up on repeating the exchange. Now, though, I had to admit that had probably been for the best. Our exchange had been consigned to oblivion, but I shuddered to remember the way I'd prattled on at her. Emi had probably been thinking: *What on earth is this randy little high schooler on about?* But because I was the Chairman's grandson, and the President's nephew, she couldn't just laugh in my face, and had instead gracefully extricated herself from the situation. The more I thought about it, the more I felt myself cringe. I really was glad the day had been reset.

After Ryuichi left, I decided to emerge from my hiding place. My heartbreak even seemed to be taking a toll on my own physical strength, because my crouched position was becoming painful. Not only that, but after listening to so many other people eat, I was ravenous.

I'd just crawled out and was stretching when Runa walked in.

'Oh. Morning, Kyu-chan. How are you feeling?'

'Ah, I'm… er… fine. Why, wouldn't I be?'

'Well, you really hit the booze last night, didn't you… You having breakfast?'

'I am.'

'Me too. I bumped into Fu-cha—sorry, Fujitaka just now and asked him if he was coming. But apparently he doesn't normally eat breakfast?'

'That's right.' *You're the one who's practically moved in with him,* I thought. *I'd imagine you're better versed in my brother's dietary habits than I am.* I couldn't decide whether her attempt to pass this off as something she'd only just learnt was irritatingly forced or sort of adorable. 'So you've already asked him to join you in the annex, have you?'

Runa had just taken a sip of miso soup when I asked this. She sprayed it across the table and made a series of guttural choking noises. For some reason I found myself thinking about how she'd probably have one of those seductive husky voices when she was older.

'Wh-what?' she spluttered. 'But... how did you... I mean, what do you mean?'

'I was on the stairs just now.' It seemed that another after-effect of my heartbreak was that I was happy to lie to people's faces at a moment's notice. 'I heard you mention it.'

'Really? Well, someone's got *very* good hearing.' Runa was staring at me as if to say, *But I basically whispered it in his ear!* In fact, it was quite possible that they hadn't even had this exchange in the corridor, but in one of their rooms, in which case I couldn't possibly have heard it from the stairs, no matter how phenomenal my hearing was. No wonder she was eyeing me so suspiciously. 'Erm, Kyu-chan, when I said that to him—about coming to the annex—that was just because... I mean, there's nothing... It was just...'

'You wanted to talk to him about the inheritance, didn't you?'

Now she looked at me like I was some sort of monster. 'How did you know that?'

'Well, why else would two cousins suddenly need to see each other at a time like this?'

'Right. Yeah.' Runa looked relieved to have been provided with a logical explanation to cling to. 'That's right. I mean, what else could we... It's all anyone's talking about at the moment, isn't it?'

'Ah, before I forget. I found this, too.' I set the earring down on the table. 'I believe it's yours?'

'Erm. Yeah, it is. Where did you find it?'

'On the stairs to your rooms. Now, about this discussion in the annex. I actually wondered if we could join you.'

'You? …Join us? Wait, who's *we*?'

'Me, Yoshio and Mai. I feel like it's time we all had a little chat, don't you?'

'But, um, Kyu-chan… I get what you're saying, I really do. But we were actually, um, planning something a little more…'

'There's something important I want to discuss. Let Fujitaka know, would you?' Even I was surprised by how coldly and dismissively I spoke. It seemed the shock and pain of losing Emi was only growing over time. Right now, though, that was probably working in my favour. Having deduced from my serious demeanour that I really did have something important to discuss, Runa simply nodded meekly.

'I'll let Yoshio and Mai know,' I went on. 'Oh, and by the way. You and Fujitaka should keep things secret a little longer, in my opinion.'

'K-keep what secret? Wh-what are you talking about, Kyu-chan?'

'Especially Mai. Be very careful about when you let her know.'

'I'm telling you, I have no idea what you're on about.'

'Well, Runa, I'm sure you can imagine the kind of tragedy that can unfold when two sisters fall in love with the same man. Before you and Fujitaka make things public, I think you should spend a bit of time being really nice to your sister. You know, getting on her good side. Laying the groundwork. Telling Grandfather and the others can wait until later. That would be my advice.'

'Seriously, Kyu-chan, are you… okay? Rambling away about who knows what, with that miserable look on your face. You look like you've just had your heart broken or something.'

'I have. Just a moment ago, in fact.'

'Really? Oh…' Runa gave me a compassionate look as she got to her feet. I must have really cut quite a forlorn figure. I only found this out later, but it seemed that Runa, without knowing the exact cause, got it into her head that I was feeling suicidal, and ended up relaying her concerns to my mother. I could hardly blame her—after all, it wasn't so far from the truth. 'Anyway, I should get going.'

'I'll see you in the annex, okay? Remember—bring Fujitaka.'

'R-right. Yeah. See you.'

Just as Runa left the room, Mai walked in, followed by Yoshio. All according to schedule. I told them we cousins had an urgent matter to discuss, and that they should come to the annex. They took one look at me, then agreed with surprising readiness. Like Runa, they seemed a little concerned about my mental state.

Of course, gathering all the cousins in the annex was part of my plan to prevent Grandfather's murder. The idea was to detain all the 'historical' perpetrators of the killing—the Runa and Fujitaka double act, Mai and Yoshio—in one location. Now, I said earlier that simply restricting the movement of the murderers from previous loops wouldn't go deep enough in solving the problem. I still thought this—and yet, however convinced I was of the need for some ingenious new plan, I'd failed to come up with one. So when I'd spotted a chance to keep all the 'murderers' in one place, I'd decided to give it a try. After all, it might just work.

In any case, what I was really interested in were the diaries I'd taken from Grandfather's office. I'd have preferred to read them on my own, but with close to twenty volumes to get through, I simply wouldn't have the time. Instead, I'd struck on the idea of dividing the labour up among my brothers and cousins, thereby reducing the required reading time by a factor of five. If anyone stumbled across anything of interest, they would report it to me. And when the loop reset, they'd forget all about the fact that they'd been reading their grandfather's diaries, and it would be as though I'd been the only one to read them. Talk about efficient.

Feeling quite pleased with the devious intellectual crime I had concocted, I made my way to the annex, where I handed the diaries out to my assembled brothers and cousins. When I declared that we were going to read them and then share their contents, the four of them were, understandably, dumbfounded.

Even Yoshio, for whom recklessness was normally a point of pride, seemed concerned. 'Er, Kyutaro, don't you think you've gone a bit too far? This is, like, a major invasion of privacy.'

'We're the ones whose privacy is being invaded,' I replied. It looked like I had some serious persuading to do. 'Grandfather keeps saying he wants to ensure his successor is really willing to take the job, but in that case don't you think he could be bit a more democratic about all this? He could ask anyone who thinks they have what it takes to step forward and make their case—then as a family we'd consider our options and reach a consensus. That would be the logical solution. Instead, he's forcing people who are neither willing nor qualified to enter the running. I say "running", but if this were really a competition, we'd at least know who was in the lead. In the end, though, it all comes down to Grandfather's whims. If the person he picks happens to be both willing and competent, then great, but what if that's not the case? The heir will be forced to take on an impossible burden—and the people who *were* cut out

174

for the job will spend the rest of their lives rueing the missed opportunity. Under circumstances like these, can we really say he's respecting our intentions?'

'Still, I don't see why that means we get to peek in his diaries,' replied Yoshio.

'*If you know the enemy and know yourself, you need not fear the result of a hundred battles.* Haven't you heard that one?'

'…What?' said Yoshio, visibly wincing. Historical proverbs were clearly not his strong point. 'Alright, nerd. Don't start quoting things at me.'

'It's Sun Tzu,' explained Mai, her face deadly serious. 'Kyutaro's saying that knowledge is the key to victory.'

'That's right. This is a battle,' I declared with a solemnness to match Mai's. 'Our rights are being trampled. Are we really going to put up with that? If not, what should we do? I think our only course of action is to get Grandfather to abandon his current approach. Instead of choosing his successor on a whim, he should enable a free and fair competition between those with the necessary ambition and talent.'

'But… how?' asked Yoshio. 'You know what Grandfather's like. Once he's made his mind up…'

'That's why we need to learn more about him. These diaries may contain crucial information. Something we can use to make him listen.'

'Hang on, Kyutaro'—Yoshio gave an uncertain chuckle, as if he couldn't decide whether to be interested or terrified by my idea—'are you suggesting we blackmail Grandfather?'

'Maybe. Who knows? If it does come to that, he'll only have himself to blame. He's the one holding the future of *our* families hostage.'

'But these are locked,' murmured Fujitaka, reaching for one of the diaries. He was acting all calm, but I could tell the idea had piqued his interest. He seemed to have concluded that if there *was* any ammunition we could use against Grandfather, we might as well arm ourselves with it. 'How are we going to read them? Or did you manage to get the keys, too?'

'We break them open. With this.' When I held up the screwdriver I'd brought with me, the four of them backed away from me with comical speed. 'Don't worry. I'll take responsibility for locking them again and putting them back where I found them. Grandfather will never know they were gone. Even if he does find out, I won't say or do anything to get any of you in trouble. That's a promise. Please—trust me on this.'

This seemed to settle it. Fujitaka grabbed three of the diaries, wrenched the locks open with the screwdriver and began reading in silence. Yoshio, apparently wanting to outdo his brother, took five. Runa hesitated the longest, but the sight of Mai cautiously picking up three of the diaries seemed to kindle her competitive spirit: in the end, she took four.

Soon a strange, silent fervour had taken hold of everyone in the annex. The question of the inheritance was clearly weighing heavily on all our minds. I sat on the windowsill and began reading a diary from just over a decade ago. It was from the period when Grandfather and Aunt Kotono's restaurant business had suddenly taken off. The old man must have been swept off his feet in those days, because plenty of the pages were blank or contained only a few lines of handwriting. The entries themselves mainly consisted simply of comments about which dishes had sold well on the day in question.

As I flicked through the pages, something moved in the corner of my eye. I glanced out of the window and saw Grandfather heading down the walkway to the old house. He had the bottle of sake in his hand—and, of course, he was alone. That was a relief. Yoshio was safely here with us. This time, surely, there would be no murder.

'Fujitaka,' said Yoshio, tilting his head to one side as he thumbed through one of the diaries. 'Who's "Mr Kawazoe"? I feel like I've heard the name before somewhere.'

'Mr Kawazoe?' repeated Fujitaka, looking up from his own diary in vague recognition. 'What's his first name?'

'It doesn't say. Oh, wait, here we go. Shota Kawazoe.'

'Oh, that's Dad's boss. You know, the president of his company. Do you think that's who Grandfather means? Couldn't it just be someone with the same name?'

'No, it's got to be him. Look, he's written the company's name, too.'

'So Grandfather knows Mr Kawazoe? Weird, he's never mentioned that.'

'Hey, Mai,' said Runa, also cocking her head to one side as she looked up. 'Does the name Tsurui ring any bells?'

'Tsurui? Yeah. Now that you mention it…' It seemed Mai didn't get the chance to help her little sister like this very often. With a rare eagerness, she came and peered over Runa's shoulder. '*Tsurui. Tsurui…* Yeah, I've definitely heard it before somewhere.'

'Right? I just can't place it. Oh wait, look, it says Mayu Tsurui here. So it's a woman. Hmm, who could it be…?'

'Oh!' All of a sudden, Mai let out a wild shriek, causing Yoshio to drop the diary he was holding in alarm. 'Ru–Runa!'

'What? What's got into you?'

'Mayu Tsurui. She's...' Mai snatched the diary from her sister's hands. 'Isn't she that... You know. Dad's pupil... the one he tried it on with. That's her, isn't it?'

Now it was Runa's turn to howl in surprise. 'Oh my god! That's right. It's her, definitely. But... but...'

'Why, though? What's her name doing in Grandfather's diary, of all places?'

Yoshio, Fujitaka and I began reading over her shoulder. In Grandfather's familiar handwriting were the words *Agreement reached with Mayu Tsurui*. Spurred by this discovery, we each began combing our respective diaries to see if the name reoccurred anywhere. It didn't, but the diary from the preceding year contained a series of references that seemed like they might be related. Combined with those Runa had found, they read as follows:

Proving harder than expected to solve the problem with money alone. I thought that was all young girls cared about these days...

Have received an update on the situation. My connection has found a girl who's looking for an excuse to drop out of school. Will have her approached.

Suggested a fee of one million yen. Offered to pay in instalments but she wants it all at once. Communicated to her that a lump sum risks attracting attention. Negotiations ongoing.

Agreement reached regard payment of one million yen in instalments. But now she wants help finding a job. Something at the

Group wouldn't be appropriate, so have asked my connection to sort something out for her.

Her name is Mayu Tsurui. Asked if I wanted to see her photo. Not sure why. Refused.

Agreement reached with Mayu Tsurui.

Was wondering what was taking so long with the Hitoshi thing, but have now had confirmation that rumours are spreading among the pupils.

It's all going swimmingly.

To me, at least, that last phrase sounded familiar. Grandfather had written the same thing in the entry I'd read earlier, for the 1st of January this year—just after the words *No sign of either of their husbands.* Did that mean…?

'Fujitaka,' said Yoshio.

'Yeah?'

'Look at this.'

Of course, Runa, Mai and I couldn't help but join Fujitaka in reading the passages Yoshio had found.

Mr Kawazoe says in the current climate it'll be easy to find an excuse—that, if anything, he's grateful. He's been wanting to trim some of the fat among his executives anyway, so my proposal is timely. Says the 'commission' we suggested is unnecessary and that he hopes I'll help with the matter he mentioned. I agreed.

Heard from Mr Kawazoe again. Says he's increasing the number of purely nominal positions to which he can demote the company's deadwood without having to fire them. It'll look too suspicious if he only puts Michiya in a role like that, so I've asked him to do the same to a few other people if possible.

'Does this mean what I think it means?' Apparently torn between astonishment and fury, Yoshio settled on a gesture that expressed both and loudly flicked his finger against the diary. 'Grandfather secretly planned Dad's demotion?'

'Not just his demotion,' replied Fujitaka, who seemed to be still trying to work out whether he stood to lose or gain from this development. 'He's left him with no choice but to quit entirely.'

Runa, meanwhile, had no such trouble making her mind up. She was glowing with rage. 'It's the same with our dad! Grandfather paid this Tsurui girl to ruin his life. She seduced him, then spread the rumours so Dad would get fired. He planned the whole thing!'

'Yeah,' said Fujitaka, in the same cautious tone, 'it does look that way.'

'It doesn't just *look that way*,' snapped Runa. Clearly upset by his failure to agree more vehemently with her, she had lapsed into the tone of a wife berating her henpecked husband. 'That's obviously what happened. What else could it be?'

'Still,' said Yoshio, fiddling in confusion with the broken lock of his diary, 'even if that is the case, what the hell did Grandfather stand to gain from all this?'

'Isn't it obvious?' said Mai. Her tone was cool, but it was clear she was just as enraged as her sister. 'He wanted to make the battle for the inheritance more interesting. He knew that if both our dads were forced out of their jobs, Mum and Aunt Kamiji would have no choice but to start vying for his affection. They'd be locked in a fight for survival, desperate for him to choose one of their children. Meanwhile, he could sit back and watch the fireworks.'

'Seriously? Do you really think he's that much of a sadist?' murmured Yoshio, but it was clear he wasn't entirely unconvinced by Mai's explanation. In fact, his expression seemed to suggest it was the only logical one.

I was lost for words. Yes, I'd been hoping the diaries might provide a nugget or two of useful information, but I'd never imagined we'd unearth anything this explosive. To think that Grandfather had conspired like this against our own families…

Then a thought flashed through my mind. *What if this was the motive behind the murder?* Even if Grandfather's scheme hadn't directly brought about his death, there could well be some sort of connection between the two. Until now, I'd never really thought of him as the type to incur grudges, but if someone in the family had got wind of his secret plot…

But this was as far as I could get in my thoughts. As I gazed out of the window in shock, I saw something I simply couldn't believe. My mind went blank with surprise. I had seen a figure in the walkway.

It was Mother, making her way from the main building to the old house. But why…? With my jaw almost dislocated from the shock, all I could do was gape idiotically as she walked along. *Why?* Why was she going to the old house? It wasn't in the schedule. It wasn't supposed to happen. It wasn't even supposed to be possible.

After who knows how long, Mother re-emerged and made her way back to the main building. I knew what was going to happen next. Soon enough, she reappeared, walking back towards the old house. In her hands was the vase of moth orchids.

9
THE MURDER WON'T STOP

It was Aunt Haruna who found Grandfather's body. As usual, she'd been looking for him because she wanted to discuss the will—and Mother had told her she'd seen him heading for the old house, presumably because she wanted Aunt Haruna to be the one to discover the body.

While we were waiting to be questioned, I had a conversation with Runa and Mai, in the course of which I learnt why Mother had ended up taking this unscheduled course of action. As I'd feared, the reason was me.

It turned out that, before bringing Fujitaka to the annex, Runa had dropped by Mother's room to tell her I was acting out of sorts. Instead of my usual gormless self, I had seemed strangely distressed, my eyes bloodshot. I had mentioned something about having my heart broken, though she didn't know if that was actually true. In any case, I seemed badly upset about something—in fact, I'd sounded borderline suicidal. Runa had told Mother all this, out of concern for me.

It wasn't clear how seriously Mother had taken her. It was quite possible she'd simply laughed it off, telling herself that there was no way her muddleheaded son was even capable of the metaphysical speculation that something like suicide would require. Still, perhaps spotting the chance to give me a pep talk about the inheritance, she had decided she might as well drop by and see how I was getting on. Because Runa hadn't mentioned our meeting in the annex, she'd assumed I would be in the attic. And so she had made her way to the old house.

This much I could understand. It was what came next that threw me. In the attic she had found not me but Grandfather, drinking on his own. What possible conversation could they have had that ended with her murdering him? And why had the murder weapon been, once again, the vase of orchids? It wasn't like Mother could have taken inspiration from the crime committed by Runa and Fujitaka, or Yoshio—and yet she had plumped for the exact same method. Why? It just didn't make sense.

It had occurred to me more than once, since the murder began happening, to simply ask the culprit directly. The problem was that it hardly seemed likely they'd cough up just like that. I found myself wishing that it wasn't just me who knew that the 2nd of January was stuck in a loop, but the murderers too. If they only knew they'd get a second chance at the day, I'm sure they'd be happy to tell me exactly how— and why—they had committed their crime. Once the day had reset, there would be no *corpus delicti*—the very body of their victim would return to life, and their actions would be deemed never to have taken place. If they only knew that, all of them—not just Mother, but Runa, Fujitaka, Mai and Yoshio, too—would surely have confessed their various methods and motives in a heartbeat. But to them, today was a day like any other, and they only had one shot at it. Once they committed their crime, it became a secret they might have to guard for the rest of their lives.

Which was why, loop after loop, I had refrained from asking the perpetrator directly about what they'd done. I couldn't bring myself to go up to members of my own family and say: *I know you murdered Grandfather. Now come clean and tell me how and why you did it.* It was just too emotionally daunting, even if I knew that the entire day was soon to be reset. All I could do was speculate. I'd established potential motives for Mai and the Runa-Fujitaka double act, but I still had no idea what could have compelled Yoshio or my mother to commit the crime. Indeed, I might never know. As soon as the loop reset, the crime itself was erased from the perpetrator's memory. The hunt for the truth was doomed from the start. Instead of worrying about the motive or circumstances behind each murder, it would be better to focus on preventing Grandfather from being killed in the first place.

The problem now, though, was that I was beginning to question whether I should even be trying this hard to save him. Needless to say, this was because of what we'd unearthed in his diaries—the shocking revelation that he'd been secretly pulling strings to get my father demoted to a meaningless role and Uncle Hitoshi fired for unprofessional conduct.

It was true that I didn't see eye to eye with either of my parents on a lot of things—that I had plenty of reasons not to respect them, and at times wasn't even sure if I was capable of feeling affection for them. But something told me they weren't such terrible people that they deserved to have their lives torn apart by my grandfather's scheming. Yes, Mother and Aunt Haruna had both treated their father quite coldly, and I could see why he might not feel ready to forgive them. But to put the security of their families in jeopardy seemed at best an overreaction and at worst an act of cruelty.

As a result, I was starting to wonder if it was really my concern whether a nasty old man like that lived or died. Maybe it was Grandfather's fate to be killed, no matter how much I tried to save him. And you can't argue with fate. Maybe it was time to just accept it.

And yet, in the end, I couldn't do it. My grandfather's murder was not, in fact, his 'fate', in the usual sense of the word. At the risk of repeating myself, on the original 2nd of January, nothing untoward had happened to him. The murdering had only started in the second loop. In other words, his murder was not supposed to occur on the 2nd of January. If I hadn't altered the day's established schedule, thereby introducing unforeseen consequences, it would never have happened at all. So, the murder was the product not of 'fate', but of human intervention. Luckily, in my case, that intervention could be undone. And because it could be, I had a moral obligation to make sure it was. Which meant it *was* my responsibility to save Grandfather, after all.

As usual, I was sitting there waiting to be summoned for further questioning when the clock struck midnight. I woke up in the attic, curled up in my futon with a raging thirst. For the sixth time in a row, it was the 2nd of January. Struggling to fight off my overwhelming sleepiness, I pinched my thigh and forced myself awake, as I had last time. It was three in the morning.

When I'd conducted my usual check of the stairs, by now more out of habit than anything else, I began pacing around the room, toying with Runa's earring as I devised my strategy.

What would be my approach this time? Including this loop, I had four more attempts to fix things. But because the ninth and final loop would become the definitive version of the 2nd of January, I needed to establish the method I would deploy in advance. The eighth loop would then be a test run for that method. In other words, it would be more accurate to say that I only had two chances left to try something new: this sixth loop and the seventh.

I left the old house just before six o'clock and went to Aunt Kotono's bedroom in the main building. As I'd expected, she was just on her way down to the dining room. When she saw me, she started and gave an exaggerated gasp.

'My, you're up early. Are you feeling okay after last night?'

Every single person in the family seemed oddly concerned about my hangover. I didn't think I'd drunk a particularly worrying amount at the New Year's dinner, but they all seemed to disagree. 'Oh, I'm fine. Sorry if I worried you.'

'Oh, no, Kyutaro, it's not your fault. Making you drink that much at your age... I'll have to have words!'

I seemed to remember she was actually one of the people pouring me drinks, but I decided not to press the issue. 'Actually, Auntie, I have a favour to ask.'

'Really? What might that be?'

'It's a bit of a strange one. I was wondering if I could borrow those orchids? Just for the day, I mean.'

'The orchids?' repeated Aunt Kotono, her eyes widening. 'You mean... the moth orchids?'

'That's right. The ones Emi bought you.'

'I mean, of course, but... what are you planning on doing with them?'

187

'I thought I might sketch them.'

'Really? I didn't know you were the arty type.'

'It's for my holiday assignment.' In reality, I'd chosen calligraphy for my art module, not fine art, but Aunt Kotono wasn't going to know that. 'I just remembered that I brought my sketchbook with me so I could draw something while I was here.'

'Is that so? How nice. Of course you can borrow them.'

But Aunt Kotono made no move to go and get the vase from her room.

'Oh, no, they're not in here,' she went on, seeing the puzzled look on my face. 'They're downstairs.'

'Really? I thought you said you were going to take them up to your room...'

'I meant to. But they're so beautiful that I decided I'd leave them out for a while, so that everyone could admire them. They're still in the reception room. Didn't you notice them?'

No, I hadn't noticed them. Now that I thought about it, the only time I'd been into the reception room since the Trap started had been in the previous loop, just before I'd snuck into my grandfather's study in the middle of the night. It had been so gloomy that it was hardly surprising I hadn't noticed the flowers. It was true that every loop ended with us all sitting in the reception room while the questioning took place, but that was after the murder, by which time the weapon used in it—the vase—had been taken to the attic. (Mai was the exception, having used the sake bottle rather than the vase, but perhaps I'd been too worked up over the murder to notice it in the reception room).

I realized that this explained something. I'd been puzzled by the fact that the murderers had all insisted on using the vase as the weapon, given that sneaking into Aunt Kotono's room seemed like quite a risky move. But if the vase was located not in someone's bedroom but in the reception room, which anyone could easily access, the situation was different. Each of the perpetrators had racked their brains for a murder weapon, and settled on the vase in the reception room. Mai was the only one who had used the sake bottle instead. Was that because of the intense rage she was feeling at the time?

I followed Aunt Kotono downstairs. Just as she'd said, the vase of orchids was in the reception room.

'Do you mind if I take them to the old house?'

'Go ahead. Careful with them, mind.'

My plan was to hide the vase in the storage room in the old house. Of course, simply eliminating the murder weapon was no guarantee that the murder itself would not take place. This was simply the first stage of the plan. It had gone unexpectedly smoothly—which may have been why I let my guard down. When Aunt Kotono asked if I'd join her and Kiyoko for breakfast, I agreed without a second thought. It was only after I'd accepted that I began to worry.

My joining Aunt Kotono and Kiyoko for breakfast was not part of the day's original schedule. The pair were supposed to be discussing who Aunt Kotono's heir should be. But because I was there as an interloper, that topic was never raised, and instead they just sat there making small talk. In itself that wasn't a problem, but I had a sinking feeling that altering the day's schedule like this would once again have unforeseen consequences. There was no telling where the next 'ambush' might spring from.

But I couldn't just get up and leave now. As I sat there, eating and trying to convince myself that everything would work out,

Emi walked in. Right on schedule. She began apologizing for sleeping in, using almost exactly the same turn of phrase as in the previous loop, to which Aunt Kotono responded, just as she had last time, that there was no need.

After that, though, things began to vary. The original schedule dictated that Aunt Kotono and Kiyoko should leave the dining room shortly after Emi's arrival. This time, too, it was true that they had already finished their breakfast and even washed their plates. But even when Emi sat next to me and began eating, neither of them showed any sign of leaving. Soon came the next scheduled entrance: that of Ryuichi.

'Shall we stick around for a coffee, Kiyoko?'

Hearing these words—which had never featured in the previous loop—issue from Aunt Kotono's lips, I found myself clasping my head in my hands. This was bad. Very bad. The day was drifting further and further away from its established course.

'Isn't it nice,' she went on, 'all having breakfast together like this? I think there are some pastries left. Oh, and those mikan oranges. Could you get them out?'

The presence of such relaxed company appeared to be making her unusually chirpy and talkative. This really was bad. I could only pray the consequences of all this weren't going to be too nasty.

Maybe it would be best to extract myself from the situation, after all. I stood up and, rice bowl in hand, made to leave. But Aunt Kotono stopped me.

'Say, Kyutaro. Who do you think my heir should be? Go on, be as blunt as you like. This is strictly off the record. I won't tell anyone—not even your mother.'

Right, I thought, that makes sense. It had taken a while, but the same topic had come up as in the previous loop—even if the precise circumstances were a little different. The guiding force was attempting to steer the day back towards its original course.

'I think Emi would be a good choice.'

'Ooh!' exclaimed Aunt Kotono, apparently delighted to hear me mention the exact person she had in mind. She leant towards me, her expression glowing. 'And why's that?'

I was about to reply, *Because she's the only one who knows what she's doing,* but hastily swallowed the words. Ryuichi was sitting right there and probably wouldn't have taken too kindly to a reply like that.

'I mean, it could be Ryuichi, too. The important thing is that it's someone who actually knows what they're doing.'

Aunt Kotono flashed a cheerful smile at Emi and Ryuichi, both sitting there awkwardly, before resuming her interrogation. 'What about you and your brothers, though? Or Mai and Runa?'

'Well, I think Mai would make an excellent adopted daughter.'

'Really!' This time she must have really felt like I was reading her mind. Her merry expression flickered briefly into one of vague suspicion. 'What makes you say that?'

'She seems the most similar to you. In fact I'd say she takes after you more than her own mother. Not that that's any guarantee the two of you would get on, of course.'

'So she'd make a good heir on a personal level, but she isn't cut out for running the company—is that what you're trying to say?'

'It's not just Mai. None of us would be any good at it. Fujitaka, as you know, is more suited to the academic life. As for Yoshio,

191

he's your typical corporate drone—better at taking orders than giving them. Plus I think he'd cave at the first sign of pressure. Just like his father.'

'What about you, then?'

'Auntie, I'm the type of kid who reads the latest bestseller eight years after everyone else. I'm too far behind the times to run a company.'

'And Runa?'

'Too likely to change her outlook completely once a man enters the picture. I know she might not look it, but she's pretty old-fashioned when it comes to relationships. She'll end up devoting herself to someone else—not the company.'

'My, my!' Aunt Kotono grinned as she took a sip of her coffee. 'And there I was, thinking you were just a scatterbrained teenager. I had no idea you were so *perceptive*, Kyutaro.'

'No, scatterbrained sounds about right. My days just last a bit longer than everyone else's, that's all.'

'So the cousins are out of the running, then,' she continued, ignoring my last comment, as I'd known she would. 'Emi or Ryuichi—an injection of fresh blood. That's what you think we need?'

'Something like that, yes.'

'Right, then. Well, which should it be? Emi or Ryuichi?'

'Well, it wouldn't be very gentlemanly of me not to pick Emi, would it?'

'Ooh, interesting. Very interesting.' She was smiling at me like a nursery teacher teasing a boy who's just been hugged by one of the girls in his class. 'Is she your type, then?'

'Oh, I think she's wonderful.'

'Just listen to him, the cheeky devil!' She chuckled, reached across the table and playfully patted the back of Emi's hand. 'Well, how about it? Is he *your* type?'

'I…' I'd never seen Emi so lost for words. It was understandable. She couldn't reply that she already had a lover—that would make it sound like she was actually taking the question seriously. But she also couldn't simply come out and confess that her boss's nephew wasn't really the sort of partner she had in mind. 'I… think he's, erm, wonderful, too.'

Aunt Kotono laughed. 'Oh, there's no need to pretend. I'd hardly expect you to say yes to… *this*.' By 'this' she appeared to mean me. 'Actually, I've been meaning to ask you, Emi. Do you have a boyfriend or anything?'

Emi froze for a moment, as if wondering how to evade the question, before regaining her usual cool, composed expression. It must have dawned on her that Aunt Kotono was only asking because of the inheritance. 'I do. In fact, he proposed to me very recently.'

It seemed the Trap's mysterious guiding force was not to be messed with. Once again, the conversation in the dining room had resumed the direction it was 'supposed' to take. I sighed inwardly. The rejection I'd barely managed to process the first time around had been thrust back in my face. Still, my shock was nothing compared to Ryuichi's. At least I'd known about the bad news in advance; for him, this was a bolt from the blue. I glanced discreetly at him and saw that he had frozen so completely it was almost comical. His chopsticks were still in his mouth, his eyes bulging in surprise.

'Oh.' Aunt Kotono seemed taken aback by the straightforwardness of Emi's reply, too. An excited glint came into her eyes. 'And…?'

'I plan to say yes.'

Aunt Kotono gave an emotional gasp that was clearly not just for show. 'Well, I'm sure he's every bit the dashing gentleman. If he's managed to win the heart of a woman like you, I mean.'

'It'll probably be some time until we actually tie the knot,' said Emi, smiling hesitantly. For a jilted lover it was excruciating to watch. I glanced at Ryuichi again and saw that he was practically cross-eyed with shock. He looked like he was on the verge of fainting.

'Well,' continued Aunt Kotono, 'say you *did* become my heir. Would this gentleman be willing to be adopted into the family and take on the Fuchigami name, do you think?'

'No, I don't think that would be possible.'

'Well, that *is* a problem.' Aunt Kotono glared reproachfully at Emi, as if she'd suddenly slipped back into business mode. 'What are you going to do if Father picks you?'

'I've been wanting to talk to you about that, actually. I wanted to ask if I could be taken out of the running, after all.'

'I think you're out of luck there,' interrupted Ryuichi, who appeared to have finally regained his motor skills. 'Once the Chairman has made his mind up about something, he's not the type to change it.'

'We need to solve this problem as soon as possible,' said Aunt Kotono, as if she hadn't heard him. 'If you get married while Father's alive, he can always change his will. But if—heaven forbid—Father dies first, you'll have to choose: either you break off the engagement or your fiancé agrees to join the Fuchigami family.'

'So, I'm not allowed to withdraw, then? From being the heir in the first place, I mean.'

'I suppose it's not *im*possible. Once Father passes away, that decision will lie with me. The thing is, though, I rather *want* you to be my heir.' At this point Aunt Kotono seemed to realize that Ryuichi—ostensibly just as much a candidate as Emi—was sitting there with us, and that she'd just written him off completely. 'After all, you're Kyutaro's favourite,' she added, as if by way of explanation. I felt horribly used.

Though Ryuichi was doing his best to look composed, I could tell he was anything but. Knowing that the final decision lay with Grandfather and not Aunt Kotono didn't seem to be doing much to ease his anxiety. I could see the cogs whirring as he tried to work out whether he could still secure his 'insurance policy' by somehow persuading Emi to break off her engagement and marry him instead.

At this point, right on schedule, Runa walked in.

'Morning!' she said with a friendly smile, before sitting down next to Ryuichi. Perhaps because, in his head at least, she was only his back-up option, he looked slightly guilty as he smiled back at her. Or at least he did to me. Maybe I was reading too much into things.

At this point, Grandfather walked in, and the atmosphere in the room grew suddenly tense. I glanced up at the clock on the wall. It was one minute to eight.

'Ah, so this is where you are! Kotono, Kiyoko—would you come with me a minute?'

Aunt Kotono and Kiyoko got up and followed him. I knew where they were going. The kitchen of the old house, where they'd have their usual exchange. He'd tell them he couldn't make his origami last night because he couldn't find the red paper, and could Kiyoko get him some from the stationery shop, and no, she couldn't, because the shops would be closed for the first three days of the year. He probably insisted on having the conversation in the old house because he didn't want anyone overhearing them.

Meanwhile, the conversation in the dining room had fizzled out. Emi got up, bowed and left. Ryuichi followed hot on her heels. He was probably about to tell her that an ordinary marriage would never be enough for her, that together the two of them could bring glory to the company. And, just like in the previous loop, she'd tell him to forget it.

Runa and I found ourselves alone in the dining room. 'Oh, by the way,' I said, holding out the earring as she silently munched on her food. 'You dropped this.'

Runa spluttered on her food. 'Right. Erm. Thanks…'

'Actually,' I continued, ignoring her inquisitive gaze, 'there's something I want to discuss. I think it'd be best if we all gathered in the banquet hall after this. Do you think you could tell Aunt Haruna and Mai?'

'Why, what is it you want to discuss?'

'The inheritance, obviously. I'll tell my mother and brothers. Oh, actually, maybe you should invite Fujitaka.'

Runa gave me a pained look. 'Um, does it have to be today, this discussion?'

'Yes. It has to be today.'

'But I have plans.'

'Oh, come on. Can't your little rendezvous wait?' Runa made another choking sound, but I pressed on. 'Now, whatever I say in the banquet hall, don't breathe a word about your relationship with Fujitaka, alright? For today at least, keep it a secret. Oh, and tell him to do the same, would you?'

196

Just then, Mai walked into the dining room. I'd finished in the nick of time.

'Ah, good,' I went on. 'I'll tell Mai, then.' Runa, her expression stiff, hurried out of the kitchen like someone fleeing a haunted house, without even washing her plate. As she was leaving, Yoshio walked in. I told him and Mai that I had something important to discuss and that they should come to the banquet hall after breakfast.

The day was swiftly descending into chaos, but there was no going back now. All I could do was execute whatever muddled strategy presented itself to my underpowered brain. If Mother had managed to kill Grandfather, then presumably Aunt Haruna had it in her, too. My only option, then, was to get everyone to remain in one place. I hadn't been sure Mother or Aunt Haruna would even turn up to a meeting convened by me of all people, but it seemed the inheritance was a topic they just couldn't resist. In the end, everyone from both the Oba and Kanagae families arrived in the banquet hall.

'I know we all have plenty of things we'd like to say to one another,' I began, eyeing Mother and Aunt Haruna. 'But I think now is the time for our two families to join hands and come together as a team.'

'Join hands?' repeated Mother, looking at me as if to say, *You have to be joking.* 'To do what, exactly? A spot of ballroom dancing?'

'I'm talking about the inheritance. The future of the Fuchigami family. You two can haggle all you like over whose child would make the best heir, but if Grandfather ends up choosing Ryuichi or Emi instead, we're all going down together. So doesn't it make sense to cooperate?'

'Cooperate…' said Mother, shooting an annoyed look in the direction of Aunt Haruna, who was surveying the room with her usual ennui-laden smile. 'And tell me, how's that going to work, exactly?'

'Well, for example, your children could get married.' I ignored Runa's hiccup of surprise and carried on. 'Fujitaka and Mai, for example, or Mai and Yoshio, or Yoshio and Runa, or Runa and Fujitaka—the precise combination doesn't matter. I hate to say this, but whether or not they're actually in love is secondary. It would be a marriage of convenience. We simply don't have the time for anything else. As long as there's a marriage binding the Oba and Kanagae families together, Grandfather may well change his mind about the inheritance. In fact, I'm convinced it's the only way we'll ever get him to. Just imagine what'll happen once the couple in question has a baby—a great-grandchild for the old man to fawn over. It seems more than likely that he'll decide to leave it something. That baby—your shared grandchild—will become the linchpin that finally brings our three families back together.'

'Kyutaro, you little brainbox,' said Yoshio, clearly delighted by the idea. 'Why did no one else think of that? It's genius.' He glanced at Runa, who seemed to be murmuring something to the effect that, actually, she'd had exactly the same idea. 'Me and Runa are the obvious choice, aren't we?'

'Hang on a moment,' interrupted Aunt Haruna. The smile tugging at the corner of her mouth seemed to say, *I can't believe I have to deal with simpletons like this all day.* 'I can see the appeal of a marriage of convenience. But what happens if Grandfather simply ignores it and picks Ryuichi or Emi instead? We'll be in a bit of a pickle then, won't we?'

'As long as Grandfather's alive, he can rewrite his will whenever he likes,' put in Fujitaka with unusual eagerness. The Runa effect, presumably. 'All that stuff he said about this being his final decision won't mean a thing if he decides to change his mind. And what Kyutaro's saying is, why don't we use a great-grandchild as a way of getting him to do so?'

'Exactly,' I replied.

'Goodness, Kyutaro,' said Aunt Haruna. 'Loveless marriage and a child who's basically a human sacrifice. I'm surprised you could even think of such a barbaric solution. I mean, I know you're desperate for your grandfather's money, but still...' She snorted derisively. 'And you're not even out of high school. I wonder where you got all this from—oh, wait, I think I know.'

I wasn't exactly thrilled to be called a money-grubber, but it was true that I'd been feeling a little uncertain about my future, so I kept my mouth shut. On the other hand, that didn't seem like something Mother was capable of doing.

'*That's* your reaction, is it?' she blurted. 'My son comes up with a productive solution—for the sake of you and your daughters, no less—and that's how you respond?'

'*For our sake*? Oh, don't make me laugh.' Aunt Haruna, looking unusually rattled, gave a hysterical titter of surprise. 'For *your* sake, don't you mean? You're terrified you won't get your share, and this is your last resort. Drop the mask, would you? If you want money, come out and tell us you want money. That's right, if you want it so much, just say! *For our sake*... I mean, *please*! Like you're doing us some big favour! It's *pathetic*!'

It didn't really matter to me whether this discussion came to a successful conclusion. In fact, it could reach a complete deadlock for all I cared, as long as everyone stayed put in the banquet hall until evening. But if it descended into a slang-ing match too soon, we might end up with a situation where someone stormed out of the room, and I didn't want that. And so I decided to intervene.

'Now, now, Auntie, please calm down. You're right—it is money I'm after. My father's current situation is making me a little bit anxious about the future. I would *like* to be able to go to university. Which is why—'

'Come on, Kyutaro. Where's your self-respect?' This exas-perated interruption came from Fujitaka. His entire face had flushed bright red, and his fists were clenched and shaking. I'd never seen him this worked up before. 'She's making fun of you right now, don't you see? Mocking you. Belittling you. It's obvious. So stop acting like some suck-up.'

'Alright, alright,' said Yoshio. 'Calm down. He means well. Don't you, Kyutaro?'

'True, true,' said Aunt Haruna. 'Just wants his money, doesn't he?' She grinned, as if she regretted getting her nephew involved and wanted to smooth things over with a joke.

But it seemed Fujitaka was in no mood for jokes. 'You watch it, Auntie! Anyway, you're one to talk when it comes to wanting money.'

'Fu-chan!' exclaimed Runa, apparently so unsettled by my brother's outburst that she let his pet name slip. But nobody even seemed to notice. 'There's no need to get so worked up. Mum means well, too, okay? So why don't we—'

'Why don't *you* shut your mouth?'

'How *dare* you talk to my daughter like that?' The usual sardonic smile had vanished completely from Aunt Haruna's face. Instead, she was giving Fujitaka a death stare to rival anything my mother was capable of. 'Like she's your property or something. Who on earth do you think you are? I demand an apology. Go on, get down on your knees. Right now!'

Fujitaka, it was becoming clear, was one of those people who almost never get angry but compensate by going completely berserk when they do. '*You* get down on your knees!' he yelled, spraying spittle. 'Get down on your knees and apologize to my brother, you merciless old bitch!'

'Did you just call her a… bitch?' Now even Runa was shouting, as if she couldn't help but match Fujitaka's furious tone. 'That's my *mum* you're talking to!'

'I thought I told you to shut your mouth! Stop getting involved!'

'No, you apologize, right now!' shrieked Runa, bursting into tears. I'd been watching her do that a lot recently. It seemed that underneath her breezy, devil-may-care persona, she was really just a huge crybaby. 'Right now. Or I'll never forgive you. Not until the day I die.'

'Yeah? And you think I care? Look at you, blubbing your eyes out again. That's all you know how to do, isn't it?'

'H-how can you act like this? After all those n-nice things you told me… Didn't any of it mean anything? Where's the Fu-chan I knew and loved?'

'What, you think I was just being *nice* to you for no reason? Read the writing on the wall, Runa – I just wanted to get you into bed. Yeah, that's right. You can stop playing the innocent little girl now.'

'*What* did you just say?!' Aunt Haruna leapt at Fujitaka, her face contorted with rage. 'You did *what* to my daughter?!'

'Well, you wouldn't want her staying a virgin into her twenties, would you? I did her a favour. You should be grateful.'

'Alright, you're *dead*!' shouted Aunt Haruna, swinging her fists wildly at him. Yoshio attempted to restrain her, but her elbow connected cleanly with the pit of his stomach and he collapsed, spluttering, to the floor.

'Stop it!' shrieked Mother, pouncing on Aunt Haruna and clawing frantically at her face. 'Are you deaf or something? Stop!'

Caught between Yoshio, still writhing on the floor, and Runa, who had somehow taken a pratfall in all the commotion and was bawling her eyes out, Mai looked completely bewildered. 'Are you two... okay? What should we...?'

Meanwhile, Aunt Haruna was giving as good as she got, and had Mother's hair in her grip. 'That's how you raised him, is it?' she shouted. 'The boy's like a puppy in heat. How could he? My poor innocent daughter!'

'Oh, come off it! I bet Fujitaka only slept with her because she talked him into it. All arse and tits and no brain, she is! Just like *you*! The spitting image! You whore! You hag!'

'Speak for yourself! You're the one who ran off to university and tricked some man into marrying you just because you didn't want to help with the restaurant.'

'That was *love*! I was in love! If anyone tricked anyone, it was you!' Mother grabbed a cushion and began pummelling my aunt with it. 'You were eighteen, still basically a girl, for god's sake, and you went and slept with your teacher! Practically forced yourself into his home, didn't you, you little tart! No wonder Runa turned out the same way!'

'Oh, and none of that is your fault, is it?' shouted Aunt Haruna, reaching for a cushion of her own with which to counter-attack. All the shame and anger she had bottled up for years seemed to be erupting at once. Her voice cracked; tears were welling in the corners of her eyes. 'You… you… abandoned us! You were the oldest, and you abandoned us! Ran right out of there as fast as your legs could carry you. Well, maybe *I* wanted out, too. It's your fault. It's *all* your fault. All of it!'

'All I did was get married like a normal person. What's wrong with that? A nice, normal marriage, that's all I wanted. What, didn't I have the right to be happy?' Mother was crying too now, even as she rained another series of blows down on her sister. 'Just because I'm the oldest. Just because I'm the oldest! That means I have to sacrifice everything, does it? Why? Tell me, why? I wanted to be happy, too, Haruna! I just wanted to be happy, like anyone else! Is that really so awful? Is it?'

'What on *earth* is going on in here?'

Aunt Kotono had arrived at my side, without me noticing, and was staring on in blank amazement as her sisters, their hair and clothes in disarray, sobbed and screamed and pounded each other with cushions. She was accompanied by Emi, who was watching the pandemonium unfold with similar bewilderment.

'They appear to be having a… disagreement of sorts,' I offered.

'Mum, stop it!' said Yoshio, who had finally managed to climb back to his feet and now attempted to separate the two once more. They turned and gave him a coordinated whack with their cushions, sending him sprawling backwards into the shoji screen. He crashed through its paper panels and landed in a heap on the veranda, where he lay moaning in pain.

'Please! Everyone, calm down!' I shouted. I was responsible for all this, and I couldn't very well just stand there watching. I made my own brave charge—and was immediately repelled by the two cushion-wielding women. I tripped and tumbled into the raised tokonoma alcove at the side of the room, my foot catching a decorative hanging scroll and bringing it crashing to the floor.

'Are you okay?' asked Emi, rushing over and cradling my head. 'You poor thing.' I resisted the urge to melt with happiness. Now was not the time.

Fujitaka had just tackled Aunt Haruna to the floor, but as she fell she managed to launch her cushion through the air like a frisbee, catching Mother squarely in the face. Mother fell backwards heavily onto the thin, crouched bodies of Runa and Mai. Mai, until now simply a concerned observer, found herself pinned under my mother's considerable bulk and, finally losing her temper, seized a cushion and hurled it at Fujitaka. Seeing this, Runa grabbed another cushion and threw it in the same direction. Fujitaka, stunned by this two-pronged assault, went reeling into the fusuma, tearing an enormous hole in the paper door. As the cushion fight got into full swing, my family began to resemble a group of elementary school children on a school trip who had decided to turn their dormitory into a battlefield.

Mob mentality is a force to be reckoned with. Aunt Kotono had been screeching at everyone to stop, but when she in turn received a cushion to the face, she underwent a sudden transformation and began scrabbling for weapons of her own. It seemed she had plenty of ill feeling bottled up, too. She made a beeline for Mother and Aunt Haruna, windmilling at them with her cushions. Yoshio had finally pulled himself to his feet and came tottering in from the veranda—but he appeared not to have learnt his lesson, because he simply re-entered the cushion-hurling fray. He was grinning manically, like some naughty boy who didn't quite understand what was going on but wanted in on the fun.

'No, don't,' said Emi, restraining me as I tried to get to my feet. 'You'll only get hurt if you try to stop them.'

And so, rather than take any further part in the carnage, Emi and I simply huddled together in the narrow alcove, waiting for the storm to pass. She smelt wonderful, and under ordinary circumstances this would have been bliss, but these weren't ordinary circumstances. As I watched my relatives semi-randomly battering each other with cushions for far longer than could ever have been appropriate, the comparison that came to mind was one of those paintings of the inferno. The fact that they were all wearing coloured tracksuits and chanchanko jackets, so that they also looked a bit like athletes engaged in some newly invented sport, merely made the whole thing more absurd. It was only my knowledge of what was at stake that stopped me from laughing out loud.

Soon even Kiyoko, who had arrived to see what all the fuss was about, had somehow been drawn into the free-for-all. It seemed that being hit in the face with a cushion triggered some unique, latent human desire for revenge. Once someone hit you, the only thing to do was hit them back. There was no longer any distinction between friend and foe. The purported showdown between the Oba and Kanagae families had only lasted for the first few minutes. By now it was pure anarchy. It would have been one thing if they were pounding the living daylights out of each other in an innocent spirit of playfulness, but the unsettling truth was that all their eyes were bloodshot with rage. Screams and sobs filled the banquet hall; it felt as though the ceiling might cave in at any moment.

Eventually, after who knows how long, they all collapsed onto the floor, huffing and puffing, their expressions vacant and morose. Their hair was completely dishevelled; some of them had nosebleeds. Nobody said a word. They simply gazed off into space. In any case, it seemed the violence was over for now.

The hall looked like it had been hit by a tornado. Holes had been torn in every single fusuma; the wooden lattice of each of the shoji screens had been crushed. Most of the glass door that led to the veranda had been shattered, and the light that hung from the ceiling still swung menacingly to and fro, its crumpled shade bearing witness to the numerous blows it had sustained. A thick haze of dust filled the air.

Emi fetched the first aid box and began ministering to the wounded. The combatants seemed to be coming back to their senses. They were all avoiding each other's gaze, as if the sheer childishness of this mass brawl had suddenly, belatedly, filled them with shame.

'My, my,' sighed Aunt Kotono as she applied a plaster to a scratch someone had inflicted on her cheek. 'What do you think Father would say if he saw this?'

'Speaking of which... I wonder where he is?' said Kiyoko, toying pathetically with her smock, which had been torn in the melee. 'All that noise, and yet he doesn't seem to have heard a thing. I suppose he must be resting.'

'What about Ryuichi?' I said, apparently the first to notice his absence. I was getting that bad feeling again, as though the fire that had been smouldering away inside me had suddenly roared back into life. 'Has anyone seen him?'

'I saw him just now,' replied Kiyoko. 'Heading for the old house with that vase of orchids. No idea why, though.'

For a moment, I was so taken aback by my own carelessness that I almost fainted. It was a wonder I didn't scream. *Of course.* The orchids. I'd been meaning to hide them in the storage room—and yet I'd been so focused on the idea of gathering everyone in the banquet hall that I'd completely failed to get round to it.

'Oh,' I said. 'And, erm, did you see him after that?'

'Yes, he came back out a bit later. But he didn't have the flowers with him, so I went over and asked what he'd done with them. He gave me this shocked look. You know, like he'd seen a ghost. Then he just sort of ran out of the house. Without saying a word. It was all *very* odd.'

10
THE MURDER PERSISTS

This was starting to get me down. Really? Ryuichi? Why did *he* have to go and kill Grandfather? What *possible* motive could he have had? And yet there was no doubting he'd committed the crime.

It seemed this is what had happened. While everyone was brawling in the banquet hall, Grandfather had been drinking in the attic. Ryuichi had gone up there, though it wasn't clear what could have prompted his visit. Maybe it was me he wanted to see. That would be plausible enough, given the conversation over breakfast that morning. Aunt Kotono had mentioned that the reason she wanted Emi to be her successor was that I was so keen on her—a comment made mainly in jest, of course, but Ryuichi might have taken it seriously. When, after breakfast, Emi had (presumably) snubbed his proposal, he would have been alarmed by his rapidly weakening position. He would have been desperate. If my opinion meant so much to Aunt Kotono, then maybe it wasn't too late to get into my good books. And so he had gone to the attic looking for me. Instead, he had found my grandfather.

Everything made sense up to this point. As usual, it was what came next that baffled me. What possible set of circumstances could have driven Ryuichi to kill Grandfather? In any case, he had returned to the main building to fetch the vase of moth orchids from the reception room. Kiyoko had seen him, but he hadn't noticed her. Then, having committed the crime, he had left the vase at the scene and left the old house, only to run into Kiyoko. When she had asked him what he'd done with the flowers, he'd looked shocked—presumably because he didn't know anyone had seen him carrying the murder weapon to the scene of the crime. It was only a matter of time before someone found Grandfather's body, at which point he would be easily identified as the murderer. Once the police were called, it would be game over. And so he had decided to run. This, roughly speaking, seemed to be what had happened. Still, while I could envisage all the steps involved in the crime, the most important part—the motive—remained elusive.

Upon being notified of the murder, the police immediately set up a cordon in the surrounding area. Once they caught Ryuichi, maybe we'd learn the motive—and all the other details of the crime—straight from his mouth. Or should I say, we *would have* learnt. Ryuichi never got the chance to tell us the truth, because before he could be arrested, the clock reached midnight, the 2nd of January was reset, and the seventh loop began.

As usual, I was awoken at three in the morning by my parched throat. This time, though, I couldn't be bothered forcing myself to get up, and simply went back to sleep. The truth was that I was in a bit of a sulk. However slapdash my attempts, I really had been trying my hardest to prevent the crime—and yet every time, as if fate were laughing in my face, some new and entirely unexpected assassin would spring into action and murder my grandfather. I was starting to feel fed up with the whole thing, like I just wanted it to be over.

This time I'd have to find a way to restrict Ryuichi's movements, too. But would that really prevent the murder? At this point, it felt like anything could happen. Even if I managed to stop Ryuichi, who was to say Aunt Kotono or Kiyoko wouldn't abruptly transform into his 'substitute'? Or even, heaven forbid, Emi? I didn't want to think about it, but it was a very real possibility.

I had to find a way to keep everyone in one place. As I dozed through the early hours, this thought kept swirling through my mind. Not just the members of the Oba and Kanagae families, but Ryuichi and Emi and Aunt Kotono and Kiyoko, too. Was there no way of getting them all to stay put somewhere?

But then an alarming thought occurred to me. Even if I managed to detain everyone in the house, what if some other 'substitute' somehow got in from outside? It seemed unfair, like a breach of the rules, but I had to allow for these sorts of things. For one thing, when it came to would-be murderers, my father and Uncle Hitoshi would make the perfect 'reserve unit'. If either of them had got wind of the fact that it had been Grandfather, of all people, who had secretly engineered their respective downfalls, there could be no clearer motive for committing the murder. It began to seem genuinely possible that they might have feigned illness to be absent from the New Year's dinner before hiding out somewhere near the mansion, waiting for the chance to strike. This was unbearable.

Right then, I thought, getting up from my futon. It was no use just stopping Ryuichi or Aunt Kotono or whoever. I would have to detain the whole lot of them—*including* Grandfather himself—and keep them in one place, under my supervision, until the evening. If I wanted to prevent my grandfather's murder, this seemed like the only option I had left. But how was I going to go about it?

I'd woken at eight but had been so immersed in my thoughts that it was now getting on for quarter past. I hurried out of the attic and, without even glancing at Runa's earring, made my way down to the kitchen. Even if I gave it back to her, it was only going to end up back on the stairs. Picking it up could wait until the final loop.

I found Aunt Kotono alone in the kitchen. The no-red-paper-and-the-shops-are-closed conversation must already have ended, because Grandfather and Kiyoko had returned to the main building.

'Oh. Kyutaro…' said Aunt Kotono. She seemed oddly surprised to see me. Her face showed a mixture of apprehension and remorse, like a shoplifter who'd been caught red-handed. Of course, the plaster had disappeared from her cheek. 'Ah, of course. You've been staying in the attic, haven't you?'

'Did you think there'd be no one else here?' I asked. My aunt's suspicious attitude must have sharpened my intuition. Something told me that a clue was just around the corner. 'I see. So that's why you brought Grandfather here to have your little secret chat. About the origami.'

'Ah.' The look on Aunt Kotono's face wasn't exactly one of surprise. Or rather, there was surprise there, but also a sort of relief, as though she'd finally been freed from a burden that only she (or rather, only she and Kiyoko) had known about. 'So you heard that, then.'

211

'I did. I keep hearing it, in fact,' I said, my tongue slipping. Aunt Kotono's expression stiffened slightly. Of course, it was only I who 'kept hearing' that conversation, which, in reality, had only occurred once. 'I mean… yes, I heard it.'

Something about the look of resignation on my aunt's face made her seem like she'd aged dramatically. 'So you know then. About everything.'

'You mean the fact that Grandfather has been making origami cranes? A black one'—as I spoke, what had so far been only vague supposition began to coalesce into a definite theory; it was so simple that it was absurd that I hadn't thought of it earlier—'a blue one and a yellow one. But he didn't have any red origami paper. Me, in other words. He didn't have my colour.'

'Yes,' said my aunt with a nod. 'Exactly.'

'The origami colours match the tracksuits we've been made to wear. Black for Ryuichi and Emi, blue for Fujitaka and Mai, yellow for Yoshio and Runa, and red—if he'd had it—for me. But there was never any green origami to go with the tracksuits worn by his daughters. There was no need for it. The only colours required were those of the potential heirs.'

'That's right.' Aunt Kotono let out a sigh, though again it was one tinged with relief. She even allowed herself a hesitant smile. 'You've worked it all out.'

'He wanted to use the different-coloured cranes to pick a successor, who he would then write into his will. But for some reason, my colour had gone missing, and he couldn't make the red crane. That was why he couldn't pick a successor or write his will. I get it now.'

'Are you the only one who knows all this, Kyutaro? Or do the others—'

'They know he hasn't written the will yet. Or at least Runa, Mai and Yoshio do. But I don't think they know about the origami. Even I don't know exactly how he's planning to pick his successor with it.'

'It's pretty silly, really. Almost too childish to explain.' Aunt Kotono let out an exasperated sigh, then seemed to gather herself and went on, smiling cheerfully. 'He puts all the cranes in two little paper boxes. One for the men and one for the women. The men's box contains four colours: black, blue, yellow and red. The women's contains three: black, blue and yellow. There's a fist-sized hole in the top of the box. He closes his eyes, reaches into the two boxes simultaneously, grabs one crane in each hand, then pulls them out one after the other. That's all there is to it.'

Of course, I'd seen one of these boxes in the study. Perhaps Grandfather had given up on making the other one when he realized he was lacking the red origami paper and would be unable to carry out his little lottery.

'Wait, so he's picking *two* successors?'

'Yes. One male, one female.'

'I don't get it. At the New Year's dinner, when Grandfather told us he's been picking a successor every year for the past five years, he only gave one name for each year. Runa, Runa again, Ryuichi, Fujitaka, Emi.'

'Yes, but he was only telling us about the first crane he pulled out. The truth is that there was always another name. He just wanted to keep it a secret that he had chosen two successors until the official announcement. I suppose he wanted to give everyone a nice surprise. He even got it into his head that the whole experience might somehow lead to the two heirs getting married.'

I was too curious not to ask. 'So who did he pick as the other successor each year, then?'

'Let's see. It went Yoshio, Ryuichi, Mai, Mai again—and then last year was you.'

In other words, Emi's designated 'partner' had been me. Of all people. And our pairing had already been lost to the winds of time. A relationship that was doomed before it could ever begin: the description was apt in more ways than one... But this was no time for getting sentimental.

Considering the gravity of the decision he was making, Grandfather's method did seem pretty infantile. When I'd been hiding in the dining room (was that the loop before last?) I'd overheard Aunt Kotono lamenting to Kiyoko that she hadn't expected him to 'come up with an idea like that'. Kiyoko had tried to soothe her by reminding her that old age was a sort of second childhood. Emi's arrival had cut their conversation short, but the point was that they'd been complaining about precisely this: the childishness of Grandfather's method. Aunt Kotono's comment about how you couldn't 'even call it gambling'—that 'at least with gambling there's a bit more to it'—made more sense now, too.

'Right,' I replied. 'But there's something I don't get. The colours assigned to us are the same every year, aren't they? For example, my colour's red, and it always has been. So why does he still insist on us wearing the coloured tracksuits at every one of these New Year's gatherings?'

The smile disappeared from my aunt's face. She grimaced and shook her head. 'He's losing track. He can't remember which of his grandchildren is which. It's not just that, either. His memory's going, too. So even with the origami method, he has to have you all around so that he can remind himself which colour means who.'

I recalled the joking comments Fujitaka had made shortly after we'd arrived at the house—and his anecdote about Grandfather getting him mixed up with Yoshio.

'In other words, he's going... senile?'

'Well, yes,' replied my aunt, an unexpected edge of irritation coming into her voice. 'What else would it be?'

'Is it that bad?'

'He's fine most of the time. It's very intermittent. That's why hardly anyone notices.'

'Are you the only one who knows about it?'

'Me and Kiyoko. That's why she was with us just now.'

'Right. I suppose I should keep all this to myself, then.'

'That would be best. Of course, there'll be no hiding it eventually, but we really don't want people finding out before he's written his will. Otherwise Kamiji and Haruna might start kicking up a fuss about how he wasn't *compos mentis* and so on. Which could get really messy.'

'Absolutely. The secret's safe with me.'

'Thank you, Kyutaro. I really appreciate it.'

'Now,' I went on, secretly jumping for joy as I spotted my chance. Up in the attic, I'd been racking my brains over how best to get my way. 'I don't want to use the words *quid pro quo*, but I do have a favour to ask.'

'And what might that be?'

'I was wondering if you might help arrange something for me. I'd like us to have another gathering in the banquet hall today. All day long, or at least until the evening. With everyone in attendance, of course.'

215

Aunt Kotono gave me a slightly bewildered look, as if to say, *Are you really that desperate to hit the bottle again—at your age?* But then she smiled again. 'Certainly, I can... arrange that. It's not as though anyone has any other plans today.'

'Thank you. That's a promise, then? I'd like everyone to be there—Ryuichi and Emi and Kiyoko, too. And Grandfather, of course.'

'Right. Just... don't let Father drink too much,' she replied with a frown. 'He's got enough going on as it is. Things you probably don't know about.'

'You mean when he blacked out for a few minutes and you were all worried about it and asked him to see a neurologist?'

'Oh. You knew about that, too? Just where *are* you getting all this information from, Kyutaro?'

'From Grandfather, of course,' I replied, hurrying on before she could quiz me any further. 'There's absolutely no need for him to do any drinking. The important thing is that he's there. Until the evening.'

'Alright, then. This is all very mysterious, Kyutaro, but I'll do as you say. Kiyoko can get cooking right away.'

'Oh, and please don't tell anyone I put you up to this. If you could make it sound like it was all your idea...'

'Your wish is my command.'

'Thank you. If we could get started this morning, that would be wonderful.'

'Right. Then I'd better get a move on.'

'By the way, Auntie,' I went on, thinking I might as well clear up all my doubts at once, 'does the name Shota Kawazoe mean anything to you? Or Mayu Tsurui?'

'No, not ringing any bells. Who are they?'

She sounded like she was telling the truth. In other words, Grandfather must have been working alone when he plotted my father and uncle's downfall.

'Oh, no, never mind.'

Watching Aunt Kotono make her way back to the main building I felt, for the first time in a long time, like a weight had been lifted from my shoulders. I was almost out of the woods. There was no way the murder could repeat itself. As long as I gathered everyone in the banquet hall and discreetly kept an eye on them, my grandfather would be safe. As I mentioned earlier, the eighth and penultimate loop would have to be a sort of test run for the final one, which meant this seventh loop was my last chance to try something new. And, with perfect timing, I'd hit upon what seemed like a definitive strategy—one that involved, unexpectedly enough, enlisting the assistance of Aunt Kotono.

Still, best to be on the safe side. I went to the reception room and retrieved the vase of moth orchids. After making doubly sure no one was watching, I took them to the old house. Inside, conscious that someone might see me through the windows, I proceeded, with an almost absurd degree of caution, to hide the vase in the storage room. There. I had eliminated the murder weapon. I had nothing to fear now. No matter what unexpected events transpired, the one thing I felt utterly sure of was that Grandfather would not be murdered.

I was so giddy with joy and relief that I hardly knew what to do with myself. In the end, I made my way to the banquet hall, where I waited for the others to arrive. The hall was deserted. Of course, the fusuma and shoji and windows were all intact, as was the hanging scroll. Even for someone so used to the day being 'reset', there was something about this miraculous restoration that brought a grin to my face.

Soon Kiyoko appeared and began arranging the food on the table. I cheerfully lent her a hand. Emi also arrived to help, presumably having been so instructed by Aunt Kotono. Next came Aunt Kotono herself. Then the more excitable members of the family—in other words, those who fancied a drink at this time of the morning—began to trickle in. Yoshio, then Runa, followed by Fujitaka and then Mai. Next was Aunt Haruna, and then my mother, accompanied by Ryuichi. Now we were just waiting for Grandfather.

The minutes went by, and the most important member of our gathering still hadn't arrived. Ryuichi went upstairs to get him but immediately returned saying that he wasn't in his room, and had anyone had seen him?

I glanced at the clock, then got to my feet. It was getting on for the time of day when he usually made his way to the old house. I announced that I thought I'd seen him heading that way and would go and have a look. Of course, what I really wanted to avoid was Ryuichi or indeed any of the others going to find him. Experience had shown me that literally anyone could become the 'substitute' murderer. Leaving any member of our group alone with Grandfather, thereby giving them the chance to commit the murder, would be the height of folly. I would have to go myself. After laying the groundwork so carefully, the last thing I wanted was for some careless blunder to ruin everything.

I made my way down the walkway to the old house. I had passed through the kitchen and was about to climb the stairs when I froze on the spot. Someone was staring up at me from the floor.

It was Grandfather. He was lying face up, his legs pointing up the stairs. His head alone protruded into the kitchen. Both his arms were flung upwards, as if in celebration, while his grey hair was stained a dark red. The eyeballs staring up at me were cloudy and white.

I reeled backwards and landed on my bottom. If anyone had seen my face just then, they might well have thought I'd lost my mind completely.

This was like a bad dream. There was something absurdly funny about the way in which, despite my stupefaction, I still bothered to check Grandfather's wrist for a pulse.

He was dead. Of course he was.

11

THE MURDER'S LAST GASPS

I must be cursed, I thought. My plan had been flawless. Infallible. Foolproof. I had succeeded in making Grandfather's death an impossibility—with the exception, it seemed, of one tiny detail.

That tiny detail was none other than Runa's earring. All I'd needed to do was pick it up on my way down to the kitchen in the morning. If I hadn't skipped that tiny step, Grandfather would still be alive.

You've probably guessed what happened by now. Grandfather hadn't been murdered by anyone this time. He'd simply been sneaking up to the attic, alone, for his usual drinking session. Just as he was nearing the top of the stairs, he had stepped on the small cylindrical earring and slipped, tumbling down the perilously steep stairs and smashing his head on one of them. And, just like that, he had died. It was as simple and as ridiculous as that. If I didn't have the 'reset' to fall back on, it would have been the most pathetic of all endings.

The rest of the day passed in a blur of self-flagellation and regret. Then the 2nd of January returned to its starting point and the eighth loop began. It was three in the morning. This time, I was so angry with my own idiocy that I didn't even need to pinch myself on the thigh. I was on my feet in no time. I went straight to the stairs and retrieved the earring. When it struck me that an insignificant little object like this had been the undoing of the brilliant—no, the downright *perfect*—plan I had devised in the previous loop, my regret yielded briefly to the urge to burst out laughing.

Anyway, here I was. In the eighth loop. As I said, this penultimate loop was my test run. I would get no second chances in the final loop, which meant I had to practise every part of the routine this time around. It was a sort of rehearsal. Instead of trying anything new, I would have to conduct a practice run of the fail-safe strategy that would enable my 'performance' in the final loop to go without a hitch.

The problem was that the only *proven* strategy I had for preventing Grandfather's murder was to spend the afternoon drinking with him. The actual effectiveness of the plan I had attempted in the previous loop—gathering everyone, including him, in the banquet hall—had not been verified. Maybe my only mistake had been to leave Runa's earring on the stairs, and perhaps if I picked it up this time, the method would work. But because I hadn't *tested* that method under perfect conditions—in other words, without the earring on the stairs—adopting it seemed unwise. I had thought my plan perfect, and in fact I still basically did. But there was always the possibility that amid the excitement of the gathering someone might even attempt to carry out the murder in plain sight. Of course, that seemed unlikely. But the previous loop had been my last chance to establish, beyond a doubt, that it was out of the question.

My only option was to spend the afternoon drinking with Grandfather. That was the only strategy I had that was completely guaranteed to work, and I would spend this loop rehearsing it.

Now, maybe you're thinking I was being a little too cautious. If I'd already established that drinking with Grandfather was a sure-fire way of preventing his murder, then why bother with a rehearsal at this late stage? I could spend this loop testing another approach, saving the original strategy as my last resort for the final loop. Why bother repeating—not once, but twice—the excruciating process of getting blind drunk and spewing my guts out?

And maybe you have a point. Maybe I *was* being a little paranoid. But then I had good reason to be. If there's one thing the Trap has taught me over the years, it's that nothing in this world is ever certain. Not even our fate. In fact, that's the biggest uncertainty of all. The idea of an incontrovertible destiny, that everything happens to you for a reason and there's nothing you could do about it, might have the veneer of truth. But to someone like me, who has seen in the Trap how myriad possible futures branch away in front of us at all times, the idea is less convincing. It wasn't my *fate* to pass the entrance exam for the Kaisei Academy. I could just have easily flunked it, if I'd chosen to do so. The fact is that, within the Trap at least, I'm the one in charge—the 'game master' steering the course of events. That's what makes it so terrifying.

Before that New Year's holiday, I'd altered my fate—or if that sounds like too grandiose a term, the life I led and how it affected those around me—on plenty of occasions. Often, acting on a whim, I had altered a day's events so that they bore almost no resemblance to those of the original loop. I justified this self-centred and arguably downright reckless approach by telling myself that a few tweaks to the life of a deadbeat like myself were never going to matter in the grand scheme of things. I'd never been in a situation where those tweaks might mean the difference between whether someone lived or died. But now I could no longer afford to be reckless.

This wouldn't be the first time that, after tinkering about in the intervening loops, I had ultimately decided to make the events of the day follow their original schedule. But because the stakes had always been so much lower, I'd always been pretty casual in my attempts to do so, without worrying about whether every single detail matched the original. My 'restoration' of the day had always been a fairly rudimentary one, since all I was after was the same basic outcome. And that had always worked out just fine.

But this time was different. Something told me that if I wanted to save my grandfather, I needed to ensure my every action matched that of the original loop, right down to the tiniest detail. In other words, it wouldn't be enough for me to simply spend the day drinking with him. Unless everything— from the precise time at which I got up and made my way to breakfast, to every word of my conversation with Grandfather— conformed to the original schedule, it was all too likely that the day would once again stray from its established course. There was nothing to guarantee that even the most minor discrepancy might not lead to the very major 'anomaly' of my grandfather being murdered. Which is why this loop could only be one thing: a rehearsal.

If that was the case, I realized now with a start that I had already made my first mistake. In the original schedule, I hadn't picked up the earring at three o'clock in the morning. But this time, in my frustration at the previous loop's failure, I'd jumped straight up from my futon and gone to retrieve it. It was only now that I'd returned to my futon, telling myself I needed to sleep until later in the morning to adhere to the original schedule, that I noticed my error.

The day had barely started and I'd already messed up. I once read somewhere that when we make a mistake, the blood rushes to our heads, causing us to make even more of them. Maybe something like that was happening. In any case, there was no going back now. All I could do was hope that this discrepancy would have a negligible effect on the day as a whole, and press on with my rehearsal.

Shortly after eight in the morning, I went down to the kitchen and patiently listened to the entire conversation about red origami paper. After that, I went back up to the attic to sleep again, as I had in the original loop. This time, however, I was so preoccupied with the day ahead that in the end I simply lay there worrying myself sick. Finally, just before noon, I made my way to the main building.

As I paced down the walkway, I felt a wave of unease. Something felt off, though I didn't know what.

I ate my late breakfast alone in the dining room, trying to reassure myself that everything I'd done since waking up again had been in line with the day's schedule. What, then, was the source of my unease? I shovelled down my cold rice and racked my brain, and then it hit me.

Emi.

I spluttered in panic, sending grains of rice across the table. According to the original schedule, I was supposed to bump into Emi in the walkway. I was supposed to tell her, absurdly enough, that if she was the heir she could always marry me in order to avoid my mother's wrath. Why hadn't that conversation taken place? *Why hadn't I bumped into Emi?*

I felt the blood draining rapidly from my head. Had I misjudged the timing? I was sure I'd walked to the main building at almost exactly the same time as in the original loop. But 'almost' wasn't good enough. I must have been slightly too early or late and, as a result, our paths had failed to cross. I had met no one on the walkway and instead come straight to the dining room.

After the earring incident, this was my second mistake. This was still the eighth loop, thankfully. But if I messed up like this in the final loop, the consequences could be irreversible. The thought filled me with dread. *This* was why the rehearsal was so important.

'Ah, Kyutaro,' said Grandfather, arriving in the dining room. So far, so good. But at his next words, I felt a fresh wave of unease. 'Perfect. Come with me a moment. You can eat later.'

As he retrieved his bottle of sake and bustled me out of the room, I felt the beginnings of what can only be described as unbridled panic.

He was saying different things. Grandfather had deviated from his script entirely. But why? How could this be happening? The basic schedule appeared to be intact: he had found me alone in the dining room and invited me to join him for a drink. But he had also dramatically abridged the entire conversation he was supposed to have with me first, in order to simply make a beeline for the old house. It appeared some slight discrepancy in the schedule was, once again, giving rise to unforeseen consequences.

The surprises didn't end there. As we made our way down the walkway, someone called out to us from behind. I turned to see Runa and Fujitaka.

'Um, Grandfather?' said Runa in her most fawning voice. *No. She can't possibly be...* 'Could we have a word? There's something we'd like to discuss.'

'Ah, good timing,' said Grandfather with a chuckle, waving the sake bottle in the air. 'Why don't you two join us?'

It was enough to make me want to burst into tears. The day was drifting further and further off course.

Runa and Fujitaka wanted to speak to Grandfather: that much made sense. After all, they would have just finished their steamy rendezvous in the annex, after which they would have discussed their plan to get married, take the Fuchigami name and live happily ever after. Fine. But why didn't my presence seem to bother them? Why hadn't they decided to postpone their discussion? At this rate, it was going be the three of us drinking with him, instead of just me. And that *really* wasn't the plan.

'Well, then?' asked Grandfather once we'd arrived in the attic. Sitting cross-legged on the futon I'd left out, he poured his sake into a large glass and began glugging away. He made a show of offering us the bottle, but it was clear he intended to drink most of it himself. 'What was it you wanted to talk about?'

'Erm... well...' began Fujitaka. I remembered how fired up he'd been as they left the annex. Now that he'd come face to face with Grandfather, he seemed to have lost his nerve slightly. Finally, prompted by a sharp jab from Runa's elbow, he went on. 'Runa and I are thinking of getting married.'

'Ah.' For a moment I thought Grandfather was going to explode with rage. In the end, though, a broad smile spread across his face. 'I see. And?'

'We were, erm, wondering if that was something you'd be okay with.'

'Why would you need my permission? If the two of you are in love, then you're free to do whatever you want.'

'There's... something else. We were also thinking that maybe, if we *did* get married, we could be the ones to carry on the Fuchigami family name.'

'Oh.' I'd assumed this would be the point at which Grandfather would start yelling at them. But now he was leaning forward with what looked like deep interest. Was this just the calm before the storm? 'Go on, then, spell it out. What exactly are you proposing?'

'We think it would work out best for everyone. Our mothers would save face, and it would be a chance for the three families to finally come together again. Everyone would be a winner. Three birds with one stone... sort of thing.'

'Just how close *are* you two? Right now, I mean.' Grandfather drained his cup, then grinned at Runa. 'Go on, I'd rather hear it from *you* than Yoshio.'

'Erm, Grandfather,' put in my brother, 'I'm Fujitaka.'

'Ah, so you are. Yes, of course, with the blue... Anyway, Runa, go on.'

'Um, I don't really know what to say.' Runa had turned bright red. Her expression was that of someone deeply in love. I thought back to the mass brawl in the banquet hall, and the semi-demonic look on her face after she'd pounded Fujitaka in the head with a cushion. It was hard to believe I was looking at the same woman. 'I, um, go around to his apartment every now and then. Do his cleaning and laundry. Make him meals.'

'Ah. I see, very nice. Yes, very nice. Good, good...' Grandfather seemed delighted. Or maybe he was just drunk. 'You know, I was secretly hoping someone might suggest just such an idea. Yoshio and Runa, eh? Who'd have thought it.'

'Grandfather, like I just said, I'm *Fujitaka*. Not Yoshio.'

'Actually,' continued Grandfather as if he hadn't even heard, 'just between you and me, I'm choosing two successors, not one. A man and a woman. And I was thinking it would be best if the two I picked ended up getting married. Say I chose Ryuichi, for example. I'd want Runa or Mai to marry him. You know, keep the bloodline going—if only just. And if it was Emi, I'd want her to marry Fujitaka or Yoshio.'

'But,' I interrupted, unable to stop myself, 'what if you picked Ryuichi and Emi? That could have happened too, couldn't it?'

'Sure, it could have happened.' Runa and Fujitaka, who knew nothing of Grandfather's 'lottery', were staring dubiously at me as if to say, *What are you on about? Grandfather would never have chosen a pair like that.* 'Black and black, you mean? It was a possibility, yes. But I'd have crossed that bridge when I got to it. Like I said, I'd rather keep the bloodline going, but I'm not going to make a fuss about it. If the Fuchigami family dies out, then so be it. It'd be... fate, I suppose.'

'Fate?' Right now, that was the one word I didn't want to hear. 'More like a gamble that went wrong, wouldn't you say?'

'Sure, if you like. I mean, Edge only exists in the first place because I hit the jackpot that one time.' Grandfather seemed completely unfazed by my knowledge of his lottery method. Presumably that had something to do with how much sake he'd consumed. 'So, I thought to myself, why not gamble on its future, too?'

There was a brief silence. Runa and Fujitaka were gawking wordlessly at Grandfather and me. I couldn't quite bring myself to explain about the origami.

'But I do care about the family, you know. There are things I'd like to fix. I thought about patching things up with Kamiji and Haruna, but I couldn't bring myself to suggest a reconciliation. Instead I got to wondering if I couldn't discreetly ensure that one or even two of their children carried on the family name. That was when I had the idea of Kotono adopting an heir who would eventually take over the company. Still, much as I wanted it to be one of my grandchildren, that felt like playing it a little too safe. The old gambler in me had reared his head, see, and he wanted me to up the stakes a little. So I added Ryuichi and Emi to the list. Like you said, that meant there was a chance I'd end up passing over my own grandchildren in favour of two complete outsiders. Still, I figured I'd always work something out—and more importantly, I trusted my luck. It would be just like that ticket I bought at the races, back when Kotono and I were at the end of our tether.' Grandfather downed his glass with alarming vigour. 'Something told me a gamble like that would bring about the best result possible. It didn't matter what I or anyone else wanted to happen. Whoever came out on top, the cranes wouldn't lie.'

Whether out of drunkenness, senility, or both, Grandfather was talking as though Runa and Fujitaka were just as familiar with his origami lottery as I was. The pair appeared to be so engrossed in what he was saying that they didn't even think to interrupt.

'But if two of my grandchildren are willing to get married and take on the Fuchigami family name, then there's no need for all this gambling business. Like I said, part of me has been hoping someone would come up with just such an idea. So, if the two of you are in agreement, I'm happy to make you Kotono's heirs in my will.'

For a moment, Runa and Fujitaka were speechless. More than delighted that their plan had come to fruition, they seemed almost baffled by how smoothly things had gone.

I was pretty stunned myself. This was *not* the direction the conversation was supposed to go in, not at all. If this was its outcome, what possible reason could there have been for Runa and Fujitaka to murder Grandfather? Instead, what appeared to be the epitome of happy endings was on the cards. What had happened to that emotional flare-up they were supposed to have? Had my presence as an interloper somehow steered the conversation in the direction of a more harmonious resolution?

Just as I was wondering what on earth to make of all this, I heard a bizarre noise, like a loud snore that had been immediately cut short. By the time I realized it had come from Grandfather, he had keeled forwards. Before I could catch his expression, he was face down on the floor.

His left arm slid under his chest, like he had tried and failed to grab someone. His right hand was grasping at the tatami. Grandfather had collapsed. And now he had stopped moving entirely.

No one said a word. Still, while Runa and Fujitaka simply gaped in shock, I found myself checking his wrist for a pulse. I'd done it so many times by now that it was almost becoming a reflex.

Grandfather was dead. Just like he always was.

12
MAYBE NO ONE DIES

'Wait,' said Runa. 'We can't leave him like this.'

Fujitaka had finally roused himself and was hurrying me out of the door so that we could call for help. Runa, on the other hand, seemed oddly composed.

'Leave him like this?' Fujitaka asked sharply, clearly unsettled by the sight of his lover sitting there calmly in front of their dead grandfather. 'What are you on about?'

'Think about it,' replied Runa. She sounded like a nursery school teacher patiently remonstrating with one of her pupils. 'Grandfather's dead.'

'Yeah, I can see that.' Fujitaka's voice was growing increasingly high-pitched. 'That's why we need an ambulance.'

'Just listen to yourself. I thought you were a scientist. If he's dead, what's the point in calling an ambulance?'

'But,' said Fujitaka, aggrieved by her mocking serenity, 'what are you saying we should do? Just leave him here?'

'The opposite. We need to sort this out before we tell the others.'

'...Sort it out?'

'Fujitaka, look. Grandfather's dead. From a heart attack or

something. Whatever it was, it was sudden. Do you honestly not see what that means for us?'

'What it means for us… Well, we don't have a grandfather any more.'

'Oh, come *on*,' said Runa, clasping her head as if she were beginning to doubt her choice of husband. 'The inheritance. Edge. If Grandfather's dead, what happens to the company?'

'Er… Aunt Kotono takes over.'

'And after her?'

'Like we were just saying, the two of us will get marr—oh.' As the penny finally dropped, Fujitaka sank back onto the floor in a stupor. 'R-right. He didn't put anything in writing just now. There's no… proof. It's not l-legally binding.'

'Exactly. Just when we got him to agree to it, he drops dead. Making everything he said null and void. *Everything*.'

'Right… so…' The shock appeared to be taking its toll on Fujitaka's mental faculties. He stared at her defencelessly, tears welling in his eyes, as if to signal that he would do whatever she told him. 'What… what should we do? What should we…?'

Runa sighed as if to communicate, in return, that she'd had no idea Fujitaka was going to be this useless in a pinch. 'Well, there's another problem, isn't there? If Grandfather's dead, that means he's not going to be writing any new wills.'

'Right. Because he's dead.'

'Stop interrupting,' said Runa, slapping Fujitaka on the arm in irritation. 'The point is that he hadn't written the new will yet. He was going to do it after the New Year's dinner, but he couldn't make his mind up, so he didn't write it. Which means his most recent one is still valid.'

'His most recent one… You mean, like, from last year?'

'Exactly. He was only going to get rid of it once he'd written the new one. Now that he's dead, it's the only one that's valid.'

'Wait. Does that mean…?'

'Exactly. Who did Grandfather name as his successor last year?'

I stifled a gasp. Forget Fujitaka—it turned out I'd been pretty slow to grasp the implications of the situation myself.

'Emi.'

'That's right. Emi.' By now Runa's tone was so spiteful that I felt like covering my ears. I wondered what she'd do if she found out that the person Grandfather had chosen as Emi's partner was none other than myself. Punch me, probably. 'That *woman* gets everything. Control of Edge, the Fuchigami estate, the whole package. A complete outsider without a drop of Fuchigami blood in her veins, and she runs away with it all. We're left with nothing.'

'But what can we do? I mean, he's already dead. That's the hand we've been dealt. We just have to accept it, don't we?'

Fujitaka appeared to be slowly regaining the ability to think. Maybe it had dawned on him that, as Grandfather had mentioned, *he* still had the option of marrying Emi and being adopted into the Fuchigami family—and leaving Runa by the wayside. Runa might not have suspected him of such a pathetic scheme, but she still looked like she was about to bite him with rage.

'*We just have to accept it?* Seriously? That's all you can say at a time like this? Some man you are… What about actually *doing* something?'

'Like what, though? What am I supposed to do? Bring him back to life?'

'No. Stop that woman from getting a single yen.'

'What?'

'Listen, if it turned out Emi was a murderer, she'd be auto-matically disqualified from the inheritance. In which case the estate would be divided up among us, the family. It's civil law. So all we have to do is set her up. *Make* her a murderer.'

'B-but... Hang on... Wait, what? How are we supposed to...? I mean, framing someone for murder is—'

'We've got all the ingredients we need. A body, for one thing. Look,' she said, glancing carelessly at Grandfather's body, as if it were some pebble she was about to send flying with a kick. 'We just need a weapon.'

'A weapon? What are you—'

'Smashing him in the head with something should do the trick. Bingo. Murder.'

'Runa, are you even serious right now?' Fujitaka seemed to have shaken off his earlier timidity. 'Do you think the police are a bunch of amateurs or something? Ever heard of some-thing called forensics? Or the coroner? Oh, wait, there isn't one in Atsuki, is there...' I couldn't see what this had to do with anything, but Fujitaka, ever the scientist, seemed intent on getting the facts right. 'Well, there's a medical university, at least. When *they* open him up, they'll see right away that he died from natural causes. Right away. There's no point trying to make it seem like anything else. I can't believe you don't know that.'

'Wow. You really are slow, aren't you?' replied Runa, brushing aside this counter-attack like it was a bit of lint on her tracksuit. Fujitaka was way out of his depth. 'The cause of death doesn't matter. As long as it *looks* like he's been smashed in the head with something, the police will have to investigate. Even if it turns out not to have been the direct cause of death, there's still plenty of grounds for assault. If we're lucky, they'll say it was the assault that caused the heart attack and she'll go down for bodily injury resulting in death; and even if they don't, we can still get her on attempted murder. As long as there was intent to harm Grandfather, there's no way she gets to keep the inheritance. That's how we keep it out of her grubby hands. Simple.'

'But... the weapon,' said Fujitaka, who seemed to be coming around to the idea even as he continued to put on a show of reluctance. 'What about the weapon? You saying we should use *that*?' He jerked his chin in the direction of the sake bottle that Grandfather had drained almost single-handedly.

'Are you stupid? How are we going to frame Emi with that?'

'Then what?'

'Something linked to her, obviously. Think. In the reception room.'

'The reception room?'

'The moth orchids. That big vase.'

'But... those are Aunt Kotono's.'

'Yes, but Emi gave them to her, didn't she?'

'But why would that make people suspect Emi and not Aunt Kotono?'

'Oh, come *on*, keep up. Whose fingerprints are on the vase?'

Fujitaka gave a little gasp, which Runa greeted with a sadistic, mocking smile.

'Exactly,' she went on. 'Emi's. At this point, she's the only one who's touched it. Aunt Kotono hasn't taken it up to her room yet. Emi showed her the flowers, then put them in the reception room herself. So all we have to do is bring the vase here without leaving our own fingerprints on it.'

'How do we do that?'

Runa gave him a look as if to say, *You really are incapable of thinking for yourself, aren't you?* 'Or maybe we wipe them off afterwards. The main thing is to avoid fingerprints. Got it? Then hurry up and fetch that vase.'

As the truth behind my grandfather's death finally came into view, I felt a strange wave of exhaustion. It seemed that, with the exception of Mai, each of the earlier 'murderers' had arrived at the same conclusion as Runa—and carried out the same act of deception. In any case, one thing was clear: his death had not been murder.

Grandfather's body had never been subjected to an autopsy. Every time, we had simply been presented with what *appeared* to be a murder—then, before a forensic examination could reveal the cause or estimated time of the death, the loop had returned him to life.

Of course, I didn't know the real cause of Grandfather's death, but it seemed likely to be a stroke brought on by alcohol consumption. His excessive drinking had literally been the death of him. 'Excessive'—that was the important word. He'd been drinking in the original loop, too, and yet he'd survived. If he only started dying from the second loop onwards, the reason had to lie in the specific amount of alcohol he consumed. In the original loop, he'd made me drink plenty myself—how much exactly I couldn't recall, but we must have split the bottle about half and half. Whatever the medical details, it seemed that drinking only half the bottle wasn't enough to kill Grandfather, whereas polishing off almost the entire thing was more than his body could bear.

My basic assumption—that Grandfather kept dying because I wasn't there drinking with him—had been correct. But the cause of death had not been murder. He had died because, left on his own, he had ended up consuming far more alcohol than in the original loop.

His death had been a natural one, and yet every single person who had discovered him had decided to frame it as murder. That was the source of all the confusion. They had done so, of course, because if Grandfather died at this point—in other words, before he'd written his new will—the one from the previous year would prevail. Emi would be officially designated his successor and would walk away with his company and entire estate, while we, his actual relatives, would be left with nothing. That was what each of the 'murderers' had so feared.

I cast my mind back to the second loop, when Grandfather's body had been discovered for the first time. Runa had laid into Aunt Haruna for trying to touch him. I'd been wondering why the 'murderer', of all people, would have been so intent on preserving the crime scene, but now it was clear she'd been desperate to ensure Grandfather's spontaneous death *was* treated as a murder. If the others were to start carelessly handling the vase, Emi's fingerprints, which she'd been so careful to preserve, would be ruined.

After the Runa and Fujitaka double act, Yoshio, Mother and Ryuichi had all arrived at the same conclusion: that if they could only frame Grandfather's death as a murder at the hands of Emi, she'd be stripped of her rights to the inheritance. Now that I thought about it, the culprits all had one thing in common: they had been informed by Runa that Grandfather had not yet written his will.

Mai was the exception: she had chosen to frame Runa rather than Emi for the 'murder'. That much was clear from the way she had deposited Runa's earring at the scene of the crime. She had been seeking revenge on her sister for stealing the man she loved. In fact, though it pained me to imagine it, she might have been the only one to actually commit the murder. As she reeled from the shock of heartbreak, Grandfather might have made some insensitive comment that only exacerbated her feeling of inferiority—it was possible that this scenario, which I'd vaguely surmised earlier, had really taken place. Panicking in the wake of her impulsive crime, she had decided to make use of the object she happened to be carrying at the time—her sister's earring. Of course, all this had been consigned to oblivion once the reset occurred, and I would never know the truth.

Though Fujitaka had yielded control of the situation to Runa, he still seemed hesitant to fetch the vase. Eventually, losing her patience, she declared that she'd get it herself.

'That all sounds very ingenious,' I said as she was about to leave. 'But you're forgetting something. What if I tell the police?'

Runa looked completely taken off guard, as if she'd forgotten I was even in the room. Something about her flustered expression came as a relief. She was human, after all.

'Wh-what? You're… not going to take our side, Kyu-chan? You're—you're joking, right?'

'Of course not. Why should I take your side?'

'*Why?*' she exclaimed, grabbing me by the lapels and shaking me. 'Come *on*. You've got as much to lose here as we do. Don't you get it? That woman's going to take everything from us. Everything. And you're just going to let her get away with it?'

239

'That's the hand we've been dealt, isn't it?' I said, shooting my brother a look as I borrowed his turn of phrase. 'And I wonder if you could stop calling her "that woman". She has a name, you know.'

At this, Runa abandoned her appeal to my emotions and started simply yelling at me. 'What the *hell*, Kyu-chan?' Her mouth flared open demonically; her eyes bulged threateningly in their sockets. 'You're taking *her* side? Seriously? What's wrong with you? Go on, tell me why! I want an answer right now!'

Deception wasn't going to get me anywhere. I decided to tell her the truth.

'I can't help it. I'm in love with her.'

'*What?*'

'And if you're going to make me choose between her and my family, then I choose her.'

Runa abruptly released her grip, as if freed of the demon that had possessed her. Her expression had turned blank with astonishment.

'Oh… right,' she murmured. 'Right. I guess you really *don't* have a choice then. I mean… love trumps everything, doesn't it…'

'Erm,' interrupted Fujitaka, anxiously peering at her. She seemed to have fallen into a sort of beatific trance, like a nun praying to an image of the Virgin Mary. 'Runa, I hope you're not going to suggest we, er, silence the witness or something.'

'Of course not!' shouted Runa, her look of rapture instantly yielding to a scowl. 'What do you take me for, some kind of cold-blooded murderer? An axe-wielding, chainsaw-swinging maniac? Forget all that scary stuff I said before, alright? All of it. I… got a little carried away, I guess. Let my tongue get the better of me. I'm sorry, Kyu-chan,' she said, abruptly wrapping her arms around me and rubbing her cheek against my tracksuit as if to dry her tears on it. 'Just… forget it all, okay? I wasn't serious. About any of it. I'm not *like* that. I'm a good person. I promise. You believe me, don't you?'

'Hey, erm, Runa… what are you…?' asked Fujitaka, looking—unsurprisingly—a little alarmed by this sudden display of affection.

'What? I couldn't *live* with myself if I turned Kyu-chan against me.'

'Right. So it's *his* reaction you're worried about…'

For a while, Runa and Fujitaka simply sat there in a sort of idiotic daze, as if they'd forgotten all about the dead grandfather lying face down in front of them. Maybe they couldn't quite bring themselves to tell the others and so face the reality not just of Grandfather's death, but of what would come afterwards—the despair of being left empty-handed by the old man.

In any case, we eventually reported his death to the others, this time without the slightest bit of subterfuge. It had taken eight loops, but finally Grandfather had avoided being 'murdered' (or killed in a ridiculous accident). Still, that didn't change the fact that he was dead.

'I must have warned him about the drinking a hundred times,' lamented Aunt Kotono when she learnt how he'd died, 'and yet he had to keep at it. If he'd only listened, he'd still be with us.'

So it seemed that all I had to do to save Grandfather was stop him from drinking. Of course, it probably wouldn't be long until he popped his clogs anyway. Still, anything would be better than this sudden death during the New Year holidays.

And if he died before he could clear up the matter of the inheritance, things would get really messy. It wasn't as if Emi and I wanted to run the company, after all—in fact, you'd have been hard-pressed to pick a less enthusiastic pair.

My grandfather's unexpected death swept the Fuchigami mansion into a panic. Before long, the clock reached midnight, I woke up in my futon, and the 2nd of January started all over again. At long last, the final loop had begun. The Trap had never felt so long.

I waited until eight in the morning, then made my way downstairs, stopping on the way to collect the earring, and peered into the kitchen. I listened as Grandfather—his voice hale and hearty as always—began his exchange with Aunt Kotono and Kiyoko about the lack of red origami paper.

'Excuse me, Grandfather,' I interrupted. 'There's something I'd like to talk to you about.' I glanced at his two companions, who were both staring at me wide-eyed. Of course, they had forgotten I was staying in the old house. 'It concerns Aunt Kotono and Kiyoko, too.'

'Bit early for that sort of thing, isn't it, er…' Grandfather peered at me with a peculiar intensity. 'Ah, Kyutaro. How are you feeling today? Really went to town on the drink yesterday, didn't you?'

Here he was, the man who kept drinking himself to death, implying that *I* was the one who needed to cut down on my boozing.

'Actually, that's what I wanted to talk to you about. I know this might sound a little sudden, Grandfather, but I promise this'll be the most important favour I ever ask you.'

'Ooh, very dramatic. What's this favour, then?'

'Do you think you could give up drinking?'

'Wh-what are you talking about?' Grandfather had turned uncharacteristically timid, maybe because he was painfully aware of Aunt Kotono and Kiyoko at his side. 'Me? Give up? Why, I, er, barely even drink as it is. Hardly a drop. I'm very careful in that area. *You're* the one who needs to cut down, wouldn't you say?'

'Grandfather, there's no use pretending. I know all about your plan to hide in the attic later and spend the whole afternoon drinking sake.'

'Wh-what? Where did you g-get that idea?'

'You can't hide it from these two forever. Otherwise I'm prepared to take the necessary action myself.'

'What on earth's got into you? Oh, I see—this is your hangover talking. You're taking it out on me…' Grandfather seemed uncertain whether to give me an earful or adopt a gentler tack. 'Oh, for heaven's sake. It's the New Year. Can't I have a bit of fun?'

'No, you can't. Anyway, I'm not just asking you to pack it in for the New Year. I want you to swear off the bottle forever.'

'Listen, you. You can't just… You're being very cruel, you hear? Trying to strip me of my one pleasure in life…'

'That's a promise, then? You'll never go near a bottle again. Not a single drop.'

'Do you… even realize what you're saying? And who you're saying it to?'

'Aunt Kotono, Kiyoko, I'd appreciate your assistance with this,' I said, ignoring Grandfather's angry remonstrances and bowing to them instead. 'If Grandfather breaks his promise, do let me know.'

'Now, wait a minute, you. Wait a damn minute. I haven't promised anything. Why would I make a promise like that? You little...'

'Tell me, Grandfather, how is Mr Kawazoe these days?' The insinuation in my voice was so strong that it gave even me chills. 'Or Mayu Tsurui—I wonder if you've heard anything from her?'

A deathly silence descended, as abruptly as if someone had flipped a switch. Grandfather's eyeballs looked like they were about to pop. His jaw was shaking. His mouth opened and closed several times, but no words came out. Again and again, he tried and failed to speak. I began to worry that he'd taken too strong a dose of his medication. If he went and died on me now— not from drinking but from the shock of this conversation—I'd really be in trouble.

'Of course, I'm the only one who knows,' I added hurriedly. 'So I suppose it's up to you whether I tell the others.'

'What's he talking about?' interjected Aunt Kotono, who was staring worriedly at us. Even without knowing the details, she had grasped that this was serious. 'Tell me, Father. What's he talking about?'

But Grandfather was still struggling to get a single word out. His shoulders heaved up and down; he seemed to be having trouble breathing. He was staring at me, but his gaze kept drifting off to one side, as if even focusing on a single point was too much effort.

'Alright, I promise,' he murmured, finally breaking the long silence. 'I'll quit drinking.'

'Well, you all heard that, didn't you? Grandfather made a promise. Aunt Kotono, Kiyoko—make sure he keeps it, would you?'

Aunt Kotono opened her mouth as if to speak, but Grandfather cut her off. 'Is that it, then?'

'Do you mean, is there anything else I'd like you to promise? If so, there is one thing, actually. I'd like you to remove my name from the list of candidates for the inheritance. And Emi's, too. That's what she wants.'

'Right. Done.' Grandfather seemed to be gradually regaining his usual composure, perhaps because he'd resigned himself to doing whatever I asked. He even managed a vague smile. 'Kotono, Kiyoko—sorry, but would you mind giving the two of us a minute?'

Looking relieved to see Grandfather back to his usual self, the pair obediently made their way out of the old house without another glance.

Grandfather turned to me. The look on his face was less one of contrition and more that of a man finally freed from a terrible burden. In fact, he almost looked cheerful. 'I'm not proud of what I did to your father and Hitoshi, you know.'

'Then why did you do it, Grandfather? Did you really hate my mother and Aunt Haruna that much?'

'I think I was just feeling a little reckless. Got to thinking nothing was beyond the pale if it meant revenge for me and Kotono—for the way those two treated us. But none of that matters. There's no justifying what I did. Please, Kyutaro. Forgive me.'

'I think my father and Uncle Hitoshi are the ones you should be asking for forgiveness.'

'I know, I know. It really was foolish of me. I can't even believe it myself.'

'You got a little carried away.'

'Yes.'

'Happens to the best of us.' I was thinking of Runa's manic state in the previous loop. 'You got a little carried away, and it just so happened that there was nobody at your side to stop you, and so fate branched off in an unexpected direction. Does that sound about right?'

'It does.'

'I won't tell a soul about all this, Grandfather—that's a promise. I can see you already regret what you did. Telling the family isn't going to achieve anything. All I'm asking in return is that you keep *your* promise, okay?'

'About the drinking? Yes, I'll stop. I swear it.'

'Until your dying day.'

'Well, that's a cheerful way of putting it… Yes, Kyutaro, until my dying day.'

Finally, I get to go home. This was the first thought that struck me, with a rush of emotion, as I followed my grandfather towards the main building. As long as he kept his promise and stayed off the liquor, he would make it through this loop—or rather, given that this would be its definitive incarnation, the 2nd of January—alive. Probably. I was only human, after all. I couldn't guarantee anything. I wasn't familiar with the specifics of Grandfather's medical condition. For all I knew he might keel over the next day instead. Still, for the 2nd of January at least, he would be safe, and we'd all be able to go home without incident. Of that, at least, I felt sure.

In the early afternoon, as if to prove that my confidence was well founded, we were asked to gather in the banquet hall, where Grandfather announced to everyone that, as promised, he would now reveal the contents of his will.

I didn't even feel like I needed to listen. In accordance with the schedule, Runa and Fujitaka would have approached Grandfather, told him about their plan to get married, and asked to be made his successors. He would have agreed, and the new will would reflect that decision.

And that really was what Grandfather announced—that he would bestow the Fuchigami family name on Runa and Fujitaka on condition of their marriage, and hand them full control of the Edge Restaurant Group. Not only that, but when it came to the estate, he would, after discussion with his lawyer, distribute it evenly among the entire family. In a final surprise, he even declared that my father and Uncle Hitoshi were to be offered management roles at Edge.

Reactions to the announcement were varied. Mother and Aunt Haruna, while clearly disappointed that one of their own children hadn't been given full control, looked relieved to have avoided a complete washout—in fact, their reactions were so comically similar that I had to stifle a laugh. They also looked delighted to have their husbands back in gainful employment. For all the rancour between them, the two sisters even managed to exchange a smile. Yoshio and Ryuichi, meanwhile, were obviously disgruntled at being passed over, both believing that they were far more qualified for the role, but eventually seemed to resign themselves to this new reality. Emi didn't show much of a response, but I knew that inside she would be breathing a sigh of relief.

My biggest concern was how Mai was going to react. The revelation that the man she'd secretly been in love with was going to marry the sister she'd always felt inferior to was bound to come as a shock, and I discreetly braced myself to subdue her in the event of some violent outburst. And yet, surprisingly enough, she remained calm. Maybe the fact that Grandfather had already made his decision was helping her remain philosophical about the whole thing. It turns out the same shocking piece of news can trigger very different responses depending on how and when you choose to disclose it.

After that we were served a lavish meal. Perhaps because the problem of the inheritance had finally been resolved, the mood was a lot merrier than at the New Year's dinner. As he'd promised, Grandfather stuck to oolong tea, but that didn't stop him from excitedly getting out the karaoke set and treating us all to a serenade. Next, of course, was Yoshio, who began belting out a few favourites of his own. The atmosphere in the banquet hall was so jubilant that it was hard to believe these were the people responsible for the almost funereal gathering on the 1st of January.

Eventually it was time to bring the festivities to a close. After repeatedly bowing goodbye to Grandfather and Aunt Kotono, Aunt Haruna and her daughters cheerily set off home. My family and I climbed into Yoshio's car—though, as he'd been drinking, Mother had to drive.

I'd wake up tomorrow—the real tomorrow, that is—in my own home. This long, long 2nd of January would finally be over. As I let that sink in, a wave of exhaustion washed over me. I tried to relax into my seat, telling myself I no longer had anything to worry about.

But a strange tension lingered in my chest. As if I were forgetting something. Something crucial. What, though?

I tried to tell myself I was overthinking things. It really had been a long day, and in a sense I'd spent it all alone. My nerves were clearly frazzled.

But it was no use. The gnawing feeling wasn't going away; in fact, it was getting worse by the second. *Something's wrong*, the alarm bell ringing in my head told me. *Something's very wrong*.

The car began to move. Grandfather, Aunt Kotono and Kiyoko were standing in the entrance to see us off. As I gazed at the three of them, waving as we drove away, it finally hit me.

That was it. That was what was bothering me.

The lawyer. Mr Munakata.

Where *was* he?

13

THE MURDER STRIKES BACK

When I woke up, I found myself in my bedroom at our family home. The familiar old ceiling seemed to smile beneficently down at me, saying *Welcome home*. For a moment I simply rolled around in my bed, savouring the reality of this brand-new day. It was over. After my lengthy ordeal, the 2nd of January really was over. Finally, it was the 3rd.

Before long, though, that gnawing feeling began to rear its head once more. Yes, that long day had ended. But could I be happy with the final version of it I'd produced? Grandfather hadn't died, at least: he'd even waved us off with a smile for once. That was enough, wasn't it? I'd managed to 'fix' the day, right down to every detail—hadn't I?

And yet I couldn't stop thinking about Mr Munakata. I simply couldn't shake the lawyer's face from my mind. In the original version of the 2nd of January, as we had been getting ready to go home, we had bumped into him in the entrance. The man in the grey suit. In other words, he had been visiting the Fuchigami household that day. Grandfather had told me as much himself. That he'd asked his lawyer to come and collect the will—but not having written it yet, and not wanting to send Mr Munakata home empty-handed, had given him some other documents to go through. The lawyer had looked a little irritated, perhaps because of the extra paperwork that had been foisted upon him instead of the will—or maybe, I'd thought, because he always looked like that.

In other words, Mr Munakata was supposed to have spent almost the entire 2nd of January at the Fuchigami mansion. And yet in the final loop, when Grandfather had announced Runa and Fujitaka as his successors in the banquet hall, Mr Munakata hadn't been there. Nor, of course, had he attended the meal afterwards. He'd also been absent when we left the mansion. What on earth could all this mean?

The man had definitely been at the house that day: that seemed like an unshakable fact. The day's original schedule included him visiting the mansion at my grandfather's request. So where had he been? While we'd been merrily carousing in the banquet hall, could he have been sitting in Grandfather's study or some other part of the house, silently getting on with his tedious work in solitude?

But no, that didn't make sense. The meal was one thing, but the idea of him missing Grandfather's announcement was absurd. Whoever else might have been absent, he was the one person you might expect to drop everything and come running. That was basically his job. And yet he hadn't been there—and neither Grandfather nor the others had seemed to think that strange. Why? However preoccupied by the meal everyone might have been, it seemed unthinkable that they had simply forgotten that he was visiting. Even if it had slipped Grandfather's mind, Aunt Kotono and Kiyoko would have remembered. But if nobody had forgotten, that only made the situation even more peculiar.

Something had gone wrong. I was sure of it. Restless with unease, I made my way down to the living room, where I could hear Mother, Father and Fujitaka chatting and letting out occasional bursts of laughter. I hadn't heard my father laugh in a long time. Last night, when we'd got home and Mother had told him he'd been offered a job in the accounting department at Grandfather's company, he'd simply stuck out his lower lip morosely, as if not yet able to cast off his hard-done-by persona. But this morning he seemed to be slowly returning to his usual cheerful self. After his period of resembling Fujitaka, he was firmly back in Yoshio mode.

Speaking of which, I could see no sign of my other brother.

'Where's Yoshio?' I asked, half-expecting them to tell me he was still in bed.

Mother gave me a look. 'Oh, he went to work ages ago.'

'Really? He's back in the office already?' I'd always thought companies gave their employees the first three days of the year off.

'That's working life for you,' said Father, looking at me and Fujitaka with a worldly-wise expression. It seemed he was finally back in a place where he felt comfortable lecturing his sons. Good for him, I guess. 'You two should brace yourselves. It's nothing like being a student, I can tell you that.'

I nodded respectfully, then made my way to the phone in the hall. I dialled the number for the Fuchigami household and got through to Kiyoko.

'Thank you very much for hosting us,' I began by way of greeting. 'By the way, is Grandfather well?'

'Oh, very. I'm afraid you've missed him, though.'

'Ah. Where's he gone?'

'Why, to the office, of course. Ms Fuchigami, too.'

'I see.' So it wasn't just Yoshio's company that cut the New Year's holiday brutally short. What a way to live… 'So, he hasn't been, erm, sneaking a tipple when you're not looking or anything? After our conversation, I mean.'

'Oh, don't you worry!' A peal of merry laughter issued from the receiver. I couldn't remember ever hearing Kiyoko laugh out loud before. 'Ms Fuchigami and I are keeping a very strict eye on him. You can set your mind at ease.'

'Much obliged. Well, I'm grateful for your help.'

I hung up, then paused to think. So Grandfather was alive and kicking. I'd half expected to be told that he'd suddenly collapsed after we'd left the mansion, but it seemed nothing that dramatic had happened. Everything really was fine. I finally felt the tension in my shoulders begin to ease.

It had been a long and lonely fight, but in the end it had been worth it. For a moment, I decided to bask in the satisfaction of pulling it off—a satisfaction that, like so much of the previous nine days (or loops), was mine alone to experience. Grandfather dying, coming back to life, dying again, and then coming back to life once more: the day had looped around and around, as if sketching a circular line that returned, unfailingly, to that same event. And yet no loop had been exactly the same as the last. Each time, slight discrepancies had emerged. Gaps had arisen. The circle had slowly veered away from its prescribed trajectory, so that it came instead to resemble a spiral. And every time, at the same point in the spiral, Grandfather would die. No matter how much I tried to fix things, he just kept dying, and dying, and dying. Then, just before I emerged from the spiral forever, I had finally averted his death.

Of course, nobody else was aware of any of this. I was the only one who knew how many times Grandfather had shuffled, however briefly, off this mortal coil. For everyone else, the only 2nd of January that year had been the final, definitive loop, and no other version of the day even existed. Grandfather's successor had been decided without a hitch, and the old man had stayed very much alive. The day had reached its undramatic conclusion and then, like any other day, it had smoothly given way to the next—the 3rd of January. What no one knew was that I was the one, of all people, who had made that happen. I was the one who had prevented the day from descending into tragedy, and no one had a clue. And so, much as it went against my modest nature, I decided to take pride in my own accomplishment. To give myself a firm pat on the back. If no one else was going to lavish praise on me, I'd have to do it myself.

Even as I felt contentment wash over me, though, the question of Mr Munakata continued to bother me, like a tiny fish bone caught in my throat. I tried to convince myself that he was some eccentric misanthrope who liked nothing more than holing up in a room and getting on with paperwork. After all, it takes all sorts. Yes, that had to be it. I must have been overthinking things again.

Back in my room, I lay back down on my bed. I still hadn't entirely recovered from the exhaustion of my time in the Trap. After all, I'd been at the mansion for a whole eight days—a total of 192 hours—longer than the others. I had barely pressed my cheek into my pillow when I felt myself drifting off.

I had no idea how long I slept. It might only have been a few seconds. But in that short time, I had a glaringly vivid dream.

The setting was one I knew well. The Fuchigami mansion. Face after familiar face seemed to shimmer in the air. Ah, yes, I recognized this room. That's right. The one by the banquet hall—

I woke with a loud gasp. In my surprise, I fell right out of my bed.

Mr Munakata hadn't been there. That was what had so unsettled me. I had been dreaming of the second loop, after we had discovered Grandfather's body for the first time. The police had arrived and asked us to gather in the reception room. Aunt Haruna, who had discovered the body, had been first up for questioning, while the rest of us had waited.

Back then, I'd felt a strange unease, as if I'd forgotten something important. I didn't know what it was, but I'd had a feeling it had something to do with one of the people in the reception room. That strange sense that something was amiss had persisted, and yet I'd been unable to identify its source. Now, finally, I knew what it was.

Mr Munakata hadn't been in the reception room. In fact, there had been no sign of him anywhere. And that didn't make sense. Why would he be absent? A murder had occurred, or at least we thought it had, and the victim was none other than Mr Munakata's own client. In the midst of such a major incident, it would have been ludicrous for him to have been beavering away in the study or some other room—no matter how much of a misanthrope he happened to be. Even if he'd tried, the police would never have allowed it.

Then I remembered something else about that scene. The officer who had gathered us all in the reception room had turned to Emi—apparently deeming her the most reliable—and asked whether this was 'everyone'. And after looking around the room at everyone, she had given him a decisive nod.

In other words, at that time, Mr Munakata *had not been* at the Fuchigami mansion. He simply can't have been on the premises. But why? How? How could the man who was *supposed* to be at the mansion have vanished like smoke from the stage? I just didn't see how it was possible.

As I paced around my room like some bewildered bear in a cage, there was a knock on the door.

'Kyutaro?' asked Mother, peering into the room. 'Telephone.'

I went downstairs and picked up the receiver.

'Hello?' came a silky-smooth voice. 'It's me.' It was Emi.

'Oh.' I felt the blood rush to my already confused brain. For a moment I could hardly hear myself speak. 'It's, er, very nice to hear from you.'

'I'm calling from the office. I had a spare moment.'

'Right. I... hope you're not working too hard.'

'Do you have any plans this evening?'

'This evening? Er... no. Nothing in particular. Probably just watching TV.'

'How about getting dinner together? There's something I want to talk to you about.'

'Oh. Right. I mean, yes, absolutely, I'd be, er, delighted. Really delighted.'

Once we'd arranged to meet at a French restaurant in town at seven that evening, I replaced the receiver. I couldn't for the life of me work out what she might want to see me about, but dinner with Emi was dinner with Emi. The restaurant was a fancy one. I should probably wear a shirt and tie. And it wouldn't do to let her pay the bill. I'd have to remember to take the otoshidama money I'd received from Aunt Kotono. In my head, this little meeting was beginning to feel a lot like a date—until I remembered the partner Emi had mentioned. Best not to dwell on all this, then. I told myself that just seeing her would be enough.

I ended up arriving at the restaurant an hour early, at six o'clock. Oh well. An hour was no time at all. I was shown to the table Emi had reserved, and had only been waiting for ten minutes when, lo and behold, she appeared.

'Here you are, just as I thought,' she said, sitting down with a chuckle. 'Knowing you, Hisataro, I had a feeling you'd be here way ahead of schedule.'

To be honest, though, I hardly heard what she said, because I'd fallen into a sort of trance. Until now, I'd only ever seen Emi in a black tracksuit and chanchanko, a combination that was beyond unflattering. This evening, she was wearing a dark green suit with a broad-collared white shirt and striped tie—a dapper, masculine look that somehow also managed to accentuate her feminine charms. She was jaw-dislocatingly beautiful.

'You look wonderful,' I managed to splutter after who knows how long. Something told me I'd been gawping at her for far longer than was acceptable. 'What an outfit.'

'Thanks. You're not looking too shabby yourself. I've only seen you in those silly tracksuits before.' Emi paused, as though lost in thought, then gave a wry smile. 'You know, you'd never guess you were a high schooler.'

'I get that quite often. People call me Gramps.'

'Actually, *I* always assumed you were at university.'

'You... did?'

'No one told me otherwise, see, and I never asked. And do you remember at the New Year's dinner, when the Chairman asked if you were willing to become his successor? Your mother said that you were, as long as your grandfather didn't mind waiting until you'd graduated from university. She made it sound like it was just around the corner—like you might even be graduating this spring.'

'I guess it's quite common for people to look older than they are.'

'So today when the President happened to mention how old you actually are, it came as quite a shock. I mean, just look at you. I'd have thought you were my age, maybe even slightly older. And—' As if realizing that she had come perilously close to revealing her own age, Emi stopped short, then gave a mischievous shrug of her shoulders. 'Anyway, it's just a number, isn't it? I mean, it doesn't change the fact that you're a very nice person, Hisataro. Much nicer than most so-called adult men.'

It was only some time after we'd placed our orders—at which point I was still blushing from Emi's compliment—that I realized something was off. I had the impression Emi had said something deeply illogical, but I couldn't put my finger on what it was. All we'd talked about so far was the fact that I looked a lot older than I really was. What could have been illogical about that? I was mulling this over when the hors d'oeuvres arrived.

I had just taken my first bite when I let out a gasp. In my surprise, I managed to swallow a mouthful of smoked duck without even chewing it.

'Emi. What did you call me just now?'

'What's that?'

'Just now. What name did you use?'

'Your name? Why, would you rather I didn't call you Hisataro?'

'Right. Hisataro. Not Kyutaro.'

Emi set her knife and fork down with a puzzled expression. 'But that's what you told me, isn't it? That the correct pronunciation is Hisataro, not Kyutaro. You specifically asked me to call you by your real name.'

Of course I had. I remembered it well.

But for Emi to remember it, too—that didn't make sense. In fact, she wasn't *supposed* to remember it. After all, I'd had that conversation with her during the first loop of the 2nd of January, which had been 'reset' a long time ago and was just one of the many iterations of that day destined to be forgotten by everyone but me. So why did Emi remember it? It simply wasn't possible. Something was wrong. Something was terribly wrong.

Gone was my giddy excitement at this romantic encounter. Under the dimmed lighting of the restaurant, the objects around me seemed to twist and warp, their outlines buckling like so many melting lollipops. I felt so dizzy I couldn't even taste the food in my mouth.

Then a thought occurred to me. I'd been so preoccupied with seeing Emi today that I'd had no time to watch television or read a newspaper.

'Sorry, this is going to sound a little odd, but…'

'What is it?'

'Today's date. It *is* the 3rd, isn't it? I mean, obviously it is, but—'

'Nope,' said Emi, with a brief shake of her head. 'It's the 4th. The 4th of January. The first business day of the year.'

14

ESCAPING THE SPIRAL

When I came to my senses, I found that I had embarked on a long explanation of my 'condition' to Emi. I was telling her about the nature and rules of the Trap, the entire sequence of events that had followed the New Year's dinner at the mansion, the fierce and clandestine battle between myself and the 'murderers' over the course of the nine loops—and Grandfather's secret scheme, which I'd promised never to reveal. In fact, I was telling Emi all sorts of things I'd never confessed to anyone, not even my closest friends and family.

Soon enough, I began to wish I wasn't. This could only end badly. The things I was telling her—with a straight face no less—were so outlandish that she was bound to conclude I was some madman losing his grip on reality, a dangerously unhinged individual who should be given as wide a berth as possible. And yet no matter how much my rational self panicked, my mouth just kept forming sentences. Before I knew it, I'd told her everything.

'Of course,' I hastily concluded, noticing the way Emi was staring at me without blinking, 'this is all just... I mean, please think of all this as a weird fantasy of mine. A silly little story. Maybe some science fiction I'm thinking of writing.'

'But…' said Emi, finally blinking. She leant forward without taking her eyes off me. 'That conversation you mentioned—in the dining room, between Ryuichi and me. That was what he told me. Word for word. That if he was made the heir, he wanted to make me his wife. That's what he said. So you can keep telling me this is all just a fantasy, but I'm going to have a hard time believing you.'

In other words, in the final and definitive loop, Ryuichi must have approached Emi at breakfast with the marriage proposal that was really an insurance policy, just as he had when I'd been there to overhear it. He'd felt confident Grandfather was going to pick him as his successor—without knowing, of course, that just a few hours later that honour would go to Runa and Fujitaka.

'But I could have just overheard that conversation by hiding somewhere in the dining room, couldn't I? Knowing what he said doesn't somehow prove that I was stuck in a time loop.'

'True, true. I'll admit it's preposterous, what you're telling me. In fact, if anyone else tried to spin me a story like this, I'd probably tell them to get their head checked out. At the same time…' At this point Emi's blank expression abruptly relaxed into a grin. I'd never seen her smile like that. There was something audacious, even defiant, about it. 'I'm not saying I believe you *just* because it's you. I'm not stupid enough to unconditionally believe every single word, no matter how absurd, that comes out of someone's mouth just because of who they are. But as I was listening to you just now, I thought of

261

something. A way to prove, using logic, that what you're telling me is true.'

'L-logic?' At this point I began to resign myself to the idea that Emi might simply be playing along—that she'd taken the absurd things I was telling her as a sort of elaborate joke which, using her trademark wit, she was about to turn back on me. 'You mean… prove I fell into the Trap? But… how?'

'First, how about we remind ourselves of the sequence of events? See, I'd like to correct a certain misunderstanding on your part. The New Year's dinner was as you remember it. The problem is the next day. You spent the afternoon of the 2nd of January drinking with the Chairman in the attic, didn't you? And what happened after that? You got in your brother's car and went home. Or you thought you did. When you woke up, you were back in the attic at the mansion. Naturally enough, you assumed that you were back in the Trap—that the 2nd of January had begun all over again. But you were wrong.'

'I was?'

'Yes. Hisataro, you never left the Fuchigami residence on the 2nd of January.'

Having only just learnt about the Trap, Emi should really have been the one in a state of shock. But here I was, completely lost for words.

'But I… I definitely remember being helped into my brother's car.'

'That's right. You all got into the car. And you really were about to drive home. Another few moments and you'd have been on your way. But tell me, do you actually remember the car pulling off?'

262

'…Now that you mention it, I'm not sure. I mean, I was pretty drunk. I think I just sort of blacked out the moment I sat down.'

'That's exactly what happened. You fell fast asleep. Then, just as your brother was about to put his foot down, the Chairman called out for him to wait.'

'Grandfather did?'

'That's right.'

'Why?'

'He promised that if you all stayed another night, he'd announce his successor the following afternoon.'

'Wh-what?'

It felt as though the ground underneath my feet had just given way. *He'd promised to announce his successor the following afternoon.* The following afternoon… I felt the pricking, once again, of that tiny yet stubborn needle of doubt buried deep within my memory. The content of Grandfather's will was only to be revealed upon his death—or so he had declared at the New Year's dinner. If he had suddenly changed his mind, he must have done so after eleven p.m. on the 1st of January, when I'd retired to my bedroom. Then, when I'd eavesdropped on Runa and Fujitaka in the annex, my brother had mentioned that Grandfather was going to make the announcement 'today'— meaning, of course, the 2nd of January. And yet Emi was telling me that on the *evening* of the 2nd, Grandfather had declared that he'd make the announcement the next day.

'The… following afternoon, did you say?'

'Yes,' replied Emi. 'It was a proposal guaranteed to get every-one's interest. In the end, we all decided to stay another night. Now that I think about it, the real reason for the Chairman's proposal was that he hadn't actually written the will yet. Of course, normally there'd be no need for you all to be present while he wrote it. But, as I believe Ms Fuchigami informed you, your grandfather is getting a little... well, forgetful. Without you all at the house, he finds it hard to associate each of the colours with the individuals they represent. That's partly where his habit of writing his will during these New Year's gatherings came from: it's the one time when the whole family gets together, meaning he can carry out his little lottery. But on the night of the 1st, he couldn't find the red origami paper—your colour, in other words—and so was unable to pick a successor. When Mr Munakata showed up on the 2nd, the will was still unwritten. At first the Chairman probably thought he could still work something out during the course of the day—even if he didn't have all the colours he needed. So he foisted some unrelated paperwork on his lawyer to keep him busy, the plan being to draw up the will and hand it to Mr Munakata before you all went home that evening.'

'But he never said anything about writing the will that day to me,' I said, casting my mind back to the conversation I'd had with Grandfather when we were drinking in the attic. 'In fact, he told me he'd given up. That he'd do it another day.'

'That was probably because he'd already started drinking by that point—with you at his side to spur him on. I imagine he figured that at this rate, with the amount of sake he was consuming, he'd probably never get around to it. In other words, he was making excuses for himself in advance.'

'So in the end, he didn't manage to write the will on the 2nd, either?'

'That's right. Mr Munakata went home empty-handed. Dismissing him for the day must have been the Chairman's way of admitting defeat—of accepting that he really would only get around to it at a later date. Then, when you were all leaving, he had a sudden change of heart. He decided he'd get you all to stay another night, and write the will as soon as he could.'

'And that's why he stopped us from driving off.'

'Yes, by offering something he knew we'd all be unable to resist—the announcement of his successor the very next day. You were out for the count, so your family carried you out of the car and up to your attic room, changed you out of your ordinary clothes and back into your tracksuit, and tucked you into your futon. Not that I, er, saw that part, of course—I simply heard about it later.'

I could glimpse the truth coming into view now—together with a feeling of pure astonishment at the delusion, almost comical in its childishness, into which I had fallen.

'So you're saying that when I woke up the next day and assumed that the 2nd of January had started all over again, it was actually the 3rd?'

'It would seem so. Now, normally, the next day would have been the 4th, and you would have realized your mistake. But as chance would have it, the 3rd of January began to repeat itself—which only reinforced your mistaken assumption that it was the *2nd of January* that was caught in a loop.'

'But it *was* caught in a loop. On the morning after the 2nd of January—in other words, what I perceived to be the second loop, though you're telling me it was actually the third—I went down to the kitchen in the old house and heard Grandfather,

Aunt Kotono and Kiyoko having the exact same conversation as the morning before. Literally word for word. If it was really the 3rd of January by that point, then why were they repeating everything they'd said on the morning of the 2nd?'

Emi paused for a moment, as though reluctant to answer, before quickly gathering herself and continuing in her usual calm, firm tone. 'I think that may have had something to do with the Chairman's... condition.'

'His condition?' Then I saw what she was getting at. It was simple, really—so simple it was bizarre I hadn't thought of it earlier. 'Ah. Right. His condition.'

'After failing to write his will on the night of the New Year's dinner, he hadn't managed it on the 2nd of January, either. The repetition must have had a confusing effect on the Chairman's mind. On the morning of the 3rd, he told the President and Kiyoko the exact same thing he had told them on the 2nd—without even realizing that he was repeating himself. Ms Fuchigami and Kiyoko were aware of his condition, and so they played along, acting as though nothing was the matter.'

I cast my mind back to the seventh loop, when Aunt Kotono had asked me whether I'd overheard the conversation about the red origami paper. In a slip of the tongue, I'd replied that actually I *kept* overhearing it. I remembered her expression stiffening slightly at the time. I'd been referring to the Trap— but for my aunt, the conversation really *was* one she'd been forced to go through more than once.

'But... I don't get it. When Grandfather stopped us from leaving on the evening of the 2nd, do you think he really intended to reveal his successor the next day?'

Now I was thinking of the exchange that had taken place between Aunt Kotono and Kiyoko in the dining room. My aunt had asked Kiyoko if she thought Grandfather really intended to make the announcement later that day, and Kiyoko had replied that it was hard to say—but even if he did, he'd probably end up putting it off again. Then there was Grandfather's diary. In his entry for the 3rd of January (that date, of course, being no mistake on the part of Grandfather, as I'd assumed) he had written: *Everyone's staying over* (an additional night, that is), *but I've decided to postpone the will until at least the 4th.* In other words, by the early morning of the 3rd, it seemed Grandfather had already given up on writing the will. After all, he didn't have the origami paper he needed for his lottery and the 'shop'— the stationery shop, that is—wouldn't be open until the 4th.

'I mean, if he had no intention of writing the will,' I went on, 'then he couldn't very well announce it. So why did he go to the trouble of getting us to stay the extra night?'

Emi tilted her head to one side and pressed her fingers to her temples as if deep in thought. 'You're right: at that point, he may have already given up on making the decision himself. At first he'd told himself he could do the lottery without the red paper, but in the end it just didn't feel right without all the colours. But remember what you told me just now. When Runa and Fujitaka explained to the Chairman that they wanted to get married and take on his name, what did he reply? That he'd secretly been waiting for someone to suggest just such an idea.'

'So Grandfather was hoping that, if he gave it another day, someone might put themselves forward?'

'Either that, or'—Emi winked at me mischievously—'he just wanted his family around a little longer. Even if it was only for one more night.'

At first, I found it hard to believe that my grandfather—the man behind that dastardly scheme to deprive my father and uncle of their very livelihoods—could really be capable of such noble feelings towards his family. But the longer I gazed at Emi's smiling face, the more plausible the idea began to seem. As Grandfather had aged, the frustration of losing control of his body and mind had only heightened his cantankerous suspicion of everyone around him. But it must also have made him lonely. Even his sabotage of my father and uncle's careers might really have been motivated not by a thirst for revenge, but by a desire for his stepsons to take their rightful places at Edge. Maybe he envisioned a future in which, by filling his company's senior ranks with his relatives, he would be able to bring his family closer together—if not out of love, then at least out of a self-centred desire for a more harmonious relationship. And wasn't the tendency to hurt the very people you subconsciously wanted affection from a contradiction that lurked within all of us, and not just Grandfather?... Anyway, now was not the time to be guessing at the inner workings of the old man's mind. I had other matters to get straight.

The original loop had been the 3rd of January, not the 2nd. It was a possibility I'd never even considered, and yet it explained all sorts of things. First of all, my grandfather's death. Why would something that had not happened in the original loop suddenly start happening in the second? I had tried to answer this question with the far-fetched theory that by not joining him for a drink, I had created new and unpredictable consequences for the day, but in the end it had remained a mystery.

But if what I'd assumed to be the second loop was in fact a brand-new day, the 3rd of January, then there was no mystery at all. On the 3rd of January, Grandfather drinking on his own was not an anomaly. I'd convinced myself that by failing to accompany him, I'd caused the day to deviate from its schedule, but for him to be quaffing sake alone in the attic was all part of that predetermined course. In other words, after spending the 2nd of January there with me, Grandfather had decided to return to his new favourite hiding place on the 3rd.

Nor was there anything strange about the fact that one culprit after another—first the Runa and Fujitaka double act, then Mai, then Yoshio—kept trying to frame Grandfather's death as a murder. Again, it was part of the schedule of the original loop (that is, the 3rd of January) for his death from natural causes to be framed as murder for reasons relating to the inheritance. The Trap had simply been exerting its usual guiding force, causing events to adhere to the day's original schedule as closely as possible.

It was the same with the unease I'd felt after Grandfather's body had been discovered and the police had gathered us all in the reception room. I'd traced its cause to the fact that Mr Munakata was nowhere to be seen, but in fact his absence made complete sense—for the simple reason that he had visited the mansion on the 2nd of January, whereas it was already the 3rd.

Similarly, it must actually have been on the afternoon of the 2nd that Runa had learnt that the will was still unwritten. She hadn't secretly read Grandfather's diary. She'd heard him telling me when she eavesdropped on us in the attic.

As for why she was eavesdropping in the first place, she must have spotted Grandfather leading me in the direction of the old house and decided something was afoot. At the time, I'd been convinced I'd briefly glimpsed something yellow— the colour of Runa's tracksuit. Intrigued by the low voice in which Grandfather, wary of Aunt Kotono, had murmured to me as we walked, she had followed us all the way to the attic. Listening from the top of the stairs, she had learnt not only that Grandfather hadn't written his will, but also that he planned to keep the old one until the new one was complete—a detail she must have included when reporting her discovery to Mai, Yoshio and the others. This was why, when she happened to be present at the moment of Grandfather's sudden death, she immediately grasped that last year's will would become binding.

When I'd heard Runa telling Fujitaka about this in the annex, I'd been impressed at how quickly she'd found out—but in fact that conversation had taken place on the 3rd of January, so that, if anything, she'd been a little slow in reporting it to him. It had been on the night of the 2nd that she told Yoshio, Mai and the others. While I was deep in an inebriated sleep, she'd invited anyone who felt like it to join her for a few drinks. (Of course, when Mai had told me about this gathering, I'd assumed it had taken place late at night after the dinner on the 1st.) Fujitaka, meanwhile, had gone to bed early, and only learnt the news the next day.

Of course, it had also been on the afternoon of the 2nd that Runa had dropped her earring. While eavesdropping on our conversation, she heard me getting up to go to the bathroom, and rushed back down the steps. In her panic, her earring had somehow come loose and become wedged in the stair. When I'd deduced that she must have dropped it between eleven p.m. on the 1st of January and three a.m. on the 2nd, there had been nothing wrong with my logic. My only mistake was to assume that it *was* the 2nd. If it was the 3rd, everything made sense.

I also now knew why everyone I met in the morning seemed so concerned about my hangover. I'd found this a little odd—I hadn't gone *completely* overboard at the New Year's dinner, after all—but of course, they'd all been worrying how much I'd drunk with Grandfather on the 2nd of January. By the time I'd attempted to get into the car that evening, I'd been so intoxicated I resembled some kind of barely sentient mollusc. I could see why they might have been concerned. When Aunt Kotono, one of the many people to have poured me drinks at the dinner, had mentioned that she would 'have to have words', she hadn't been blaming the very group she'd been a member of, but my grandfather.

And when, in the eighth loop, I had failed to encounter Emi in the walkway, the problem hadn't been my timing, but the fact that I'd originally bumped into her on the 2nd of January, not the 3rd. This also explained why, shortly afterwards, when Grandfather came into the dining room and invited me to join him for a drink, he'd been so abrupt. The longer conversation I'd been expecting had already taken place the day before. Everything came down to my misguided assumption that the loop began a day earlier than it had.

'There was another reason for your confusion: the clothes we were all wearing. If the Chairman hadn't made us wear those tracksuits, we'd all have been wearing different clothes

271

on the 3rd, wouldn't we? Runa, for example, loves dressing up. Normally I bet she switches outfit several times in one day, never mind two. You would have noticed a thing like that at once, wouldn't you? That everyone was wearing completely different clothes, when you thought you were stuck in a time loop.'

'R-right.'

Emi's thorough exposition of the entire situation had left me slightly stunned. It was as though she already had a better understanding of the way the Trap worked than I did.

'The Chairman's impulsive behaviour, his forgetfulness and the tracksuits he made us all wear: these coincidental factors only served to deepen the illusion.'

Emi had carefully unravelled each of the mysteries that had been weighing on my mind. It was all incredibly convincing. But just as our conversation seemed to be drawing to a close, it struck me that there was one thing she hadn't explained. The biggest mystery of all.

'This all makes a lot of sense. It really does. But…'

'But?'

'The day is only supposed to repeat itself eight times. In other words, there are supposed to be nine loops. Now, if you're right, and I mistakenly assumed it was the "second" 2nd of January when in reality it was the "first" 3rd of January, then that should have created a sort of lag between my perception and the reality. What I mean is…' I was getting more and more confused as I spoke. I held my head in my hands as I attempted to make sense of what I was saying. '…I *counted* them, Emi. The loops. And "yesterday" was the ninth and final loop. I'm completely certain. I've been through this enough times in my life. I always make sure to count them.'

'Oh, I'm sure you do,' said Emi with a reassuring smile. 'It's all just as you say. In fact, this is where that logic I mentioned comes in.'

'Wait, wh-what? Listen, I'm already having trouble keeping up. Before you confuse me any further, can I just get one thing straight? If I really did mistake the "first" 3rd of January for a repetition of the day before, my calculation should have been thrown out by one loop. When what I assumed was the final loop ended, the day should have begun to repeat itself again—from my perspective, once more than it was supposed to. At which point I would have finally figured out that I'd got the starting point wrong. That's what should have happened, right? I should have noticed my mistake.'

'Exactly.' Emi seemed completely unfazed. In the meantime, I was growing increasingly uneasy.

'But… that means I should have woken up at my grand-father's house this morning. If I didn't count the loops wrong—and I'm sure I didn't—then today should have been the final loop. And yet this morning I woke up at home. You called me on the phone. We're sitting here having dinner. Which means the Trap *has* ended, after all.'

'Exactly. It has. Listen, Hisataro, I know this is confusing. I know it doesn't make sense. I bet you're even beginning to wonder whether the number of loops might somehow have switched, for the first time in your life, from nine to eight—in other words, if there might have been some sort of change in your "condition". Am I right?'

'Yes.' It was true that I'd jumped to the conclusion she'd just outlined with a readiness that was pathetic. 'I mean, that's the only explanation I can think of.'

'And who's to say that isn't what happened? I mean, this time loop thing is still basically a mystery to us, isn't it? Without a clearer understanding of its inner workings, we can't rule anything out. Still, I think there's a different explanation.' Emi looked deep into my eyes, as if gently rebuking me for my hasty assumptions. 'A more logical explanation. One that doesn't require us to believe in some abrupt change in the number of loops.'

'Really? But... what?'

'Don't you see?'

'See *what*?'

'I had an idea while you were explaining all this to me. But the very nature of the idea makes proving it impossible. It'll never be anything more than conjecture. Still, something tells me it's the truth.'

'Conjecture is fine by me. Please. Tell me.'

'Of course. But there's one condition, okay?'

'Go ahead.'

'Remember what I said when I got here? That I thought you were much older than you were. Which is why—and you might think this is stupid—I was convinced I wouldn't have to wait too long. You know, until your suggestion became a reality.'

My suggestion. It took me an absurd amount of time, so long I felt like kicking myself in the backside, to realize that she was referring to the conversation we'd had at around noon on the 2nd of January. It dawned on me, finally, that our exchange that day had never been 'reset', never rendered null and void. In other words, it was still very much... in effect.

'Does that mean,' I replied, 'that when you turned Ryuichi down, it was because...'

'What, when I told him my heart already belonged to another man? Yes. I meant you, of course.' She giggled, as if this was all highly amusing. 'Fate works in mysterious ways, doesn't it? If we hadn't had that conversation on the 2nd, I might well have reacted a little more enthusiastically to Ryuichi's proposal. I'm not saying I would have accepted, but I might at least have entertained the possibility. But by the 3rd of January, the only person on my mind was you. I practically had to stop myself from laughing in his face.'

'Wow.' I didn't know what else to say. 'So… I was just in the nick of time.'

'Anyway, let me tell you why I asked you here today in the first place. Like I said, I was convinced I wouldn't have to wait that long for you. I'd even persuaded myself you might have finished university by this time next year. But if you're still in your first year of high school, that changes things. You're going to have to put your studies first. It made me start wondering just how long I could wait. I mean, we're talking six or seven years at least, aren't we? I'll be in my thirties by then. And at university you'll barely be able to move for all the eligible young women. You might have a change of heart. So what I wanted to ask you today was: just how serious are we about this? But then all of a sudden we were talking about time loops and murder. You know, for a minute I thought it was all just some long-winded way of breaking up with me. Trying to get me to pretend our conversation never happened…'

'Breaking up with you?' I said, slightly taken aback. 'But we're not even—'

'Then I realized that someone as honest as you would never beat about the bush like that. No, you had to be telling the truth, I thought. Still, that wasn't the only reason I believed you. There's the other thing. The part you just don't get.'

'The part I just don't get?'

'You know—about today being the 4th of January, instead of the final loop of the 3rd. You just can't get your head around it, can you? But, see, that's how I know you're telling the truth. I mean, if all this were just some clever story of yours, you wouldn't have made all that fuss. If your condition wasn't real, the idea that the 3rd of January had somehow "disappeared" would have been a pointless addition to what was already a fabrication. In fact, the idea would probably never have occurred to you. You would have simply explained everything to me neatly and methodically, and that would be it. There'd be no need to act all confused about a possible mistake.'

As much as I wanted to be convinced, I wasn't sure this qualified as the 'logic' Emi had promised. Yes, if you assumed my confusion was real, then her theory made a kind of sense. But it fell apart entirely once you allowed for the possibility that the confusion itself was all part of the act. After all, adding unnecessary detail to your story to make it more convincing is one of the oldest tricks in the con artist's book.

'Anyway,' she went on, 'like I said, I'll tell you where I think the missing loop went, Hisataro. But on one condition.'

'Yes?'

'I want you to trust me. I want you to trust me when I say I believe everything you've told me. I'm not just humouring you because you're Hisataro: I mean it from the bottom of my heart. I genuinely believe you, and it's that belief that's allowed me to work out what happened here. Will you trust me on that?'

276

The truth was that by now, it didn't matter to me how shaky her logic was. I felt a strange joy, laced with guilt, as it dawned on me that Emi had seen right through me. She had worked out exactly what I feared—that even as she helped me make sense of my predicament, she might secretly be viewing all this as some elaborate joke that she would ultimately shrug aside—and she was reassuring me that she believed my every word. Here was confirmation that Emi really was every inch the wise and beautiful woman I'd thought she was. No—she was even wiser, and even more beautiful, than I had known.

'It's very simple, really.' Emi watched me nod slowly, then settled back into her chair with an air of satisfaction. 'You were convinced it was the 2nd of January that was caught in a loop. When the loop ended, you expected to wake up on the 3rd; instead you seemed to have skipped ahead to the 4th. That was because the Trap only started on the 3rd, and what you thought was the first loop was in fact an ordinary day. But if that was the case, you should have been shocked, on waking up after the so-called final loop, to find yourself still in the Trap. But that didn't happen. The Trap ended just when you expected it to. Somehow, everything had worked out just as it was supposed to. If you got the starting point wrong, how was that possible? Well, I'll tell you. Because you missed one of the loops entirely.'

'Hang on a second. I just told you I counted them all. I'm sure of it.'

'Of course you did. But there was one loop when you were in no position to count.'

'In… no position to count?'

'Yes. In fact, you were incapable of doing pretty much anything.'

'Incapable? Why?'

'Because, Hisataro, you were dead.'

I instinctively clenched my fists and held them over my ears. I heard someone at one of the other tables chuckle at my bizarre pose, but I had bigger things to worry about.

'Sorry... what?'

'You were dead. Deceased. Departed.'

'D-dead? But, erm, Look at me. I'm sitting right here. All... alive.'

'Of course you are. Don't act so surprised. Whatever happens during a loop, it eventually gets reset, doesn't it? I mean, look at the Chairman. He died over and over again during the course of that long 3rd of January, but right now he's alive and kicking.'

'But then... when are you saying I... died?'

'I'll give you a hint. Cast your mind back to the seventh loop. What happened then?'

'The seventh? Well... er... that was when I asked Aunt Kotono to get everyone together for another meal in the banquet hall, as a way of making sure they all stayed in one place. And then just when I thought nothing could go wrong, Grandfather had his... accident.' I heard my voice growing hoarse all of a sudden. 'He... fell down the stairs.'

'Exactly,' said Emi, nodding. 'The same thing happened to you. Think back to what you thought was the "third" 2nd of January. In other words, what was actually the "second" 3rd of January. When Mai was the culprit. When that loop reset, you woke in the attic. Then, still half-asleep, you wondered whether you should get up and check whether the earring was on the stairs.' More than anything, I found myself marvelling at the fact that I'd gone into this much detail during my earlier explanation. 'In the end, however, you failed to rouse yourself and fell back to sleep—or so you believed. In fact, however, you *did* make your way to the stairs to look for the earring. Then, in your semi-waking, barely conscious state, you slipped on it. You fell down the stairs, banged your head and died. Of course, *I* have no memory of the loop in question—which is obviously a good thing. I mean, if I'd come across your dead body, I… well, let's say I'd have made a bit of a scene. Probably would have gone half-crazy with shock.'

I thought I detected a gleam in Emi's eyes as she spoke these words. As I gazed at her, I cast my mind back to the 'dream' I'd had on the night in question. It was all coming back to me now. That was right—I'd had the impression of falling from some great height.

'You spent the rest of the day dead, and then midnight came around and the loop reset. You were back in your attic—and, in your drowsy stupor, mistakenly assumed yourself to be in a continuation of the previous loop. Had you already been to check the stairs? No, you told yourself: that must have been a dream.'

It was true—I'd assumed I'd been dozing, and that the shock of hitting the ground in my dream had woken me up. Now I saw that it had been no dream.

'You convinced yourself you had simply fallen back to sleep, when in fact you'd spent the entire previous loop dead. And because you remained entirely unaware of that fact, you "lost" a loop. That's what I think happened, Hisataro. The thing is, we'll never be able to prove it.'

TIMELINE

Objective passage of time	Protagonist's perception
2nd January	2nd January (first loop)
3rd January (first loop)	" (second loop)
" (second loop)	" (third loop)

" (third loop)
Protagonist spends the day dead

Objective passage of time	Protagonist's perception
" (fourth loop)	" (fourth loop)
" (fifth loop)	" (fifth loop)
" (sixth loop)	" (sixth loop)
" (seventh loop)	" (seventh loop)
" (eighth loop)	" (eighth loop)
" (ninth loop)	" (ninth loop)
4th January	3rd January

15
TIME'S SPIRAL NEVER ENDS

This is where the story should end. There isn't much else to tell, and as for what happened between Emi and me, I'd like to follow the time-honoured tradition of leaving that up to the reader's imagination. The problem is, there was an unsettling epilogue to the whole story—one I should probably relate here.

That April, I began my second year of high school. Fujitaka, meanwhile, abandoned his doctorate, in order to officially become Aunt Kotono's son and begin his induction at the Edge Restaurant Group, the company he would one day control. To celebrate his adoption, Grandfather invited Edge's top executives, together with an array of prominent local figures from the political and business worlds, to the biggest hotel in Atsuki, where a grand ceremony was held to mark the occasion. Grandfather even took the opportunity to announce his retirement as the company's Chairman. It seemed that, mellowed by old age and his newly found sobriety, he intended to simply potter about and tend to his bonsai until a great-grandchild came along.

It didn't seem that would take too long, either. All that needed to happen now was for my brother—formerly Fujitaka

Oba, now Fujitaka Fuchigami and technically my cousin—to marry Runa. Everything was going smoothly. Then, just when we were preparing to celebrate, an unexpected development upset all our plans.

Just before their engagement was officially announced, Fujitaka and Runa had a huge fight. The precise reasons for it remain unknown. In any case, after tearfully exclaiming that she could never live with 'a brute like that', Runa brushed aside Aunt Haruna's hasty attempts to make her reconsider and ran away from home.

Grandfather was furious. His choice of Fujitaka as successor had been conditional on the marriage to Runa. If she intended to renege on her promise, then the inheritance was off. He made it known that he wasn't going to budge an inch. It was possible his worsening 'condition' had made him even more stubborn than usual.

Of course, all this sent Mother into a panic. She'd assumed that once her son had the Fuchigami name, he'd be able to act as he pleased. Surely it didn't have to be Runa he married—after all, women would be queuing up to marry him. But now Grandfather had declared that without Runa, the adoption itself would be annulled. Mother ended up joining forces with Aunt Haruna in a last-ditch attempt to change Runa's mind. But even after she was persuaded back to the family home, Runa was adamant that she would never marry Fujitaka—that actually she didn't ever want to see his face again.

Mai, meanwhile, saw this as her chance. She put herself forward as a substitute, apparently convinced that as long as one of the Oba sons married one of the Kanagae daughters, Grandfather would have nothing to complain about. And maybe she wasn't too far off the mark, because the old man did at least consider the idea. In the end, though, she only succeeded in adding fuel to the fire.

The problem was Fujitaka, who threw a huge tantrum, asking how on earth he could be expected to marry someone 'that grumpy and ugly'. He seemed to think he was entitled to someone at least as beautiful as Runa, though I wonder if he ever stopped to consider his own merits in that area—or just how fragile his own position was. In any case, we found ourselves no nearer a solution.

Next it was Yoshio's turn to enter the fray, and with all the delicacy you'd expect. He proposed nonchalantly that if Fujitaka's adoption was off the cards, he'd be happy to take the Fuchigami name instead—adding, with headache-inducing flippancy, that he'd be perfectly happy with either Runa or Mai, thank you very much.

Mother and Aunt Haruna were growing increasingly desperate. Their carefully laid plans for a leisurely retirement had been going so well—and now their selfish children had thrown a spanner in the works. They seriously discussed the idea of Yoshio taking his brother's place, only for both Runa and Mai to declare that they'd rather jump off a cliff. Yoshio could only be thankful for his ability to rise, phoenix-like and undaunted, from the ashes of even the most harshly worded rejection.

In the end, everyone reconverged on the idea of getting Runa to change her mind. But that horse had already bolted. It seemed the disagreement in question had been Fujitaka and Runa's first big fight. In other words, they were one of those lovey-dovey couples whose entire relationship goes up in smoke the moment they have a proper falling out. Not that this came as much of a surprise to me—after all, the writing had been on the wall plenty of times during the Trap.

I told myself, a little optimistically, that since Fujitaka had already been publicly announced as the successor to the Fuchigami name, there was a limit to how serious things could get. It might take time, I thought, but eventually the dust would settle. In fact, part of me saw all this as entirely unrelated to me—the proverbial fire on the other side of the river. But it wasn't long until an unexpected gust of wind sent that fire leaping across the water.

With Mother and Aunt Haruna pestering her relentlessly in stereo, Runa ended up announcing something truly absurd: that though she would never marry Fujitaka or Yoshio, she could 'just about see herself' with 'Kyu-chan'. Now, this was obviously the spur-of-the-moment raving of someone at the very end of her tether, but two drowning women will clutch at straws, and so Mother and Aunt Haruna began actually trying to talk me into the idea. Then, in what seemed an attempt to really spite Fujitaka, Runa herself turned up at our house with a suitcase and forced me to run away with her. She seemed to have some sort of elopement in mind, but the hiding place she'd come up with turned out to be a business hotel about ten minutes' walk from her house. Still, when Mother and Aunt Haruna saw the note she'd left before leaving home, they panicked, assuming some sort of abduction had taken place, and both reported it to the police as such, so that what should have been a family quarrel ended up in the pages of local newspapers in a shameful debacle that seems certain to sully the name of all three families for generations to come. (As an aside, this was how I became reacquainted with Inspector

Hiratsuka of the Atsuki Police. Of course, my grandfather's 'murder' had long been wiped from his memory, so for him, this was his first encounter with the family.)

In any case, the chaos showed no sign of abating. In fact, it still doesn't. Runa and Fujitaka don't seem like they'll be making up any time soon. It turns out that, in his despair at what seems to be an irredeemable situation, Fujitaka has been trying to get back together with a young office worker he once dated.

The whole thing has become a complete quagmire—one that seems unlikely to improve by the time our next New Year's gathering comes around. And right now, I'm worried sick. What if Grandfather loses his patience and declares that he's ditching the latest will for a new one—that as far as Fujitaka and Runa are concerned, it's back to square one?

That's not the only thing on my mind, either. What if there's some fresh mix-up over the inheritance? And what if, as chance would have it, I fall back into the Trap on the day when all hell breaks loose?

To be honest, it doesn't even bear thinking about.

AVAILABLE AND COMING SOON
FROM PUSHKIN VERTIGO

Yukito Ayatsuji
The Decagon House Murders
The Mill House Murders

Boileau-Narcejac
Vertigo
She Who Was No More

María Angélica Bosco
Death Going Down

Piero Chiara
The Disappearance of
Signora Giulia

Frédéric Dard
Bird in a Cage
The Wicked Go to Hell
Crush
The Executioner Weeps
The King of Fools
The Gravediggers' Bread

Friedrich Dürrenmatt
The Pledge
The Execution of Justice
Suspicion
The Judge and His Hangman

Margaret Millar
Vanish in an Instant
A Stranger in My Grave
The Listening Walls

Baroness Orczy
The Old Man in the Corner
The Case of Miss Elliott
Unravelled Knots

Edgar Allan Poe
The Paris Mysteries

Soji Shimada
The Tokyo Zodiac Murders
Murder in the Crooked House

Akimitsu Takagi
The Tattoo Murder

Josephine Tey
The Daughter of Time
The Man in the Queue

Masako Togawa
The Master Key
The Lady Killer

S. S. Van Dine
The Bishop Murder Case

Futaro Yamada
The Meiji Guillotine Murders

Seishi Yokomizo
Death on Gokumon Island
The Honjin Murders
The Inugami Curse
The Village of Eight Graves
The Devil's Flute Murders